THE LEAVING YEAR

BY

KATHRYN A. KOPPLE

First Printing, 2017

Mirth Press
PO Box 231137
San Diego, CA 92123
www.mirthpress.com

ISBN: 978-1-936869-90-9
Library of Congress Control Number:

First Edition
10 9 8 7 6 5 4 3 2 1

Dedication

A dedication can't possibly express my gratitude to Monika Weikel. A writer could not wish for a more generous friend.

CHAPTER ONE

MYRIA

Myria went to college at a place that looked more like a summer camp than a campus: cottage style dorms, the red barn where classes were held, a swath of lawn that led to a steep drop down into the thickets. Students called it "the Edge of the World." In the distance, topping off the view, the mountains: thrilling green in summer, followed by gorgeous fall, the rainy days of November, after which bristling cold winter, the melting season, and at last spring, blossom-wonderful.

Myria majored in Spanish. She was assigned books no one but Spanish-speaking people seemed to have heard of: *El Cid, El libro del buen amor, La celestina.* Her public high-school Spanish wasn't up to the task. Profesora Storni suggested Myria purchase the dictionary: *Pequeño Larousse Ilustrado.* 91 thousand words. 230,000 definitions. 5,200 illustrations. The *Larousse*, although compact, easily weighed a pound or more. Myria believed it contained the entire Spanish language. If she could memorize every verb, adjective, adverb, all the parts of speech found in the *Pequeño Larousse*, she was convinced she would speak Spanish better than any native speaker. Her Spanish would be the best anywhere. A vain hope since learning to speak a second language fluently took many years.

Her sophomore year she met Sheffield. He came from the Sheffields of Braintree. Originally, the name referred to the River Sheaf. Sheaf, too, as in paper, and the many poems she wrote about him. In one poem, she compared him to Ben Franklin because he liked to fly kites in stormy weather. In another poem, she called him reckless because on their many tramps up mountain sides he'd find some outcrop, where he'd stand dangerously close to the brink.

"You'll fall one of these days."

"I'm testing the wind," he would say.

"You're testing fate."

After graduation, Sheffield broke it off with her. They'd been at the formal lunch with the parents, exchanging toasts over cold-cuts and cheese wedges. He asked her to walk with him. They traipsed across campus and down a carriage road that was used as a horse trail. Horse shit smelled up the air; avid flies crawled over fresh mounds of manure. Under a hickory tree, he told her he couldn't go out with her anymore. "It's over."

Myria stretched out her arms, trying to lasso him around the waist. Her repeated why's and what if's got mixed up with her tears. She reminded him in snuffles of their summer plans. A plan to go road tripping to the Grand Canyon was in the works. Many destinations bored Sheffield but not the Grand Canyon, its geological wondrousness. Sheffield spoke eloquently about "geological time" and "metamorphic rocks" and, gracious, so many other marvels. When it came to the Grand Canyon, Sheffield was passionate. He was racing towards great discoveries. He was chasing the sublime. It never occurred to Myria that he would make the trip without her. She thought they would experience the great canyon together, spending days scrambling across ledges and analyzing rock formations. Come night, they would snuggle under swarms of stars, whispering a future of adventures and world trekking to each other until they fell asleep. Now, the trek had screeched to a halt. Just like that, Myria's visions of sharing a sleeping bag with

Sheffield turned out to be delusions.

Sheffield unlatched himself from her grasp. She buried her face in her hands. He was saying something about the hickory, the peeling bark, spooky, that it reminded him of witches, the shaggy gray hair.

She lifted her head. "You got that from me."

"Got what?"

"I told you that hickories always looked like crones to me, and that they used to scare me as a kid."

"You did, didn't you?"

"It's mine, my memories, and you can't speak to me like that, not when those are my words."

What had he said? She saw danger everywhere. So many things scared her: heights, highways, hickory trees. He was tired of it, her.

"What is this? Some kind of object lesson?"

"It's just a tree, Myriam, but not to you. To you, it's a witch or ghost. A lot of the time, I think you really believe it when you say those things. But it's just a tree, that's what I'm talking about."

"I know what a tree is, Sheff. I grew up around here. I should know what a stupid tree is." She glared at the hickory.

He stuck one hand in the pocket of his trousers, the other he used to support himself against the hickory. It was a very macho pose. Sheffield was all guy.

"You're always telling me to be careful."

"And you don't like it," she said. "You don't like that I care about you. I care so much I don't want you to get hurt."

"It's more like you keep trying to hold me back."

Hold him back. There was more than one way to parse that phrase. He might have said, "I'm too young to be tied down." Instead, she held him back. Sheffield was a legacy, an Anglo-Saxon pure blood, and rich. He didn't often talk about his enviable position in life because to do so made him appear utterly gauche. He had so much and she had so little, but to mention it would make her appear utterly gauche.

And her people? They made the voyage to America in the 1800s, fleeing Germany on a freighter carrying among its cargo bakers, butchers, brewers.

Her poor grandmother. She spent her childhood sharing a cold-water flat with her mother and brother in the Bronx. In a voice drenched in sorrow, she told Myria that she slept on a mattress bloodied by bedbugs. The bedbugs were horrible, much worse than the cold, even worse than going hungry. Her grandmother told Myria how her brother found work in the Diamond District when he was twelve. Neither of them had gone to school. "What choice did he have but to work?" she would say. Her father had cracked up, vanished into an asylum. He left his family destitute.

A sad story, one that Sheffield must have found vaguely distasteful. His prejudice. What about her pride? Pride was all she had, and it wasn't enough to elevate her to the high plateau where the Sheffields resided.

"We should get going," he said.

Myria sobbed.

"Myriam, I have to go. My parents will wonder where I went."

He started walking. She didn't follow. He turned around. "Are you coming?" She didn't respond, leaning against the hickory tree, the old witch.

"Are you all right?"

Myria sniffed. "I'm fine, Sheff. It's just that I have horse crap all over my shoes."

She moved back in with her parents. She slept on the living room sofa. While away at college, the house had been sold. Her mom and dad were in a two bedroom condominium now.

If she wanted to get off the couch, Myria needed a job. Her degree didn't specify what it was that she was qualified to do but there was plenty of work for receptionists. She bought a blue skirt and a crisp, blue blouse to match. She showed up at nine on the dot her first day at a local real estate office where her duties were summarily explained to her: answering the phone, photocopying, sorting the mail.

Such a mingy existence of un-entitled drudgery struck Myria as unbearable. She filled her journal with aphorisms, quotes and bitter commentary. She wrote letters, dozens, never sent. And the terrible poems, the dark night of the soul poems.

Months passed. At some point, Myria decided to put down her pen. Something, a voice inside her said. Just do something. You have to do something because he's not coming back.

She quit her job. Whatever she could sell, she sold. She sold her VW Bug for a thousand dollars. The owner of a used bookstore pulled several ten notes from his pocket for her English translation of *The Ingenious Nobleman Don Quixote of La Mancha*. A signed copy of a Salvador Dalí print given to her by Sheffield brought in some more cash. She emptied her savings account. She begged her parents for a loan. She took out a government loan.

After all the scrounging for cash, she sat down and wrote a note, addressed it to Sheffield, and mailed it to his New York address. She couldn't be certain it would reach him. Where he was, she had no idea.

✉✉✉

Sevilla in August was an inferno. The native Sevillanos, having bolted their doors and closed up shop, flocked in tremendous migrations to the sun coast.

Myria rented a room in a women's residence in a built-up area of the city. The room was tiny. It barely fit a flimsy cot. The cot had been wedged under a window. A cupboard had been converted into a closet of sorts. There was no space for a desk.

Her cramped quarters were separated from the kitchen by a double-handled frosted glass door. She was paying rent to live in what was once a pantry.

When in need of fresh air, Myria sat on the cot, and stuck her head out the window. Sheets flapped like so many colored flags from the clotheslines that ran from one rooftop to the next. From her perch, she felt as if she were the sole occupier an abandoned city. Once, one of the white sheets slipped the clothesline; it fell six stories before landing in a heap on the ground. Myria waited to see who would risk the volcanic heat of the afternoon sun to fetch it. No one did. By the end of August, there was quite a pile of sheets strewn about the alley.

Myria spent hours on her cot. Sevilla certainly wasn't what she had imagined. She came to the city expecting adventure. She imagined flamenco dancers on every corner, cafes brim-full of customers sipping wine, music everywhere. She had heard that the Spaniards were festive people. Myria was the festive type.

Olé, Olé, Olé.

Who was she kidding? She had come to forget Sheffield. Instead of Sheffield, she had the dueña, a Spanish widow of tremendous girth who wore starched, black dresses. The dueña spoke very little, never more than a word or two to Myria. The dueña arrived at 7:00 in the morning, prepared breakfast and lunch, and left at 12:00. She returned in the evenings to clean up.

Myria's classes began the end of September. School couldn't come fast enough but it didn't. Time crept along as if too were suffocated by the heat.

And then September came. Like a castaway rescued from a deserted island, she almost leapt for joy when seven other women moved into the residence.

"Soy Espinosa."

"Me llamo Myria."

"Soy Dolores."

"Soy Myria."

On it went. A brief salutation before each woman hauled a suitcase to one of the three bedrooms and closed the door behind her.

The following morning, Myria put on her robe and slippers. She shuffled past the dueña and her pans of frying smelts into the dining room. Her roommates had already left, and in a hurry from the looks of the mess left on the table. Among the debris, two jugs, one for coffee and one for milk. Myria poured her *café con leche*. Spaniards ate buttered rolls for breakfast. Myria picked up a roll and dunked it in her coffee.

The television, a vintage set with rabbit ears, took up a good deal of space against the wall next to a long, dimly lit passage that ended at the front door. Myria put down her roll, got up, and turned on the ancient TV. Spanish television morning broadcasts aired current events, documentaries, and round-table discussions.

In the news today: ETA. In the news yesterday: ETA. ETA was the news, the news ETA. More than two decades of abductions, shootings, and bombings attributed to Basque militants. *Euskadi Ta Askatasuna*, E.T.A. for short.

Myria turned from the television to stare at the clock on the wall, an oval carved from walnut, the large Roman numerals, the black minute and hour hands. Nine o'clock. Hours to go before lunch.

CHAPTER TWO

LA SOLITA

Over smelts, potatoes, and bread, Myria listened as the women talked among themselves. She did her best to follow the conversation, translating their laments, jokes, and pronouncements in her head.

"*¡Dios mío!* This heat is intolerable."

"It is enough to asphyxiate you."

"I drank three Fantas and I'm still dying of thirst."

"Three Fantas?"

"How could you?"

"You will get fat."

"It is not healthy."

"I never put on weight. I spend all day at the hospital running. Who has a smoke?"

"Take one."

"Gracias."

"Put on the tele. Cristina is about to start."

"Did she tell the *novio* yet?"

Novio. Spanish for fiancée. What was the word for dumped girlfriend?

After the meal, cigarettes, and soap opera, the Spanish women went to their rooms to take a siesta. Siesta was the worst part of the day for Myria. She would lie in a sweat, eyes wide open, on her cot. She began to regard the siesta as a cruel custom, a way of further crushing her spirits because she could never sleep. She might have gone out. After one or two forays, and finding every café, kiosk, and store locked, Myria gave up. Spaniards observed the siesta with an absolute and universal Catholicism, she told herself. Myria spoke a lot to herself, particularly during siesta. Her soliloquies brought out her inner Shakespeare: to stay or not to stay, love's labor's lost, as luck would have it. Four hours every afternoon of every day nothing moved. She didn't move.

Nothing would make her happier than returning to the States.

Or rather she wanted to go back to Sheffield. With so much time on her hands, Myria couldn't resist doing the thing that hurt most, which was thinking of him. Sheffield. Her misery was increased by the realization that many of the Spanish women had *novios* to whom they returned on the weekends, when the residence experienced a mass exodus, and Myria was left stranded. Sundays were unbearable. With everyone gone, even the dueña, Myria wandered the residence like a character from a Lorca play, one of those morbid spinsters who make a cult out of longing and rejection.

A corset of loss laces
Her torn nightgown

A corset of loss laces
Her forlorn nightgown

A corset of loss laces
Her gray nightgown

Myria, *la solita*. Myria, the unwanted. Myria, the discarded, alone and pining in a strange and remote city. Sheffield. Sheffield. Sheffield. She would have taken any excuse to board a plane.

She decided, after many pensive hours on her cot, to call home rather than get on a plane. She considered her options. The only way to contact the States by phone meant going to the *Telefónica*— not so different from a post office but for making phone calls. A call to the States was expensive, and there was the seven hour time difference between Sevilla and home to consider. Calling Sheffield was out of the question. Obsessing about Sheffield was one thing and calling him was another. She couldn't—and not because she wished to preserve whatever shred of dignity she had left. She feared he would pick up and hearing his voice she would sob into the phone. Besides, she didn't know how to reach him.

She decided to call her mother instead. Her mother answered with that panicked voice people have when the phone rings in the middle of the night.

"Who's this?"

"It's Myria."

"Myria!"

"Yes, Myria, your daughter."

"Really, Myria, it's after midnight. Is anything wrong?"

"Everything is fine," she lied.

"What time is it there?"

"It's 7:00."

"It must be 1:00 in the morning here."

"I would have called earlier but the *Telefónica* is closed in the afternoon."

"The what?"

"It's hard to explain. Did you get my letter?"

"We got a postcard."

"The one of the Giralda?"

"I think so. Are you having a good time?"

"Yeah, it's great. Classes haven't started but they will soon."

"I'm glad you're having a good time."

"Sevilla is a beautiful place."

"It must be very exciting."

"Couldn't be better."

"Write again soon."

"I will."

"Take care of yourself."

"I will."

Myria hung up and slid out of the booth. She walked past dozens of other booths occupied by gesticulating Spaniards and out the front door.

In Sevilla, not everyone owned a phone. Phones were ridiculously expensive. It was a privilege to own a phone. Myria sensed the Spaniards viewed her in much the same way. She was privileged and somewhat ridiculous. She was beginning to find out something about herself that the Spaniards already knew: she was an American. They could see it in her face, casual dress, and faltering speech. They saw that she wore sneakers, t-shirts, and little makeup. They understood without asking that she took telephones for granted, ate hearty breakfasts, and indulged in long showers.

Myria also sensed that they disliked her American ways—or rather the ways of America, as she learned from her housemates.

"Reagan! What an ass!"

"He is the worst of them."

Either Dolores or Espinosa (usually it was Espinosa) instigated these exchanges.

"Americans love their cowboys. They even elect them president."

"Reagan's not a real cowboy," Dolores joined in. "He's too old."

Espinosa puffed on a cigarette. "Do I look like a Marlboro man? Maybe the Yankees will make me president."

Myria did find her glamorous. She wore a new shade of lip color every day. Coral, pearl, ruby. Whatever lipstick matched her couture.

"That's the problem. The Yankees want to be president of the whole world," opined Dolores.

Not nearly as pretty as her friend, Dolores was still attractive. The Spanish women, even if plain, were well schooled in the arts of make-up, hair-styling, and jewelry. They understood the complexities of beauty care. They understood the differences between creams, lotions, scrubs, and how to apply them. They tweezed, waxed, and moisturized. No aspect of their appearance was left to chance. Beauty could not be left to mere chance.

Dolores pushed a large ashtray across the table toward Espinosa. "You smoke too much."

Espinosa shrugged. "Now you sound like an American."

"Americans smoke," Myria said.

Espinosa pointed her cigarette at Myria. "Spain has enough problems without OTAN."

OTAN. Myria saw it all over the newspapers. She saw it on billboards. The letters graffitied on sidewalks, in bold colors, with a black X spray-painted over them.

"And besides," Espinosa continued, "Reagan is crazy."

"What is OTAN?" Myria asked.

Dolores fell back in her chair, mouth open, arms dangling at her sides. "What is OTAN? It is a big, big problem."

"A headache." Espinosa took a final puff, exhaling loudly, let her cigarette drop to the floor, and crushed it under her red leather shoe.

"OTAN is not good for Spain," another woman said. Amelia, who had green eyes, a musical voice. "But enough already. Put on the tele. I do not want to miss Cristina because you two want to talk politics. What is the point? Better to watch Cristina."

She smiled as if in pity at Myria. "You like Cristina?"

"Very much."

"It is the greatest." Amelia turned her back to Myria and faced the television.

CHAPTER THREE

A ROSE

The Río Guadalaquivir separated Los Remedios, the modern section of the city, where Myria's residence was located. Myria had begun to familiarize herself with old Sevilla, exploring far and wide on foot.

Before leaving the States, she received an envelope from the Spanish Institute in Sevilla. The letter bore the insignia of the Royal Academy of Language: a pale blue oval of intertwining laurels on a white background and the motto "Limpia, fija y da esplendor." Whatever did it mean? She showed it to Amelia.

"Those words are centuries old. They describe Castilian. Castilian is pure, enduring, and elegant."

Myria read the centuries-old words again. "I still don't understand."

"It means that Castilian is the official language of Spain."

"Of course, it is."

"Not in Andalucia."

"But you speak Spanish."

"It's what they teach you in school."

"What is the language of Andalucia?"

"*El andaluz.*"

The envelope sent by the institute also contained Myria's class schedule, a list of "helpful tips" and "warnings," and a map of the city.

Helpful Tips: how to obtain lodging, post office hours, send a telegram, where to cash travelers checks, what to do in case of a stolen passport, being prepared for the weather.

Warnings: beware of pickpockets, don't go out alone at night, valuables should be locked in a safe place.

Schedule: classes were held from 9:00 in the morning until noon. She was "matriculated" (as the Spanish would say) in Advanced Spanish Grammar, Spanish Conversation, and Golden Age Literature.

Myria smiled at the list of "Helpful Tips" and "Warnings." The Institute might have warned her about Sevilla in August.

With dreary August behind her, she rose early to breakfast with her housemates. By now, she learned all their names: Dolores, Espinosa, Amelia, Estrella, Maria Celeste, Patricia, and Esperanza. Each woman claimed a seat at the table set with café, milk, bread and butter. Myria sat whenever possible next to Amelia. Unlike lunch, which was leisurely and noisy, breakfast yielded mostly yawns, coffee downed quickly, and a cigarette or two smoked in silence. Afterwards, the women scrambled back to their rooms to dress, scolded anyone who took too long in the bathroom, and then marched out the door, their heels clacking on the tiled floor.

Myria stayed behind. She had the bathroom to herself. Novelty was everywhere, even in the bathroom, where Myria learned to do without toilet paper and used the bidet. Sieged by five years of drought, the government restricted the city's water supply. The dueña told her no more than two showers a week. She had held up her fingers, as if Myria, who spoke Spanish so poorly must be equally ignorant when it came to math. In order to make her point, the dueña repeated the injunction no less than five times. Myria nodded, saying, *"por supesto,"* which she was fairly sure meant "of course." Her roommates used the phrase often.

Satisfied that Myria understood her, the dueña had returned to her pans smoking of olive oil.

The drought also explained the bucket of water in the bathroom. The women used it for washing panties, bras, and stockings. They hung their underwear, soaking and dripping, on a wooden rack to dry. What belonged to whom, Myria had no idea. She wasn't alone. Arguments broke out when, say, Espinosa thought Maria Celeste had taken her panty hose. Maria Celeste accused Espinosa of being too cheap to buy her own panty hose. Patricia came out of her room one morning, a bra in hand, asking where it had come from. Esperanza could never seem to find her socks. Myria managed to stay out of the fray. Unlike the other women, she had a clothesline. She shared it with the tenant across the alley. It ran on a pulley, the rope threaded in a long loop. She hung out her nylon briefs and other clothes. She had packed seven pairs of underwear, primarily white but two in black. The synthetic fabric dried in a flash but it didn't breathe the way cotton did. Myria found herself perspiring in places she never imagined before.

"You wear old ladies' panties." Espinosa laughed. Dolores also laughed. The other women laughed.

Either Espinosa could see the clothesline from her window—entirely possible—or she'd been in Myria's room while she was out.

"How do you know?"

"All of Remedios can see your underwear."

Myria threw up her hands. *"Por supuesto."*

Epinosa gave a wry smile. She looked at Dolores. "I think her Spanish is getting better."

"A little, yes."

"Miss, Miss. I got a hundred *pesetas* that says you're an American," a man called out in English, so natural and confident, as if there were no other language in the world worth speaking.

Myria had become adept at ignoring men who ogled, whistled, and hooted. Another custom of Andalucía. Men flirted with women. They whistled if they liked a woman's legs. They yelled out "*bella*" if they thought her pretty. They broke into song if they really wanted to impress her.

I adore the shine of your eyes,
The sweetness there on your red lips,
I adore the way you look at me,
And even when you sigh. I adore you.
You are my life.

Myria sort of liked it. The men flirted without being lascivious or too aggressive. If anything, they saw it as their duty to catcall. Shopkeepers, construction workers, young men out for a walk: they all flirted. Every man was a poet, a troubadour.

The man calling out "Miss" wasn't a troubadour. But he spoke her language. Among friends in short sleeve shirts, khakis, with bottles of beer at hand, he and his crew occupied a table at a riverside café.

"You just won a hundred *pesetas*," Myria said.

"See? What'd I tell you." He knuckled the guy sitting next to him in the shoulder.

"I wouldn't be so sure. She looks German to me." The doubter had straw-colored hair cropped close to his skull, like a patch of shorn wheat. "I'd get more intelligence if I were you."

"That's right. You can't be too sure of these things." He was a southerner. Pure molasses came from his mouth.

"Never can tell." There were several empty bottles lined up before this one, and another in his hand. He didn't look a day over sixteen.

"Exactly," he chimed in.

"I'm American," Myria said.

"What's the address of the White House?"

"Address and phone number?"

"Address, phone number, and nearest airport?"

Myria hadn't the faintest idea. How could she not know these things?

"I told you she was an American," the man said, the one who had first called out to her. The joke was on her. Still, there wasn't a hint of meanness in his voice. He told his friends to pull up a chair for her.

"By the way, the name's Neil. Can I buy you a beer?" He snapped his fingers at a passing waiter. "*Una cerveza para la señorita.*"

A beer for the young lady.

Myria tried not to notice the waiter winking at her.

"What's your name señorita?" Neil reached for a potato chip. She noticed the wedding band on his finger.

"It's Myria."

"Nice to meet you, Myria. What brings you to Seville?"

"I'm a student."

"You're studying Spanish?"

"I study literature."

The waiter placed an amber bottle wrapped in gold foil decorated with an eagle on the table, together with a tall glass and a plate of fresh chips. He set down a napkin, leaning in close enough to catch her eye while he poured beer into the glass. Myria blushed.

"Literature," Neil said. "Now that's something. Your Spanish must be really good."

"I wish."

"I studied a little Spanish. Read Cervantes, Calderon, that kind of thing."

"Then you've read a lot."

"Guess you could say that."

Snorts from the peanut gallery. A hoot or two. The southerner shook his head.

"So what brings you guys to Sevilla?" Myria asked. "I guess it's not literature."

"We're on liberty and thought we'd have a look around," Neil said.

"Liberty?"

"That's right," he said. "Time off for good behavior."

The others cheered. They were a rowdy bunch. Drunk.

When they settled down, Myria ventured, "Let me guess. You're in the military?"

"The military?" Neil winced. "No, señorita, we're Navy."

"There's a difference?"

"No other country in the world can do what the United States Navy can do," he said.

"Damn straight."

"Balls to the wall."

"Bad ass."

"Fucking right."

"Watch it," Neil said. "There's a lady present."

"So what is it you do in the Navy?" Myria asked.

"We do what our superiors tell us to do," Neil said. He looked around the table. "And that goes for you guys too."

"Aye aye, captain"

"Whatever you say boss."

"You don't hear me complaining."

Neil looked at Myria. "We're in charge of the bombs."

"Bombs, as in…"

"That's right," the southerner said, casually. "We load missiles onto the aircraft."

"Isn't that dangerous?"

Laughter erupted all around her.

"It's no different from any other job," Neil said, after the har-de-har calmed down. "When they tell you to work faster, you do." He smiled, one that concealed more than it revealed.

She lifted her glass. The cold beer ran easily down her throat.

Neil tossed a few hundred *pesetas* on the table. "I'm going to walk this lady home."

Home. Was the residence Myria's home now?

"Really, you don't have to," she said.

"I'm walking you to your place. Let's go." Neil was on his feet. "I trust you squids won't wander off?"

"No sir."

"Don't worry about him. He can barely walk."

"I'd say that calls for another round."

"Make that two."

The bridge to Remedios was crowded with cars, pedestrians, and gitanos. The gypsies roamed the city, selling fans, brown bags of roasted chestnuts, cigarettes, roses—whatever they could manage. Neil stopped to buy a rose.

"Not interested," he said, when the gitano offered him another.

"*Cigarrillo?*" The man reached into a tattered bag and offered Neil a beat-up cigarette. "*Cien pesetas.*"

"Get lost," Neil said. He continued across the bridge with Myria on his arm.

"It's pretty at night here," he remarked. Behind them, Myria could hear the gitanos hawking their wares.

"Where are you stationed?"

"Rota. We'll be shipping out soon."

"Where?"

"Don't know yet."

She didn't believe him. "Don't know or won't say?"

"Same difference," he said.

"I'm not sure I could do what you do."

"Serve your country?"

"More like, take orders."

"It's part of the job."

"You don't worry you might get killed?" Myria asked.

"Never think about it."

"How is that possible?"

"It just is."

He was a cool operator—or sailor, she was certain of that much. "The Spaniards don't like having our bases here."

"No? Where'd you hear that?"

"You know what I'm talking about."

"I may have heard some things on the news."

"It doesn't bother you?"

"Why would it bother me?"

"Something bad could happen."

"That's why we're here, to make sure nothing happens. Keep the peace."

They turned onto Virgen del Monte, the street where the residence was located. Neil made a crack about her living on Mount Virgin Street.

"Not funny," she said. "Actually, I do live in a convent, sort of. It's an all-female residence."

"I like the sound of that."

"No men allowed."

"Can't say I like the sound of that." He reached out to shake her hand. "Nice meeting you, Myria."

"Thanks for walking me."

"My pleasure. It helped me sober up. We've a long drive and it's going to be a fast one," he said. He placed the rose in her palm.

Myria looked at the long-stemmed flower, the drooping red petals. "I can't take this."

"It's just a rose, Myria."

"You're married."

"Doesn't mean I can't give a nice girl a rose."

"How do you know I'm such a nice girl?" For the love of god! Where had that come from? Was she flirting? She was.

"I was also thinking that you seem kind of sad."

"I see," Myria said. "You thought I needed cheering up."

"Something like that."

"Am I so pathetic?"

"You just seem sad is all," he said.

She rummaged through her knapsack for her keys. "I'll try to look less sad."

"Be safe."

"You don't have to worry about me. What are you waiting for?"

"For you to get inside."

"Whatever you say, captain."

"It's lieutenant, actually."

"So where does that put you on the chain of command?"

"No time to explain. Get inside or else you'll be responsible for my court martial."

"I'm going." Myria let herself into the residence.

"She comes carrying a rose," Espinosa said.

"A rose can mean only one thing," Dolores said.

"It cannot mean another," Amelia said.

"You must put it in your hair, like the Spanish women do during *feria*," Maria Celeste said.

"A true flamenca always wears a rose in her hair," Esperanza said.

"You mean in her teeth," Espinosa said.

Esperanza ignored her. "Do you know flamenco?" she asked Myria.

Maria Celeste began to clap, a deliberate rhythm. Esperanza stood up, arms raised, elbows arched over her head, wrists and fingers in a swirl, like a butterfly pinned to the air.

"You should give Esperanza the rose," Amelia said. "So she can put it between her teeth."

Esperanza grabbed at her skirt and began to beat her heels on the floor. She circled the table, pausing in front of Myria, hand held out. Myria let her have the rose. Biting down on the stem, Esperanza continued around the room.

"Ay! Esperanza, please," Dolores cried, and then to Myria, "She really is terrible."

Espinosa agreed. "She is no flamenca."

Esperanza paused to take the flower from her mouth. "Quiet or you will frighten the spirits away."

Maria Celeste stopped clapping.

"What spirits?" Myria asked.

The women glanced at one another; their expressions solemn or quizzical or at a loss.

Amelia broke the silence. "The *duende*."

"Do not bother. She would not understand," Espinosa said. "She can barely speak Spanish."

"I want to know," Myria said. "I want to know... how did you call it?"

"*Duende*?" Amelia closed her eyes a moment before speaking in English. "It is very deep in our culture."

"Do not speak to her in English," Epinosa scolded. "She needs to learn Spanish."

Never one to contradict Espinosa, Dolores said: "She has been here for a month and can barely speak."

"You two! You are two *malas*," Amelia scolded. She turned to Myria. "The duende is... the souls of the dead. To know flamenco is how we call the dead to help us. We don't see them or hear the dead every day. It's a gift. Only the greatest artists possess duende. When a singer is of this tradition, has traveled to this realm, in dreams or by some other way, then it comes out, in the voice and the body. What you see about flamenco is for tourists. There are still masters out there. You must work to find them."

"Go on," said Espinosa, also speaking in English now. "Tell us where we find them. Tell her."

"It's not for me to say," Amelia responded.

Espinosa snapped at Dolores to give her a cigarette. "Go on, Amelia," she insisted. "Tell her."

Amelia kept silent, her lips tense, frowning.

"Look at her." Now Espinosa was speaking to Myria. "She is so dark and haunted and maybe a little crazy, like a gypsy."

"You don't know me," Amelia said. The rose lay on the floor next to her, where Esperanza let it drop. Amelia reached for the flower. She brushed the petals against her lips. "You are a silly girl."

"Why do you hide it?"

"You are the one full of secrets," Amelia responded.

Espinosa drew heavily on her cigarette and released a stream of smoke into the air.

"I don't understand," Myria said.

"You do not understand," Amelia said. "How could you? It is something only we Spaniards know."

"Do not say we know as if everyone agrees with you. Many Spanish people do not believe in duende." Espinosa erupted. "It is ridiculous! It makes us look superstitious!"

"She speaks like this because she is not from the south." Amelia's impatience was evident. "She is from Madrid. She is so cosmopolitan. She is not a dirty peasant."

"No, I am not."

"So be careful."

"Of the duende? Or the fact that you are a gypsy?"

Myria's eyes settled on the rose. The gitano who sold it to Neil kept pulling things out of a sack that seemed to contain everything, like some magician's hat. Had a dove flown out of it, she wouldn't have been surprised.

Well, the gitanos, subject to so many myths, feared and despised by many. Beware when it came to the gypsies. Every pocket they pick; every tourist a target; every woman and child prey. They keep company with the living and the dead. Stretch out your hand and they will grab it, holding it close to the face, and you will feel their breath on your palm. You aren't able to hide from the truth; from birth, there, you see it? The hand speaks all; it shows all and where all leads. You need the gypsy more than you know. Come to my shop. Come to my home. Come, come. You look frightened. You are not well. Darkness surrounds you. An amulet or medallion of St. Teresa might fix the problem. What problem you ask? Do you not see it? Do you not feel it? Say no, and the gitanos will give you the eye-of-the-fortune-teller, the evil eye of the spurned. Never stare into the eyes of a gypsy. You could go blind or mute or lame. Yes, by a mere look, that quick tongue, scurrilous laugh, curses you never dreamt of.

"Tell us about your novio?" Amelia asked. She pressed the rose to her lips once more before returning it to Myria.

"He's not my boyfriend."

"You take a rose from a man you do not know?"

"I, uh-" Myria's vocabulary failed her.

"Amelia, why bother," Espinosa said. "Her Spanish is horrible."

"Espinosa is right," Amelia said. "You'll never learn how to speak if you don't open your mouth."

"If you don't want to speak Spanish, why come to Spain?" Dolores asked.

Round the table they went, each woman badgering her about her poor language skills. Amelia let the harangues run their course before she asked Myria again who had bought her the rose.

"A man."

"A Spanish man?"

"No, not Spanish."

"I did not think so," Amelia said, in Spanish now. "He was an American, maybe a sailor?"

"He's an American. It's not what you think. He wasn't flirting. He was being friendly. He bought me the rose out of generosity." At least, that's what Myria thought she said, having given her answer in Spanish, and apparently had because Amelia responded that she knew it all along.

"How?" Myria asked.

"Because she is a gypsy," Espinosa said. "She can read your mind."

"Espinosa, you are like a chicken. *Cloc, cloc, cloc.*" Amelia gave Myria one of her sympathetic smiles. "I am not able to read your mind but you are not happy here."

"She is right," Maria Celeste said. "If you want to be happy, you need to spend more time with Spanish people."

"You will feel better," Amelia agreed.

"*Por supuesto,*" Myria said.

CHAPTER FOUR

SHOCK

Whether in English or Spanish, the word "happy" had for Myria a foreignness to it; it carried a promise of morning glory skies, light heartedness, a buoyancy of spirit, an airiness of being, an easy manner, a gentleness about the mouth, smiling eyes and rosy cheeks, harmony among friends, contentment.

She knelt on the cot, the old casement windows in her room opened, her arms crossed before her on the ledge. Sevilla didn't settle down at night; it awoke, the heat subdued by winds from the Gulf, the streets lively as any carnival. Had the residence been better situated, she could be looking at the famous Cathedral or the trumpeting angels of the city's baroque fountains. The terra-cotta rooftops made for a pleasant view during the day, the tiles bright red under the sun. At night, she was boxed in, and little light got in that box. The building across the street looked like it was in a black out. The inhabitants kept their sashes drawn or turned out their lights to save electricity.

The mewling cats in the alley were all she had for company now that her housemates had gone out on the town. Only Dolores and Maria Celeste remained behind, still seated at the living room table, smoking and watching American movies dubbed into Spanish on the tele. Did they know what Hepburn or Bogart really sounded like? She had a patrician accent, his, a street-wise growl. Or Bette Davis, her singular voice, unforgettable. It was Bette Davis who made the unlikable characters she portrayed sympathetic. Spunk, which she possessed to no end, served her well, and she was a dame. A real dame, as they used to say. These days, she would have been called a "diva." Sometimes people remarked on Myria's voice, saying it was "sultry" or "sexy." She had a deep voice, throaty, and boys seemed to like it. Whatever else she might be lacking in the way of looks, she had a voice. Not that it mattered when the on-going struggle to speak in Spanish reduced her more often than not to silence.

The overhead light had begun to attract moths, their wings the color of rotting apples. She turned off the light.

Stripped down to her underwear and bra, Myria lay on the cot, staring up at the ceiling, the moths still visible—dark thumbprints against the white stucco. She grasped at the flesh around her hips and belly, running her hands across her breasts. The constant diet of fried smelts and potatoes was making her fat. Compared to the Spanish woman—all petite—she was blubbery. To get into her jeans, she had to suck in her gut, and even then she worried the zipper would burst. She didn't have money for new clothes, and if she did she doubted she would find something in that city of skinny women that fit her.

Did it matter? How she looked? Maybe she was eight or ten pounds heavier. What did it matter? She starved herself for months at a time for Sheffield. She ate cottage cheese from the gross salad bar at the college cafeteria morning, noon, and night. Sometimes, she allowed herself a salad with Russian dressing, or a hamburger. A slice of pizza was an indulgence.

The next morning, after coffee with milk, Myria dressed in sweats and sneakers.

"Where are you going like that?" Espinosa asked.

"Running." The word had rolled off her tongue; it wasn't an

easy word to pronounce in Spanish—with its double r's.

She ran past the bar on the corner, where the waiter had already lined up demitasse cups and glasses for the morning shot of *anis con sifón* (a breakfast custom kept by a generation of men old enough to have lived through the Spanish Civil War), over the bridge and along the Paseo de las Delicias, the long avenue that hugged the Guadalquivir, where red and blue hulled ferry boats tugged at their moorings and gray tufted pelicans dove the waters in search of trout and catfish.

Winded, Myria stopped to catch her breath and bearings. The mansions along the river made for an impressive sight; tiled patios and fountains visible through wrought iron gates, and the basilica of the Torre del Oro rising above a cluster of palm trees to the sky. She'd read that its original architects—the Moors who had once ruled southern Spain—had built the fortress from the ground up out of pure gold, and even now, after conquerors stripped the diagonal structure of its precious façade, the tower, by magic or other means, retained its golden hue.

She wished Sheffield were there to see it, although she couldn't be sure it would make much of an impression on him. He'd been abroad. He would mention "Juliette" in passing, his friend from France. Or Nikko, from Italy, was staying at his parents' home for the summer. And wasn't there someone from Switzerland? He and his friend Andrew, whose family owned General Mills (something like that), spent a month in the Alps skiing. He came from one of America's great metropolises. He was a real New Yorker. She knew he didn't like, much less love, New York. He showed up on campus in workboots and flannel shirts; his version of a backwoods Yankee. Maybe that's why he liked her. She was from Connecticut, a woodsy girl, who felt right at home among the foothills and dirt roads of New England. Unlike Sheffield, she didn't have to pretend her parents weren't celebrated journalists.

She didn't grow up in a Brownstone on the Upper East Side; she knew nothing of the best private schools. She didn't have to pretend that she wasn't from money because she wasn't. She was a public-school kid who managed to get a scholarship to one of the most elite colleges in the country.

Sheffield had never set foot in a public school. He attended private school—more than one. He had been to Paris, London and Rome. He called tourists "museum rats." Whenever they were in New York, visiting his parents, he became irritable, especially if his mother recommended a place for lunch, a Broadway play, or a new exhibit at the Met. Sheffield preferred to hide out in his bedroom on the third floor, leaning out the window and looking at the street below. The thing he enjoyed most mystified her: watching crashes, or rather bashes, as a driver, wedged in a parking spot, would put the car in reverse and back into the car behind, then shift into drive, and do the same to the car in front. Sometimes, Sheffield would race down the steps, rush outside, a grin on his face, and offer the driver help. On more than one occasion, the person would hand him the keys. Sheffield never felt more at home than behind the wheel. He always managed to dislodge the vehicle, no matter how tight the space.

Did she ever complain that he never took her out? No, she never did. She never complained, not at first, but later.

The run exhausted her. She really was out of shape. A blister made her left foot tender, her shins ached. The birds, the water, the boats turned pale as limestone under the sun. She walked half an hour or more before she unbolted the residence door, limped past the dueña, and collapsed on her bed.

"You look like you just woke up," Dolores said when Myria entered the dining room, the air rank from the burnt olive oil used to fry the day's fish and potatoes. A plate of mandarins, pretty as orange garnets encased in their thin rinds, had been placed on the table. Fruit! Myria took one and put it to her nose.

Espinosa laughed. "She does everything backwards."

"You are supposed to take fruit after you eat," Dolores said.

"And siesta after the fruit," Espinosa said.

The foyer, kept in perennial darkness because to light it would cost too much, was suddenly livened by voices and the customary clack of heels on the tiled floors. Maria Celeste and Estrella arrived. Two kisses were bestowed on Dolores and Espinosa by the women, and then the same for Myria.

"Where is Amelia?" she asked Maria Celeste after offering her cheek.

"She's not here?"

"Sometimes she eats lunch with her mother," Estrella said.

Myria sighed. She always looked forward to Amelia's company.

"She is in shock," Espinosa observed. "Americans don't take their meals together. They spend lunch in the office. They pack their food in paper bags and eat cold ham on bread."

"And drink Coca-Cola from vending machines," Dolores said.

"What do you expect," Estrella said, taking a seat at the table. "Americans work so much."

"Yes," Dolores said. "Work, work, work."

"They work like robots," Espinosa said.

"Slaves to their bosses," Dolores said. "I do not think I could put up with it."

"Dolores, if you keep on like this, she will think we are lazy and no good," Estrella said.

"I don't think that," Myria said.

Espinosa sniffed at her plate of fish and asked Dolores to pass the potatoes.

"You do not think what?" she asked.

"Do you think?" Dolores smiled before a wave of laughter rolled out of her mouth.

Myria also laughed.

Espinosa said, "She's not so serious after all."

Myria wanted to say, "I can take a joke," but failing that said: "Spanish people are famous for their sense of humor." She began to peel the mandarin. "You have Cervantes."

"And you," Espinosa said, with an impish grin, "have Mickey Mouse."

Myria should have seen that one coming. Of course, Mickey Mouse, along with American football (a coward's sport because the players wore helmets), Hollywood movies, Cadillac convertibles, frozen food—the list went on.

Myria took a slice of mandarin and sucked on it until the delicate membrane broke and the flavor of the orange fruit was full on her tongue.

She swallowed.

Spaniards didn't have a word for mouse, that much she knew. To her roommates Mickey was *el ratón*, the rat.

"Not everything you read about America is true."

"I agree with you," Espinosa said. "It is mostly lies."

"Myria," Estrella intervened. "The United States is not popular in Spain for many reasons."

"Tell me."

"My English isn't as good as Amelia's."

"Tell me in Spanish."

"Do you know the Civil War?"

"Of course," responded Myria. "I read Hemingway."

"Who is Hemingway?" Maria Celeste asked.

"Ay! Don't you know anything? He is an American writer," Espinosa responded. "He came to Spain to drink and watch bullfights."

Maria Celeste shrugged, unimpressed. "Most Americans come to Spain to drink and watch the bulls."

With a disgusted look, Esperanza said, "It's impossible to have a serious discussion here."

"Not true," Espinosa responded. "But why talk about the past?"

"So tell me, Espinosa, on which side did your family fight? You are from Madrid." Esperanza leaned back in her chair, awaiting a response.

"No one fought," Espinosa replied. "We had nothing to do with the war."

"Exactly, your family did nothing."

"Can we watch Cristina, now?" Maria Celeste pleaded. "It's almost time for it to begin."

"She still hasn't told the novio," Dolores said.

"She has to tell him one day," Espinosa said.

"The poor thing," Esperanza said.

CHAPTER FIVE

KILLIAN

The first day of class Myria woke with relief. Finally, the empty hours of her mornings would be filled. She looked forward to the end of long summers at home because she would be together again with Sheffield. He went away in the summers. Myria spent her June, July, and August in New York, living in her grandmother's apartment on Amsterdam Avenue. She worked as a clerk at the God Box, a high-rise well known in the neighborhood occupied by numerous religious and ecumenical organizations. She would collate, file, and lick envelopes, and hope Sheffield hadn't forgotten her. She thought about him to a point where it seemed as if Sheffield were her thoughts.

But, she told herself, not today. Today would be different. She stowed her notebooks, full of unsent letters, poems, and scrawl—all dedicated to Sheffield—under the cot.

Myria tugged at the laundry line outside her window, pulling in her panties, a bra and a t-shirt. She skipped breakfast and, for once, was the first in the shower.

She hadn't been more than five minutes in the bathroom before she heard knocks at the door. She ignored whoever it was as she cleaned herself under the spurts of water that ran dry before she could get the shampoo out. She had thick hair that required a lot of rinsing. Her hair! When was the last time she'd had a haircut? Her hair wasn't straight but it wasn't curly. She had the kind of hair that grew any-which-way if not tamed. Under the hot sun, ash streaks made her appear more of a blonde than she really was. Back home, her hair had its seasons: frizzy in summer but lighter in color, stringy in fall and darker, flat in winter and dry, and bouncier once spring came. In Spain, the season of her hair was simply a mess.

To rinse off the shampoo, she stoppered the sink and dunked her head in the water. She used a towel to get rid of any soapy residue.

Emerging from the bathroom, she ignored the glares from Espinosa and Dolores. They yelled at her that she had used up all the hot water.

"I have class," she said.

The two women glanced at one another.

"She has class," Espinosa said.

"I have thirty minutes to be at work!"

Myria told them in her flawed Spanish that she hadn't had a hot shower in a month.

"You poor little girl," Espinosa said.

"Yes, yes," Myria said. "I'm a poor girl who will be late for class."

Myria pushed open the frosted glass door to the kitchen. She smiled. She and the dueña, who busily chopped onions, were both dressed head to toe in black. Spanish widows clothed themselves in the color of the bereaved long after their spouses had died. *La mantilla*, lacy black veils and shawls worn with stiff, cotton dresses. Black signaled to their family, friends, neighbors that they hadn't remarried, no matter how much time had passed; they remained faithful to the dead. The only ornament, a crucifix with Jesus nailed to the cross around the neck. A pious woman considered remarriage adultery. She attended mass daily, lighting a candle, asking the priest to pray for her husband's soul. The wife who outlived her husband wouldn't break her vows, not even if widowhood left her destitute.

The dueña couldn't be so very poor. She owned the residence. Myria wondered if some handsome gentleman showed her a little attention, would she cast off her mourning garments? How long had the dueña worn her widow's weeds?

Myria's grandfather died when her grandmother was in her forties. She remained a widow for the rest of her life. In her dresser, Myria, discovered negligees with plunging necklines and delicate off-the-shoulder sleeves. Myria liked the robes, silky and colorful with geishas, lily ponds, and green fronds, or pink and blue sashes to wrap around the waist. Maybe the dueña had a drawer full of lingerie stashed away? Who knew what the dueña hid under all that black cloth?

Myria waited for the dueña to look up from the stove. A platter of trout—head, eyes and gills, dusted in white flour sat within easy reach on the counter.

"I have class today," Myria said.

The dueña picked over the fish. She found one she liked and tossed it into the large, round pan, where it sizzled in hot oil.

"The *café* and *tostado* is on the table." She frowned at Myria. She was too busy for idle chatter.

"I'm going to study literature."

"You left your mother and father for that?"

"They want me to study."

The dueña bent over to examine the blue flame under the smoldering pan.

"*Literatura?*"

"Yes, literatura," Myria said.

"You should be working to help your parents," the dueña said.

"My parents want me to have an education."

"So you come here? What is wrong with your own country?"

"Maybe because Spain is a great country," Myria said.

"You are not in Spain. You are in Sevilla," the dueña said. "We are different from the rest of Spain. Ach, the Basques! The north! We keep our traditions."

"The world is changing."

"Is it? What can the world do for us?"

"Maybe not use so much olive oil," Myria said. "It isn't healthy."

"Not healthy! We use the best oil anywhere."

"I know but—"

The dueña went to wash her hands under the kitchen sink.

"You have a problem with the food? Americans always complain to me about the food."

"Do you have any eggs that aren't fried? All this fried food isn't good for me. It's too much."

"Eggs? You want me to make you eggs?"

"Can you?"

The dueña returned to the stove and turned off the burner. "One day, I will make a Spanish tortilla."

The building was equipped with an elevator, although it was so often out-of-order that Myria had gotten into the habit of taking the stairs.

Amelia called out to her. "Wait for me."

Myria held the front door open as Amelia walked down the foyer applying lipstick, no need for a mirror. If Myria tried such a trick, she would end up looking like a clown. Amelia liked pastels, fuchsia, magenta and green—but especially fuchsia. She had slacks in fuchsia, blouses in fuchsia, and scarves in fuchsia. To Myria, she resembled an exotic flower, an orchid or bird-of-paradise.

"You washed your hair," Amelia said. "It smells nice."

Two-inch stilettoes didn't slow Amelia down a bit. She must have been born in those heels to be able to walk so fast.

"You weren't at lunch yesterday," Myria said.

"Did I miss something?"

"Not much."

"My boyfriend is in town. He took me out."

"How nice," Myria said.

"He is very good to me. Loyal, you know."

"How did you meet him?"

"My mother introduced us."

"She likes him?"

"She thinks he is the perfect man for me. She was once engaged to his brother."

Engaged to her brother? How old was Amelia's boyfriend? "I don't understand."

"He was her true love."

"Why didn't they marry?"

"He died. He had a weak constitution."

"How horrible," Myria said.

"Why horrible? He was young."

"How old was he when he died?"

"Maybe eighteen."

"Only eighteen years old!"

They had gone the way of the Avenida de la República Argentina. The Guadalquivir was now in sight.

"It must be terrible to die so young," Myria said.

"To die young is less terrible than to grow old," Amelia replied. She paused to reach into her bag and pulled out a pair of pink-rimmed sunglasses. A man, coming in the other direction and catching sight of her, turned to follow them.

"No te vayas por el sol, porque los bombones se derriten."

Amelia didn't bother a look in his direction. The catcaller crossed the street.

"What did he say?"

"He said," Amelia responded in English, "do not walk in the

sun because it melts the best sweets."

"How romantic," Myria said.

"Not so romantic. Men use that *piropo* all the time."

The river behind them, Amelia remarked that her office was just around the corner. The woman gave Myria two kisses.

"Will you be at lunch?"

"No," Amelia said, "the boyfriend again."

Myria returned the other woman's kisses.

"One day you will tell me about your lover."

"I don't have a lover," Myria said, surprised that a Spanish woman would speak of "lovers." A lover meant sex, and Spanish women were reputedly sheltered. Under General Franco, during the years of the dictatorship, women weren't allowed to wear bikinis on the beach, a couple making-out in public could get in trouble with the police, there was no contraception, divorce was banned.

"Now you are keeping secrets," Amelia said.

"There's no one."

"Yes, there is. He is far away."

"How do you know?" Myria asked.

Amelia spoke very quickly in Spanish, something about Myria's soul and brokenness and her eyes, and then she said she had to leave because she didn't want to be late.

"Before I go," Amelia said. "I always wanted to tell you that you seem Spanish to me."

"I do?" Hadn't Neil and his friends picked her out immediately? Her jeans and sneakers gave her away as an American. What had one guy said? She looked German.

Amelia stepped off the curb oblivious to the dangers. Stop signs, street lights, speed limits; all of it went unheeded by drivers.

"I have no time. Later, I will tell you"

Come! Learn Spanish in Seville. The Spanish Language Institute, established in 1977, makes its home in the historic quarter of Santa

Cruz, where the ancient ambience of the neighborhood has been preserved. Our school is located in a building that will enchant with its Moorish architecture.

Affordable tuition, individualized programs, and small group classes make the Spanish Language Institute the finest Seville can offer. We teach 100% Spanish. All classes are conducted by native speakers trained in their area of specialization. Our method of teaching is based in the traditions of Spain's famous Real Academia: *Limpia, fija y da esplendor.*

Myria wondered if she had gotten the date for the start of class confused. She had rung the bell, pulled at the handle, expecting the door to the Institute to swing open and to find the halls crowded with students, waiting outside classrooms, talking excitedly among one another. But the door didn't open; the building was locked.

With the Institute's brochure in her hand, she sat on the historic marble steps of the historic Moorish building, and scanned the material she'd received in the States. There, right there on her schedule: Thursday, the 25th of September. Classes begin at 900 hours. Nine o'clock, right?

"May I help you?"

Myria looked up, startled that someone would speak to her in English. A woman stood on the bottom step, her left arm weighed down by a bulging leather briefcase, the handles so weathered they couldn't possibly last much longer. Around her scrawny neck, a clutch of skeleton keys of varying sizes hung from a silver chain.

"I'm here for class. It says on my schedule that classes begin today at 9:00."

The woman shifted the briefcase from her left hand to her right.

"Are you a teacher?"

"No, I'm the director. You are to call me Señora Blandura."

The woman referred to herself as señora but her accent was pure Queens.

"I'm Myria Hirschberg. I'm so glad you're here. I thought I got the dates mixed up." She stuffed her schedule and the brochure into her knapsack, and got to her feet.

"Welcome to the Spanish Language Institute. Doors open at 9:00 but classes won't begin for another hour. You don't have a schedule?"

Myria was in the woman's way. The marble steps were too narrow to fit both of them.

"Maybe you should go get some coffee," Señora Blandura said.

"I don't want to be late for class."

"The students always arrive late. Class begins at 10:00. The students are never on time."

"Americans are very punctual." Myria smiled, hoping her joke wasn't lost on Señora Blandura.

"When they leave the States they seem to lose all track of time."

"It's easy to lose track of time here."

"Lose track of time." Señora Blandura sighed. "In Sevilla, time moves to its own rhythm."

How poetic! Although there was nothing poetic in Señora Blandura's voice except resignation.

"Life is very different here."

Señora Blandura took a step up "I have to open the office. The café around the corner is good. Lots of Americans go there."

Myria got to her feet and let the other woman by. She was about to ask the señora if the café was expensive. Coffee would be nice but she didn't want to spend her limited budget going to an expensive café.

"The café is full of Americans."

"It sounds great."

Señora Blandura took the chain from her neck, examining

the numerous keys. She tried one and then another. Finally, she managed the lock and the door opened.

"Classes begin at 10:00," Señora Blandura repeated.

"I won't be late."

"Take your time. And besides, 10:00 is when classes are supposed to begin. You can't be late."

You can't be late. As in, there is no such thing as being late.

Myria started off, passing the mustard colored houses, carved doors set deep into the homes, some protected by elaborate grates, others with splintering wooden porticos. She entered a small plaza chock-a-block with cafes.

A man, his beat-up straw hat covering his face, dozed on one of the benches. The historic city had its share of poverty: children with stumps for feet; women wrapped up in black rags, their faces covered, hands outstretched; elderly people on crutches. She'd heard stories about mothers cutting off their children's arms or legs, sending them to beg in the streets.

She stood for a moment, trying to decide which establishment would extract the least from her purse. The price for a coffee could be two, three times what her budget would allow.

The café was a small cave of a place. Patrons stood shoulder to shoulder at the bar. Ruddy ham shanks hung from hooks above their heads, along with thick bundles of puckered sun-dried tomatoes and ropes of garlic.

Myria could always tell the Spaniards apart from the Americans by the shoes they wore. Spaniards never wore sneakers. Just as Señora Blandura said, the bar was full of sneakers, calling out orders to the waiter, who hustled to their demands.

A blonde shouted "Hey there" to her. Her name Myria soon learned was Samantha. She exuded a girl-next-door attractiveness, eyes of blue and hair of amber waves of grain. She had a natural friendliness about her.

"Just squeeze in," she said.

The girl talked. Myria listened. She was from Colorado. She was drop-dead tired from the flight. She was studying at the Institute for Spanish.

"You mean the Spanish Language Institute?"

"Is there another one?"

Myria responded that there were probably a dozen in Sevilla.

"I only just got here three days ago," Samantha said. "I had something like a five hour lay-over in New York. I haven't even unpacked." She was staying with a family and she couldn't understand a word they said. "Gosh, not one word of English? Doesn't everyone speak a little English?" Samantha's voice was full of bubbles, cheerful.

The cup in front of her empty, Samantha picked it up and leaned over the counter.

"More café, por favor."

Myria could tell from the way Samantha had ordered her coffee, without as much as a hiccup, that she wasn't self-conscious when it came to the language. Myria had been studying Spanish for four years. She could read it, write it, but those skills didn't translate when it came to speaking. Why couldn't Myria snap her fingers and say what she wanted? It was if her tongue grew a foot longer in Spanish and she was always tripping over it.

"Are you going to get something?" Samantha asked.

"Sure," Myria said. She ordered an espresso.

"This Spanish coffee is too strong for me." Samantha told the waiter she needed more milk. He'd been staring at her as though she was one of the Seven Wonders of the World.

"American coffee isn't as strong," Myria said, and to the waiter: *"¡Oye! Mi café por favor."*

"I don't even drink coffee back home."

"I'm a coffee drinker. The coffee here is better."

"Oh sure," Samantha said. "It's better than the food."

"You've only been here a few days."

"It seems like forever," Samantha said. "I haven't had a single moment to myself. The first day my host father picked me up from the airport. When I got to the house, there must have been thirty people there. All of them wanted to meet me."

"Where are you living?"

"I live with a family. They're good people. I just wish I didn't have to meet every single one of their relatives."

"I meant where are you living?"

"You mean what street?" Samantha sniffed at her coffee. Her expression! Not so different from a little girl about to dive into the deep end of the pool, all but holding her nose.

"Around the corner," Samantha said. She still hadn't taken a sip of coffee.

"You live in Santa Cruz?"

"My family owns this—I don't know what to call it. It has a courtyard and a fountain. When I saw it, I thought I must be dreaming," Samantha said. "In a million years I never imagined I'd be staying in a house that had its own courtyard."

"What's your house like back home?"

"Back home? Oh, it's not so much. We live on a ranch."

Myria smiled. Samantha, the yellow rose of Colorado, the cowgirl who lived on the range.

"No ranches where I'm from," Myria said. "There are a lot of farms."

"Where are you from?"

"Back east," Myria said.

"Really!" As if "back east" was the most exciting place in the world. "I went on a field trip to New York once. We were only there a week. Are you from New York?"

"My grandmother lives in New York." And then: "Do you have the time? Classes begin at 10:00."

Samantha hadn't the faintest idea of the time but if Myria thought they should get going then they should get a move on.

Myria called out to the waiter. "How much is the coffee?" As she expected, it was ridiculously expensive. She could have five coffees in Los Remedios for the price of one in Santa Cruz.

"Don't you worry about it," Samantha said. "I'll pay."

"No, really, I'd rather you didn't."

"My treat," Samantha said and tossed several hundred *pesetas* worth of coins onto the counter. "Do you think that's enough?"

"That should do it," Myria said.

Students arrived to the chiming bells of the nearby cathedral. The Institute, catering to its American students, had none of the restrictions imposed on the southern district of the city. As befitted historic Santa Cruz, which depended on tourism for economic survival, the Institute was brightly lit; the walls shone with dark, red resin, and the marble floors gleamed.

The director waited just inside the Institute door, the necklace of skeleton keys still in a jumble around her neck. She wished incoming students good morning, announced that orientation would be held in one of the classrooms down the hall.

Students assembled in the designated classroom, its windows open, the plaza in view. A large fan whirred from the ceiling above. Late September and the sun still raged in the unsheltered sky above the rooftops of Sevilla. The students had been all but put to sleep by the rising temperature.

Señora Blandura repeated her wishes for a good morning. She instructed her charges to make every effort to speak Spanish. If any of the students wanted a change in schedule or had any other matter of personal importance she was the person to whom they should report.

The students roused themselves, reached for knapsacks slung across the back of chairs, and began to shuffle out of the room.

Later, many years later, Myria could still recall the first thing she noticed about Killian. It wasn't that Killian had arrived late, just as Señora Blandura was winding up orientation, or how the squat desks were too puny to accommodate his height; he was easily six feet tall and willow thin. The most striking thing about him, the thing everyone must have noticed first when it came to Killian was his blue eyes; they were an ocular miracle, iridescent.

CHAPTER SIX

BREVITY

The fish had been set out, together with the rest of the meal, by the time Myria arrived at the residence.

Most days, she was first to the table, waiting for the Spanish women to return from work. They heaved sighs of relief, and eagerly shared their daily woes: the irritable co-worker Dolores couldn't bear much longer and hoped would get fired; Espinosa's manager, who wore too much perfume, a cheap scent that smelled less of flowers than urine; the obligatory meetings Maria Celeste had to sit through, taking notes by hand that she couldn't read because everyone talked so fast and she couldn't keep up; a coffee break spoiled because Patricia received one phone call after another from disgruntled clients; the lack of decent pay (a universal complaint among the women); Esperanza exhausted from her rounds at the hospital, where there were too many sick people and not enough doctors; Estrella worried about how budget cuts at the University would come to no good. Amelia would listen, nod in sympathy, and finish her meal before she joined the chorus of lamentations. She said she couldn't talk if she were hungry. "I am always dying of hunger," she once remarked.

"Yes," Espinosa had responded, "just like the rest of Spain."

Myria went to her room, dumped her backpack on the cot and

returned to the dining room.

Espinosa chatted with Dolores. They shared a cigarette between them, passing it back and forth over uneaten fish heads and other food scraps left on their plates.

"Why do you carry that ugly sack," Espinosa said as soon as Myria sat down.

"You mean my backpack?" Myria was too busy translating to take offense at Espinosa's remark. She assumed that just about every word launched in her direction contained an insult of some sort, and yet Espinosa didn't single her out specifically. She treated everyone the same and spoke whatever was on her mind. Rarely, did Myria let the people around her know what she really thought. A college friend had called her on it: "I love the way you lie. I think they call it charm."

Maria Celeste excused herself from the table and came back from her room with a fresh pack of smokes. She offered Myria a cigarette.

"I don't smoke."

Actually, Myria did smoke. She quit because it annoyed Sheffield. Smoking wasn't a habit with him. She'd seen him once, maybe twice, with a cigarette; he was drunk. Sheffield drank a lot.

"My mistake. I thought you smoked," Maria Celeste said.

"I'll try one," Myria said.

The Spanish black tobacco, very strong, no filter, made her want to retch. After the initial shock came a sense of relief. She'd been trying so hard not to do things: not to use too much water or offend the dueña or tell Espinosa off; not to smoke or drink because she worried that once she got going she wouldn't stop. The cigarette, vile as it tasted, liberated her, and an unhealthy liberation seemed better at the moment than no liberation at all. She would let herself go more. No one had locked her up in that laundry closet the dueña called her bedroom. No one made her self-conscious about her Spanish. Her instructors had never

failed to praise her. Spanish wasn't the problem. If she had studied
French, German, Dutch, Welsh, it would have been the same: her
voice in another language didn't sound like her voice; the accent,
intonation, phrasing—all of it was foreign. She wasn't herself
in another language. She would no sooner get a sentence or two
out and want to retreat back to her mother tongue, to her own
self, and that self, the Myria she knew, could only be at home in
English, with its galloping rhythms and the nasal accent common
to Yankees.

She had to smile. The Spanish women called all Americans
Yanquis. Myria really was a Yankee. Or rather, she would be a
Yankee if she could trace her forebears to the 1600s, came from
old money, and lived in some crumbling ancestral home. She'd
grown up in an old mill town, where the forest reclaimed the river
banks after the factories closed and the textile workers picked up
and moved elsewhere.

Sheffield. He wanted so much to hide his privileged New York
upbringing in those thickets, rolling hills, the bogs and logging
roads. When they first met, the day he walked up to her as she
sat reading on the lawn, he was sporting his rural, casual style:
flannel shirt, jeans, Timberlands. She assumed he must be from
New England, just like her, woodsy instead of metropolitan. Most
of the students looked as if they came from anywhere but New
England. Weeks of walks and talks, and parties, went by before
Myria learned that Sheffield's backwoods Yankee look was pure
put on.

"Myriam, are you around this weekend?"

"Why, yes I am."

"No plans?"

"I have a lot of work."

"Studying?"

"I have a lot of reading to do for Spanish."

"Who would have thought? Isn't Spanish supposed to be

easy?"

"I don't know who told you that."

"Well, I can't recall at the moment." Pause. "Myriam, I'm being summoned to New York this weekend."

"You won't be around?"

"Why don't you come with me?"

"Okay, well, yes, I would like to."

"I should let you know…"

"What?"

"You might have heard of my stepfather. Sam Judge."

Heard of Sam Judge? Who was Sam Judge? She smiled to cover up her ignorance on the subject of Sam Judge. Sheffield mumbled something about Sam being a columnist for The New York Times. He looked embarrassed. She couldn't tell if he was embarrassed for himself or her.

"I'm sorry. I guess I never read the newspaper."

"Sorry? How strange of you, Myriam, to be sorry. There is nothing to be sorry about."

Sheffield's need to go incognito became clearer to her. Myria could see why Sheffield would want to trick everyone into assuming he was a farmboy instead of the stepson of a journalist who wrote a column for a big, important newspaper. It could get uncomfortable.

Apparently, it was, because Sheffield talked very little after that about his stepfather, not to mention his mother, or his actual father.

Myria was polite and quiet around his parents. Polite and silent. Sheffield tacitly approved. The less said, the better, right?

Sheffield sometimes joked about snobs. He joked about Stilton, and how great Stilton was. Amused, he explained that Stilton was a truly great cheese. Myria didn't get the joke. How could anyone work themselves up, much less put on airs, about cheddar? Ah, but Stilton was not just any cheese. It came from England. And

Sheffield came from the Upper East Side. People on the Upper East Side could sniff out the good cheddar from the bad.

Myria drew gingerly on the cigarette, the smoke heavy in her lungs. She gazed at the faces around her. Espinosa lit another cigarette while the other women finished their food or drank coffee. None of the women knew her, perhaps with the exception of Amelia, but with her it came down to intuition. Amelia, the psychic one, the gitana.

It wasn't necessarily a bad thing she couldn't be herself in Spanish; it might be a very good thing. Maybe she couldn't be whoever she wanted to be because no one could play a part so well that they erased themselves completely. But why try so hard? She could learn something from these women if she would open up.

She stubbed her cigarette out in her fish. The problem was Sheffield, not the language or culture or the infernal heat. Missing him, sad because she wasn't with him, jealous because she wondered who else he might be with, angry because he dumped her, mortified at the way she had broken down the last time she saw him, convinced she would never experience happiness again.

In the kitchen, the phone began to ring: a beige dial-up model with a lock the dueña installed on the rotary-finger wheel to prevent the women from making out-going calls.

Myria hadn't received a single phone call. She hadn't received a letter, not even from her closest friends. Troubling to think that those she believed cared about her could carry on perfectly well in her absence.

"Myria!"

Estrella emerged from the kitchen.

"Myria! You have a phone call."

She got up from the table.

"A phone call? For me?"

"It's an American."

"Are you sure it's for me?"

"Of course, I'm sure. The person asked for you by name."

It must be her mother. Someone had died. Her mother didn't use the phone if she could help it. She didn't like it when people called and she didn't like to return phone calls. If she overheard Myria on the phone, she'd make nervous gestures, or tell her to get off. Noise bothered her mother excessively, and any call announced itself with a shrillness she couldn't bear.

"Mom?"

"Myriam!"

Myriam. Only one person called her by her full name.

"Sheff!"

"I thought you might be interested in learning that there's a seven hour difference between New York and Seville."

"Is that really you? I can't believe you called. I was just...." She was about to say, thinking of you. "It's been an adjustment I was really lonely when I got here. The city was practically abandoned. It's unbelievably hot in August here. People go to the beach. It's better now that school started. I met a girl from Colorado. She lives on a ranch."

Silence

Myria wondered if the line went dead. "Are you still there?"

"I am."

"It's great to hear your voice. How are you?"

"It seemed appropriate to call."

"Appropriate?"

"I've been reading up on Spain. Why I saw today in the paper that the temperature in Seville is a pleasant 85 degrees with scattered clouds and zero percent humidity."

"Thanks for letting me know." Typical Sheffield. He kept things cut and dry, communicating through facts and figures. He was a conduit of information as long as it didn't involve anything personal.

"How did you get this number?"

"I have my ways."

"No, really. I don't remember giving you this number."

"I'm not sure I can indulge your curiosity."

Myria leaned against the counter, receiver cradled between her ear and shoulder.

"What's really amazing is that there is a full seven hours difference between us," he said.

"I'm aware of that."

"Seven hours."

"You've done your math I see."

"Another thing, our voices are traveling across thousands of miles of underwater fiber optic cables."

"No satellites?"

"Impractible," he said.

"Did you say 'impractible?'"

"Did I? I was referring to the satellites."

"Sheff, are you drunk?"

"Now why would you say a thing like that?"

"Because you're slurring," Myria said. "Are you going to tell me how you got this number?"

"Your mother gave it to me."

"You called my mother?"

"About half an hour ago which would mean that it was 2:00 your time."

"I'm surprised she picked up the phone. How did she seem?"

"She asked how you were."

"Yes, most people do."

"Do what?"

"Ask how people are, Sheffield."

"She asked me how you were," he said, slurry. "She told me to tell you not to worry. Everything is fine there."

"I'm so glad." Myria considered lighting the cigarette. It might calm her. She found his talk about time differences and weather maddening.

"What's going on?" she asked. "Are you okay?"

"Everything is just fine."

"You're in New York?"

"Not for long I hope."

"What are your plans?"

"No plans," he said.

"What happened to the Grand Canyon?" Thousands of miles of heartache and disappointment traveling in an instant through underwater fiber optic cables.

"The Grand Canyon? It's still there as far as I know."

"Okay."

"Still there."

"Good for it."

"Maybe I'll call you again sometime."

"You do that, Sheff. We can talk more about the marvels of transatlantic communication."

She heard him laugh or maybe the connection was going bad.

"I look forward to it," he said.

"You take care, Sheff," Myria said. She could have smashed the receiver on the counter until it broke into a hundred pieces. Instead, she hung up.

Myria returned to the dining room. Espinosa looked in her direction. Before the other woman could utter a word, Myria turned on the tele. "Time for Cristina."

"She is right," Estrella said.

"Poor Cristina," Dolores said, as if the soap opera character were a dear friend.

Myria resumed her place at the table. "Has she told the novio yet?"

"Not yet," Espinosa said. "She will have to tell him sometime."

"I feel sorry for the novio," Dolores said. "He's not such a bad guy."

Espinosa said, "Then I feel sorry for you. The novio is a *bobo*."
Stupid.

"I think so too," Myria said.

"You see," Espinosa said, "even she can figure it out."

CHAPTER SEVEN

DUENDE

Myria stood outside a store that sold stationery, magazines, and books. Above it loomed four balconies whose interiors were partially hidden by balustrades of metal wrought into florid patterns. Painted in bold lettering, outlined in gold, against a black background, she read: Papelería Ferrer 1856. The wooden façade reminded her of the old oak trees back home, each gouge, line, splintering bit of timber. Two large windows, left and right of the deep-set door, displayed shelf upon shelf of leather bound books, vintage posters. There were glass blown lamps—colorful, shimmering globes that reminded her of delicate, hot-air balloons.

The walk down the Calle Sierpes to the store took Myria over the river into the center of the city. *Sierpe*. Serpent. Serpent Street. After Sheff's phone call, it seemed the perfect destination. The street held that peculiar allure for tourists where horrible events had taken place. Centuries past, Sevilla, with its fertile plains and easily accessed by the Guadalquivir, made it home to many people: Muslims, Jews, and Christians. The city was also famous for its missing children.

Infants, baby boys and girls, were taken from their beds, or snatched off the streets, never to be seen again. The Christians blamed the Jews, believing that they had taken the children, so they could cut out their hearts and drain their blood for their Passover meal. The Jews pointed to the Muslims, who no doubt took the children and sold them into slavery. The Moors blamed both the Christians and the Jews, not only for the abductions but for stealing lands that had been under their domain for hundreds of years.

"You are so deep into your thoughts," a voice whispered in her ear.

Myria smiled. The voice she recognized immediately. It was Amelia's voice, soft and preternaturally calm.

"How did you know I'd be here?"

"I did not know. I was walking home and saw you standing like a statue in front of the store."

"I missed you at lunch."

"Good! It makes me feel loved," Amelia replied.

"Did you have a good time with your novio?"

Amelia wore the same shocking pink frames she'd pulled out of her bag that morning, her eyes concealed behind black lenses.

"He is my mother's friend. She has always been in love with him. I told you that already?"

"I don't understand."

"I spend time with him because it makes my mother happy. She imagines us holding hands, the touch of his lips on mine, how he undresses me, slowly, unbuttoning my blouse one button at a time."

"Amelia!" The idea that her mother would ever think about her and Sheffield naked in bed made her cringe. Although, what Amelia described sounded to Myria like something out of Hollywood, a fiction. When had Sheffield ever unbuttoned her blouse one button at a time? He'd just climb on top of her—that was after they'd stripped to their underwear and gotten under the covers.

"You think your mother is different?" Amelia put an arm around her. "All mothers are the same. They want a hot man to fuck their daughter, especially if he is rich."

"You think!" She must seem a naïf to Amelia. How strange! Weren't Americans the sexually liberated ones?

"Be calm. I must concentrate. You know gypsies. We read minds."

"I thought you read palms."

"No, we call those people fortune-tellers."

"Then tell me. What am I thinking?"

"You are thinking about shopping." Amelia laughed. A joyful noise. Myria could listen to her laugh forever. "But that is not what brought you to this place, is it?"

"You tell me?"

"I can tell you that there are cheaper stores much closer to Los Remedios. You will spend too much money here and not get much."

"I don't mind," Myria said. Amelia was right, actually. Her budget didn't allow for much shopping. "It's just so elegant."

"This old place? It is haunted."

"The store?"

"The neighborhood," Amelia said. "It looks nice but it is a graveyard. Sacred ground. Watch where you put your feet."

Step on a crack and you break your mother's back.

"We have a saying in English. I don't know how to tell it to you though."

"Try," Amelia said.

"I don't think it translates."

"We have our sayings too," Amelia said. She ran her hand through Myria's hair. "Tell me in your own words."

"Speak to you in English? I will never get better at Spanish if I do. You told me that."

"Spanish! You use it as an excuse to avoid having to speak what you feel," Amelia said. "And we have that proverb too--you hurt your mother, right? Is that what you really wanted to say?"

How could she know? Maybe Amelia was psychic after all.

"Where I come from children are taught a little rhyme." She pointed to a crack in the sidewalk. "You walk on that and you—"

"And your mother dies," Amelia said. "How many times have you stepped on a crack?"

"I don't believe it," Myria responded. "If I stepped there, nothing would happen."

"You think it silly?" Amelia said. "Americans are rational people. They do everything according to science. Who do you think brought science to the Americas? The Spaniards."

"Americans don't know much about Spain," Myria admitted. "But they do teach us about Columbus in school."

"What do they teach you? About Colón and his glorious discovery? About La Pinta, La Niña, and La Gallega? Did you know that La Pinta was named after a prostitute? *La pintada.*"

"I was taught he sailed on the Pinta, Niña and the Santa María. I've never heard of La Gallega."

"La Santa María came later."

"You mean there were four ships?"

"No, they changed the name of the ship to make it seem more holy." She smiled. "You think I am not telling the truth? What a wonderful sense of humor those sailors had. They liked their women so much they paid to bed them. They named their ships after them."

"I thought all the ships were named after saints."

"*La santa pintada.* The Magdalena was also a prostitute. The blessed one. We see her in all our mothers."

"My mother..." Myria couldn't go on. It was as if she were being strangled. Was she crying? She was but not about her mother. Her mother stopped making her cry a long time ago.

"There is no reason to be so sad," Amelia said. "You've had a bad day, nothing more."

Myria nodded. "Nothing more," she agreed.

"Let us go shopping? It is why you are here, right?"

"I need paper and new pens," Myria said.

"Of course, you do."

Amelia held the door open for her. The narrow entrance, darker as evening came on, welling up with shadows, was less welcoming than the bright sun.

"Did I scare you?"

Myria couldn't tell if she was being teased. "You were the one who said the place was haunted."

"And you said you did not believe in those old tales."

The Papelería Ferrer contained everything its customers could have wished for, and then some. Paper of all types: construction, watercolor, glassine, carbon, wax-coated, stencil, calligraphy, marbled, Mylar, vellum; Cockerel paper, printed with glorious scenes, so that the writer could pen her thoughts on seascapes, mountains, bonsai trees. Myria liked them better than the stationery with repeating geometrical patterns. What attracted her most were the bound diaries, pages unlined, pristine. She picked one off a shelf, ran her hands over the smooth leather cover, the burgundy stitching along the edges. The craftsmanship so lovely that, for a moment, Myria worried she might not be able to write in it—as if to fill those blank pages with her own sloppy script would ruin it. That, and the fact, as Amelia warned, it wasn't cheap. Back home, she wouldn't have indulged herself and bought instead a flimsy spiral bound notebook.

"Very nice," Amelia said. "Elegant. Now we must find something to write with, a pen, one with a beautiful feather."

"A black feather," Myria said. Quill pens always came with a black feather, at least in every picture she'd seen, together with an ink pot.

"I already found you one," Amelia said. "See, this is your pen."

"Which one?" Myria asked.

There were dozens.

"It has the red feather."

"I can't really write with that kind of pen," Myria said. She was south-pawed, a lefty, and even a ballpoint gave her trouble.

"You must. It will go so well with your new writing book."

"It is lovely," Myria said. "But it's not practical."

Amelia shrugged, in that typical Spanish way—as if to say, "Oh well."

"We will find you a pen you can fit in your pocket then."

"Better," Myria said.

"But no black pens. Blue, green, yellow, rose. Every color in the rainbow. For every word a new color." Amelia removed her sunglasses. How she'd been able to see in the dimly lit store was a mystery to Myria. She'd have to be a cat.

"That's a lot of pens. I just need a few."

"You wear black. You write with black pens. You must be a duende."

"Me? I doubt it."

"Black music. Black colors. Black voices," Amelia said, looking Myria up and down. "You have a very deep voice for a woman. A deep voice that makes me think of sex and death." She leaned over and ran her nose along Myria's cheek. It tickled. If anyone else did that Myria would have flinched.

"You smell of duende."

Myria nearly responded that she if she smelled of death it was because she couldn't get a proper shower. As for sex, six months or more passed since she'd slept with Sheffield. Sex with Sheffield had never been good. She couldn't relax and just get into it, anxious that her naked body would turn him off, especially her breasts. Men liked women with small, perky breasts, and pale, flat nipples; or at least Sheffield did. Her first time with him he'd knocked at her door after a Friday night party, a bottle of Stoli in one hand, already pretty much shot. She sat on her bed while he rambled on about two girls he thought cute. They both lived in the same dorm, both dance majors. One was a blonde and the other a bobbed brunette. She didn't say much. Then he kissed her and she kissed him back, and they'd gotten undressed, and it was over in five minutes. In a sleepy voice, he said her breasts reminded him of two large pears. Pears! She grabbed at her shirt, not able to cover herself up fast enough. "Could you leave?" She vowed never to let him touch her again. The next day, he caught up with her on the way to class, asked if she'd go for a drive with him later that afternoon. "For a drive? Where?" He would only say, "You'll see."

On the counter, she noticed a pack of ballpoint pens.

"I'll take one," Myria said to the clerk. The clerk, who'd been sitting on a stool flipping through a magazine, got to her feet. "And this," she added, handing over a leather-bound diary.

"Algo más?"

"No, gracias," Myria said.

Myria watched the clerk tear a sheet of blue paper from a long roller and wrap her purchases, sealing them with Scotch tape.

It was as if she'd just bought herself a present.

CHAPTER EIGHT

GITANOS

Myria and Amelia walked over the Guadalquivir, its banks festooned with lights. The fiesta already in progress: outdoor café patios lively, streets busy, tourists lined up to board the ferry boats for a night on the river.

Amelia stopped abruptly.

"You remember this morning? You remember my words?"

"I'm not sure," Myria said. "You were in such a hurry." She couldn't think of anyone in that foreign place who made for better company. With Amelia, the hole-in-the-heart loneliness subsided, the wound sutured by the woman's glowing presence.

Amelia said: "You live in shadows."

Myria hesitated. She didn't quite understand. She took what Amelia said to mean that she didn't like to attract attention. What was wrong with that? And what would Amelia know of living in the shadows? Everyone and everything, including dogs, birds, and butterflies noticed Amelia.

"Yeah, well," Myria said, lapsing into English and bitterness simultaneously, "I'm not that pitiful, am I?"

"With that voice?"

"What voice?"

"The voice of the martyr," Amelia said.

Myria was angry now.

"You see," Amelia said. "This is better. You are angry but have pushed the shadows away. You force them away."

Myria wished Amelia would drop the whole thing. But, Amelia kept talking.

"If I let you," Amelia said, "you would take my shadow. You would keep it."

"Like follow you everywhere?" This was too much. "It's you, Amelia, who turns up every time I turn around."

"You are confused," Amelia responded. "My shadow, not my person, is what you want to take from me. You want my shadow. You feel it protects you. You feel it is safer that way."

Myria didn't get it. Maybe this was the way gypsies spoke or maybe Amelia just liked being cryptic?

Over Amelia's shoulder, she saw a group of twenty-somethings cruising the street. Spiked hair, studded black jackets, shiny metal belts swinging from their waists, heavy boots.

"You got *plata*," a girl called out, her lips painted black. "We have no money for kief."

Another punker began to rant, "*Plata, plata, plata.*"

Money.

A wire-thin guy spat on the sidewalk. "*Machas*, you like girls more than kief?"

"*Lesbias*," another snorted. "Come on. You want this." He stuck his hand down the front of his pants.

Amelia glanced at Myria, smiled, and said to him, *"Piri telemosa chi athadjol o kam."*

The crotch-grabber glared, spat some more. For a moment, Myria thought he might lunge at Amelia. Then kief girl wrapped her arms around his neck and whispered into his ear.

"Forget him," she said. "You have no money for us, there is no problem." She smiled, her teeth smudged from the black lipstick.

Amelia answered. Whatever she said it wasn't in Spanish. Kief-girl shrugged and whistling to her friends moved on, the others falling in step behind her.

The two women walked down the long avenue, turned a corner, the residence within easy reach now.

"I guess they were gypsies," Myria remarked. "I thought they were punk rockers until you began saying—what did you say? What language were you speaking? It wasn't Spanish. Was it a gypsy language? Romani?"

"Caló," Amelia responded.

"I don't understand."

"The gitanos of Spain speak Caló, not Romani." Amelia frowned.

Myria wondered at the change in her friend. She wondered at Amelia's tone—so full of pins—and if it meant she no longer wanted Myria around. She'd had begun to drain Amelia. She expected too much. She was a shadow thief.

Myria mumbled excuses in the hope that Amelia would soften.

Amelia sighed. "Gypsies exist for you as poetry, not as people."

"I'm not from here" Myria said. It was a lame defense but no other came to mind.

"You think I care if you're from the United States?" Amelia asked. "And so what if I did?"

"I'd worry you'd think—"

"You worry but why? I already told you. Inside, you are Spanish."

"I don't get it. I'm not Spanish. I'm from the U.S."

They climbed the steps to the residence.

"Don't be angry, Amelia."

"Why should I be angry? You see, there you go again. This is what I saw when we first met. Everything that has no importance you take personally and what matters most you pretend you don't take personally."

Myria pushed the door open, holding it for her friend. "Is that why I seem Spanish to you?"

"For other reasons," Amelia said. "In Andalucía, we do not fret about small things. We are busy trying to make enough to put food in our mouths."

"I think you blame us for Spain's troubles."

"Our troubles won't go away because you pity us. You are just one person. Your nationality is your own problem. When I say you seem Spanish, I am not talking nationality."

"Here I feel more American than I do at home," Myria said.

"You might feel that way but you left for a reason. Maybe you don't belong there."

They went inside. Myria expected to hear the tele, or the women squabbling around the table.

"It's so quiet," she said.

Amelia set her bag on the dining room table. Off came one shoe, then the other. Relieved of her heavy purse, she stretched, her slim arms forming an arch over her head. The slightest gesture mesmerized. Amelia could make a yawn appear graceful. She might be the loveliest person Myria had ever met.

"Much better."

Myria slid off her backpack, unzipping it, and pulled out the package she'd bought at the stationery store. Running her hand across the paper wrapping, Myria said: "I don't follow you. You speak in riddles."

"I am a gypsy. We specialize in riddles."

"You are," Myria agreed, and on second thought: "Are you really a gypsy?

Amelia cooed at her, saying she was sweet, and she was going to bed.

"Don't leave," Myria pleaded. "Could we just sit for a while?"

"And do what?

"Let's watch a movie?"

Amelia laughed, as if it were the funniest request she'd ever heard. "Yes, yes. We will sit and watch a movie together. Do you think that stingy landlady has any food left for us in the refrigerator? I'm dying of hunger."

"Me too," Myria said. "I'll go see what's in the kitchen."

"Our jailor has left for the night. The old bitch locks the refrigerator, the telephone. She would lock the bathroom if she could."

"Do you want to go back out? I could take you to supper."

"Could you?" Amelia glanced at Myria's purchases. "You spent a lot on your notebook and pens. Are you scared to be by yourself?"

"No," Myria said. Yes. "I'd really like to take you to supper."

"Another time."

"Why not?" Myria asked.

"You are tired. Tired people attract problems."

"But you're starving," Myria said. "I'm hungry too."

"Ah, I have a secret," Amelia said. "I have a key to the refrigerator. We can eat our dinner and watch a movie here."

"Does the landlady know?"

"Maybe she gave me a copy." Amelia tilted her head, and even in the dim lit room her eyes were green as ever, the sort of green Lorca adored. "Tell no one."

"I won't. I promise."

"Spanish tortilla," Amelia said after she returned from her bedroom with the key, "is marvelous served cold."

CHAPTER NINE

ADRIFT

The following week came and went, and Myria still hadn't unwrapped the notebook she bought at the Papelería Ferrer. During the siesta, she lay on the cot, her face turned to the window. At night, she did the same, not that she was unhappy. Adrift, more than miserable, bored more than troubled. She woke late. By the time she got to the shower, the water amounted to little more than a trickle. Her towel smelled rank. Instead of hanging it out to dry, it got tossed on the floor of her closet, where it lay in a damp heap. She dressed mindlessly, shoving one leg, then another, into the same jeans; pulling the first shirt she grabbed off the hanger over her head. By the time, she emerged from her room everyone had gone, and breakfast was cleared from the table.

After classes, she'd find Samantha at the café near the Institute. The Colorado pageant queen (as Myria thought of her) had every guy in the program vying for her attention. Killian paid court to her as well. The few times he bothered to show up. He turned everything he said into a joke, his accent musical, high pitched.

"You always wear black," he said to Myria. He'd never spoken to her before, not directly.

"So I've been told."

Myria tossed off the remark as though his attentions meant nothing because while those gorgeous blues of his might captivate, it was obvious that he wasn't into her. He wanted Samantha. Myria was certain.

"You're like something out of Black Flag."

"Yeah, I hear that all the time." His comment surprised her. Killian didn't look at all like a Black Flag type of guy. He wore penny loafers, for one thing, and collared shirts: groomed, preppy, and definitely not a Black Flag fan. On the other hand, neither was she. Sure, she'd heard of them, but she couldn't name one song.

From Samantha, Myria learned that Killian's family came from the Midwest. His father was a doctor. He'd been to prep school back east, and after that, went on to college. East or West, Samantha had said, she'd never heard anyone talk that way, and said so to Killian, then "felt real bad" because he got "red in the face," and insisted that if he sounded different it was because he was Irish. "But he's still American! No one in Colorado talks like that. I don't think it's because he's Irish. It's some kind of…" Samantha stopped herself, and then asked Myria if she thought she was being mean. "I don't want you to think I'm like that."

Myria assured her that she didn't think she was being mean. Samantha must have taken that as encouragement. "Maybe he has a problem? Back where I come from, you sound like that and you get called names, bad names."

Myria had lit a cigarette. She was back to smoking regularly now. "I wouldn't worry about it," she replied, and told Samantha how she'd been out with a Spanish friend and they ran into some punk-rockers who called them lesbians. The horror in Samantha's eyes! Myria couldn't restrain herself. For the first time that week, she laughed.

"Where is Amelia?" she asked, over lunch that Friday. The women looked at one another.

"Amelia?"

"She is with her mother"

"She did not tell you? Her mother is not well."

"She is very sick. I think Amelia took time away from work."

"Amelia cannot afford to take time off."

"I do not miss her. It is so nice to have the bedroom to myself."

"Why do you ask?"

Myria said she was just wondering where she went.

"Amelia goes where she wants to," Espinosa said. "Gypsies cannot stay in one place for very long. Her mother is sick? She is lying. Gypsies never tell the truth."

"It is in their blood," Dolores said.

"You mean she moved out?" Myria asked. And didn't tell her?

"Her clothes are still here," Patricia said.

"It does not mean she will be back," Dolores said.

"Why do you call her names?" Myria asked.

"Call her what?" Maria Celeste responded.

"A liar."

"*Si te queda la gorra, póntela,*" Epinosa said. "You know what it means?"

If the hat fits, wear it.

"Yes." Baffled, annoyed, Myria sank into her chair.

"You are an American," Epinosa said. "What do you know about gypsies?"

"Stop it, Espi!" Maria Celeste had heard enough.

Maria Celeste. Celestial Maria. An ethereal name for such a reasonable person.

Espinosa downed her coffee. "I say what I think. And I say out with the Americans. Spain has enough problems."

No one could shut Espinosa up. Myria bit down on her tongue.

"If they leave they will take everything." Maria Celeste glanced at Myria. "It is stupid to send the Americans away. They are the first in the world."

What any of this had to do with Amelia, Myria didn't know. Wanting to change the subject, she asked: "Where does Amelia live?"

"In Triana," Patria said.

"So close?" Triana, another one of Seville's ancient neighborhoods could be easily reached on foot.

"Patricia has no idea of what she is talking about," Epinosa said.

"We share the same room," Patricia said. "Besides, all gypsies live in Triana. Where else would they live?"

"In caves," Espinosa said.

"You are very cruel," Myria said. That woman—she was so tired of her, and her nasty remarks. "But it's okay because fighting with you only makes my Spanish better."

"How generous," Espinosa said, astringent as ever. "The American wants us to bow down to her. She comes from the first world. What is Spain to her? We are a poor country where she can live cheap. Look at her? Just look at her. She crawled out of a trashcan. *Vasura.*"

Vasura. Trash.

"*¡Hija de puta!*"

Daughter of a whore.

"*Tu madre,*" Espinosa snipped. She looked around the table and said: "She thinks she can make me cry."

"Nice!" Myria slumped in her chair. "Laugh at me. Call me trash. Go on."

"There is a lot you don't understand," Patricia said, her tone soothing. "Your government helped Franco. You know Franco?"

"Watch what you say," Maria Celeste warned. "Some of our parents supported Franco too." She looked at Dolores. "Am I wrong?"

"The Civil War is over and has been for many years," Dolores replied, irritated. "Have you noticed?"

"Franco is dead. Spain is not the same as it was," Espinosa said, and for once Myria thought she detected sadness in the woman's voice.

"I apologize," Myria said. "I don't want to argue."

Esperanza offered Myria a consoling smile. "Everything will be fine. You'll see."

"Tell it to her president," Espinosa said.

CHAPTER TEN

DON'T REMIND ME

I am off, chicas."
   "Hugs and kisses."
"Yes, give me a hug?"
"Three kisses."
"Yes, the Spanish way."
"Have a good trip."
"You too, travel well."
"Look at her running for the door."
"I think she has a new man."
"If she had one, you think she would keep it a secret?"
"It is true, she can't keep a secret."
"What will I do without you for two days?"
"And me without you."
"Has anyone seen my keys?"
"You lose everything."
"Hurry, we will miss the bus."
"The first one left already."
"I do not want to miss the second bus."
"Then go, both of you!"
"She is still looking for her keys."
"Ooh la la! Is that a new dress?"

"You are a movie star."

"She is!"

"The boyfriend will be jealous."

"I hope so."

"Ay, out of my way. I am late."

"Did she tell you she's going to the beach?"

"The beach? At this time of year?"

"How are you going?"

"How else? By car."

"I didn't know she could drive?"

"Neither did I."

"Friends are taking me."

"I wish I were spending the weekend in Huelva instead of my mother's house."

"Remember to pack your panties. I meant bikini!"

"I still can't find my keys."

"I am leaving without you."

"Found them!"

"Let us go!"

Myria rolled onto her side. Her pallet, as she'd begun to think of the cot, hard as frozen ground underneath her. Sevilla's sky still flared blue but chilly weather was setting in, normal for October even in that Mediterranean city, and back home, colder still, but there she'd have access to a heavy blanket and thick socks, not some flimsy cotton rag. The cold laid siege to her feet first, then legs, back and neck, her hands the last to succumb.

After suffering through the heat of August, she should welcome the change. No more sweating, suffocating, under the relentless sun. She wouldn't feel the need to bathe herself in Talcum powder. She wouldn't dream of burrowing into soft, cooling silt, safe from the sun. Now, that the swelter months had passed, she should relax, enjoy the respite, and would, if only she'd been prepared.

To take her mind off her shivers, she imagined Julie Andrews singing: Warm woolen mittens and scarves made of kittens, brown fuzzy flannels and sweatpants tied up with strings. These are absolutely my favorite things. When the dog bites, when I'm frothing and feeling mad, I simply remember my favorite things, and then I don't feel so bad.

If she let herself, she could remain prostrate all day, inventing dark parodies, indulging the demons, cursing her lousy luck. She could. She could do anything she wanted to because it was the weekend and she had nowhere to go and nothing to do.

"Stop wallowing," she said to the wall. "Just stop it. You ever think what people would give to be in your position? You, lounging in bed, in an exotic country…"

Oh, God! She was talking to herself, out loud. Well, so be it. She needed a good talking to, and she needed to get out of bed, not that she couldn't just lie there until the sun went down but she wouldn't. She'd get off her cot, or pallet, or rack. She would shower, dress, and comb her hair.

She wanted coffee, with scalded milk, caramelized and sweet. What she wouldn't give for freshly brewed coffee.

But first she had to deal with the dueña.

At the sight of Myria, the dueña frowned, her mottled lips disappearing into heavy jowls.

Oh, joy! *Oye vey! ¡Ay, caramba!* Oh, what the hell.

Myria greeted the widow with a good-day, and then fully aware that she would least expect it, kissed her sagging cheek.

It worked, not that the dueña smiled. She brushed her off in a gentle way.

"You have a little coffee for me? Maybe some hot milk? Some toast?"

"Of course," the woman responded. "You think I let my girls starve."

"No, dueña, no," Myria said. "You are a good woman."

The dueña pointed a wooden spoon at her. "I attend Mass two times a day, every morning and in the afternoon. At night, I say my rosary."

Mass twice a day! Myria had scarcely set foot inside a church.

Sevilla, so famous for its grand cathedral, she had yet to see it. Maybe she would go and have a look. What else did she have to do?

"You have faith and our beloved Savior provides for all your needs." The dueña talked while stirring the milk bubbling on the stove.

"It's that simple, yes?"

"Simple!" The dueña was appalled. "Nothing about the Holy on High is simple. His ways are mysterious."

"Of course they are," Myria said.

"You are Catholic I hope?"

It was best to change the subject.

"I wanted to thank you."

"For what?"

"My mother is so far away. She worries about me all the time. I tell her, don't worry. The dueña takes such good care of me."

"You talk to your mother about me?"

No, she didn't.

"I tell her that you work very hard," Myria said.

"I raised my children by myself when my husband died." The dueña put down her spoon and crossed herself. "May he rest in eternal peace. I am a mother of eight and the grandmother of ten. My work here is not difficult."

Eight kids! Her mother had half as many and felt overwhelmed. Her mother, the artist, doomed to teaching to make ends meet.

"You are blessed to have such a large family," Myria said. She was fast becoming a hypocrite, but she was famished.

The dueña took the pot of milk off the stove.

"You said you wanted coffee too? And toast?"

"How nice of you," Myria said.

"Go to the dining room and I will bring your breakfast."

"You don't have to do that. I could eat here in the kitchen,"

In a starchy voice, the dueña said, "First rule of the house, No men allowed. Second rule, No eating in the kitchen."

Myria couldn't see why. In the center of that scrubbed spotless perfection of a kitchen stood a table, its enamel muddied by age. The table could easily seat six people.

"In my country, people never eat breakfast in the dining room, always in the kitchen," Myria said. She'd grown tired of the dining room, dreary because it had no windows. She would rather eat right there, in that space made a little brighter by the glamour of the frosted glass doors behind which she could imagine not a laundry closet—not that miserable cell—but a cozy place illumed by sunny skies.

"Do you want your breakfast or not?"

"Very much," Myria said.

"Good, I will bring it to you in the dining room."

Myria chewed her scorched toast; it was like trying to eat a rock coated in butter. The coffee she couldn't complain about because it was wonderfully hot, and that was all that mattered.

She could hear the dueña puttering about. Instead of the usual for lunch, she'd gotten into the habit of preparing a light meal for Myria on the weekends: *jamon seranno*, cheese, and bread, some fruit for dessert. The dueña left the food out on the kitchen counter covered with a dish towel.

Myria finished her coffee, picked up the cup and plate, and carried them into the kitchen, the sink already filled with soapy water.

"I can wash these," she said to the dueña. "You can go."

The dueña threw on her shawl, gave her a short lecture about how to wash the dishes and where to stow them.

"May you enjoy your family," Myria said, by way of good-bye.
The woman heaved a sigh. "You should be so blessed."
Was she joking? She was! The dueña had made a joke.
"Remember to clean up your mess."
"Not to worry, dueña."
"I return on Monday morning. I expect a clean house."
"*Por supuesto*," Myria said.
Of course.

Myria stood, arms apart on the countertop, and stared at the
sink, the cups, plates, spoons sunk beneath a white foam-scum of
soap bubbles. She braced herself, assuming the water gelid as the
North Atlantic in winter. "Nothing to do about it," she muttered
and plunged both hands in to discover the basin still warm—if
not as luxurious—as a manicure bath. Fingers stiff from cold
began to relax, and a good bit of time passed before she got to
work on the dishes.

New York had its skyscrapers, Spain its cathedrals. And then
there was the Catedra de Sevilla: an amalgam of religious fervor,
artistic passion, and material brilliance said to be one of the largest
churches in the West. A gothic citadel.

People came from all over the world to pay their respects, to see
the legendary materialize before their eyes. Catholicism aside, the
cathedral offered something for everyone: the tombs of Columbus
and Pedro, the Cruel; paintings by Murillo and Goya; the gilded
altar of the main sanctuary; the glorious Giralda tower. It was all
there and more, housed in splendor: religion, art, history.

Once inside, Myria discovered Columbus's tomb, the mariner's
remains not far from the main entrance. The earnest expressions
of her fellow tourists, their gasps and whispers, would have
induced in her the same solemnity, but the sarcophagus brought
back Amelia's joke about *La pintada*, the prostitute, and she

laughed, which earned her numerous dirty looks. .

Amelia! Where had she gone? She missed her friend.

Myria extricated herself from the crowd, moving on to the nave, and further still to the main sanctuary with its images of Christ in the hundreds, his story told in gold and silver, oil and fresco. An astonishing scene before which the faithful genuflected, bowed their heads, broke down and wept. And there she was, in the middle of it, a lonely-planet traveler, who cried often enough and still couldn't work up so much as a tear for Christ.

Maybe it was enough for one day.

She retraced her steps to the residence. If Amelia were there, she'd no doubt remind her: Step on a crack and your mother dies. On those streets, cracks were unavoidable. They reminded her of the shingle beaches back home—pebbly underfoot. Lovely it was to hear the music of tumbling stones as the waves rolled in and then back out to sea. Singing beaches.

She wondered if Spain, so famous for its sun and surf, had singing beaches the way they did back home. The New England coastline. She could look out on the ocean, marvel at mast and skiff, ship and seabird, lighthouse and rock-cliff.

Memory, the great enemy, and its pincers of homesickness; memory, the trickster, it took all forms. Every bit of her ached from remembering, even the feel of rough stone underfoot made her yearn for familiar ground.

She kept walking, neared the café, the one where she'd met the sailor. Sailor was rather quaint for a man who spent his days on an aircraft carrier. No matter. He'd come and gone, probably out to sea, on his warship. Most likely, he'd forgotten her. Why should she care? He was married, not to mention in the Navy, and even more importantly, he was married, although he'd been sweet to her, gave her a rose, not that it meant anything because he was married. They could be friends, if he weren't in the Navy, and a bombardier—and married.

"Myria!"

She knew that voice. "Killian!"

The café was shut-down for the siesta but there was Killian, lounging in a patio chair, wearing Ray-Bans and taking in the sun.

"It's fabulous here, isn't it?"

"Killian, the café won't open for another hour at least. You could get arrested for…"

"Loitering? In Spain?"

"I was going to say trespassing."

"Please!"

She waited to see if he would do the polite thing and from the aluminum chairs stacked in a corner bring one to her.

He didn't, so she stood.

"I can't get enough sun," he said

"You sound positively opiated. Too much sun does that to a person."

Arms folded over his chest, head tilted back, legs spread out before him, he did seem knocked out. She noticed he'd traded in his penny loafers for a pair of brown Docksiders.

"Been here for hours," he said. "This is a great place."

"I pass it nearly every day. I've never seen you here before."

"It's my new discovery," he said. "Nice to sit here by that— whatever they call it."

"The Guadalquivir?"

"Is that how you say it?"

"It's an Arabic word. It means long river."

"Anyone could see that," he said.

"You don't sound particularly interested."

"Not really," he said, "now you on the other hand."

"What about me?"

"I was just thinking of you."

"You were not."

"I was. I was thinking wouldn't it be delightful if Myria were here so I could get a cigarette off her."

And here she thought it might be because he was delighted to see her.

"You don't buy your own?"

"Why would I?" he replied.

"Well, because you wouldn't have to spend your entire day waiting around for me." She regretted the remark immediately; it came off as serious, implied some desire on his part.

He confirmed her fears, saying, "An entire day—no, a couple of minutes perhaps."

"Well then I won't take up any more of your precious time."

"You really can't take a joke, can you?"

Myria didn't respond. She was thinking of ways to punish him, and not just any punishment, something of biblical proportions.

"I can take a joke but right now I need to go."

He nodded and then gripping the arms of the chair hoisted himself up. "I'll come too."

Come where? To the residence! "I wasn't headed anywhere special."

"Fabulous."

He made absolutely no sense.

"Killian, don't you have somewhere to be?"

"Don't remind me." He sighed, or sobbed. Myria couldn't tell. She focused her attention on the river—the to and fro of boats, the gulls cavorting overhead—while he got a hold of himself.

"My host mother is worse than a prison guard. She keeps track of my every move and reports back to my father, who tells my mother. I get a barrage of phone calls. Why don't I eat with the family? Am I staying out late? When was the last time I went to Mass?"

"You're Catholic?"

"More than you'll ever know," he said.

"Excuse me?"

"Your name—Myriam—it's a Jew's name. If you were Catholic, you'd go by Mary."

She'd never heard anyone put it so bluntly: a Jew's name.

"I really have to go," she said.

"Let's go together," he said. "Find a bar, something."

"I can't."

"At least, let me walk you to your place."

She hesitated. Sure, he had the bluest eyes, a cherubic face, but he was glib. She didn't do well with that sort at all.

"You don't have to," she said. "I know my way around."

"Where do you live?"

"Across the bridge in Los Remedios," she said and added: "in a convent."

"I doubt it."

Was he calling her a whore! She couldn't let that one slide.

"Don't be an ass."

"It was a joke, Myriam. A joke. Are you always so prickly?"

"Only when someone calls me a—"

"What? A tart?" He laughed.

Tart. Prep school-speak for "slut."

"You're quite the comedian," she said. "I do live in a convent, sort of. It's an all-female residence. No men allowed."

"No men? How very provincial," he said.

"It has its advantages."

"And they are?"

She could have said: because of Sheffield, because she was tired of boys who refused to grow up, because the rent was cheap, because she didn't want to live with a family, because her own family drove her crazy, because Sheffield drove her crazy, because he'd called and didn't bother to say he missed her, because she couldn't stop thinking about him, because anything was better than wondering if he had ever really loved her.

When she said nothing, he asked: "Are men at least allowed to walk you home?"

"If I allow it," Myria said.

"Then allow me."

He talked the entire way to her place, in that chanting way he had.

"This is it?" Killian said, less than impressed when they'd reached the door to the residence.

"It's your basic high-rise."

"How much do you pay?"

"Not much."

He volleyed more questions her way. Did the rent include board and lodging? Did she have her own room? Could she use the kitchen? How many roommates? Were they all Spanish?

Yes, yes, no, seven, yes.

"Can I call you?"

He'd walked her home. He was asking for her phone number. He'd been obnoxious, insulting even, but he was trying to make it up to her. The only problem was: "I don't remember it."

He grabbed her hand, turned it palm up. "Do you have a pen?"

"What for?" She tried without luck to take back her hand.

"You won't give me your number so I'll give you mine."

"You're going to write your phone number on my palm? What are we? Ten years old?"

"Maybe." His smile, puckish.

"I don't think it's a good idea for me to call you."

He released her. The sunglasses came off, and the sky had its competition in those blue eyes.

"How about I give you my number?"

"It's all the same," he said.

"No, because if I call you, your host mother will know and your mother will ask why some girl named Myriam is calling you."

He didn't respond, not a word out of his mouth, which usually did double-time. His silence was excruciating; the worst possible sign that he might agree. While he pondered, her mind flew to all the dark corners of insecurity: she wasn't rich enough, educated enough, good looking enough. Enough. Enough!

At last, he said: "How could you forget your phone number?" His upper lip trembled.

Unbelievable! He thought she was rejecting him. He wasn't mean, not innately, but a child; a little boy who couldn't bear the merest hint that he was anything less than adored.

"Wait. I have it written down somewhere."

"Are you certain I can't come with you," he asked, his confidence restored.

"Rules of the house, no men allowed."

"I was teasing you."

"You don't know my dueña. If I brought a—" She was about to say "boy." Instead, "a guy into the residence and she found out I'd be on the street."

"I can wait."

"It might take a while."

"I'll wait."

Keys. Door. Stairs. Kitchen. Her room.

Where was the envelope the Institute sent her, the one with all the helpful tips, a list of residences, her address and phone number?

It must have taken half an hour or more before she was running down the steps, expecting that Killian had gotten tired of waiting for her and left. He was still there, smoking a cigarette.

CHAPTER ELEVEN

KISS

Fleeting hope, the speedy transit of what the future could hold; that quick slippage of wishes; to fleet with them. Sail away, sail away.

Away from where?

She wanted to drown herself, mortified that Killian, when she offered him her cheek, had cringed. She hadn't meant for him to kiss her—not an American kiss, on the lips—but in the Spanish way. Talk about mixed messages: first, he'd absconded with her hand, insisting she give him her phone number, and after she gave it to him, he'd fled.

Her supper plate freighted with crusty Spanish pan, ham, manchego, Myria sat down to eat. It was so quiet, she could hear herself chewing. She put down her sandwich, went to turn the knob on the old television set, then back to her food.

A man in a uniform of olive gray materialized on the screen. Polished medals and ribbons of all stripes pinned to his jacket, under which he wore a white shirt and black tie, the background a tapestry of florid images. He faced the camera, two microphones to his right, his speech deliberate. He could have been made of plaster, or a wax statue, hardened and set behind a magisterial desk, only his lips moving, or eyes fixed on the written document before him as he addressed the country.

"Palacio de Congresso;" "autoridades civiles;" "mantener el orden constitucio-nal;" "proceso democracia," "por referéndum."

The Congressional palace. Civil authorities. Maintain constitutional order. Democractic process. By referendum.

Myria recognized the footage, the light orchestral preamble, the patriotic bravura of the Spanish national anthem that followed the King's speech. Juan Carlos Borbón, the night: February 23, 1981.

The Borbón king was calling for "order." In the past, order meant oppression, years of it, under General Franco, who had bided his time before the Civil War in Spanish Morocco. When the moment came, the fascists had crossed the Straits of Gibraltar, troops ripe for action, hammered Andalucía with artillery before moving north. Whether militants or not, the people lived the terror. Loyalists became rebels, rebels loyalists, right was left, or the reverse—and a grim war became a cause célébrité with the likes of Hemingway and Orwell joining the Republican front.

But that was back in the 1930s. And Franco, now dead, had designated Juan Carlos his successor. A King on the Spanish throne once more. Many thought him the General's puppet, and decades later, in the 1980s, as the left gained power, the Falangists chaffed and plotted, then struck again in the hopes that the royal groomed by their exalted leader would support them.

"The Message of His Majesty the King" had lost none of its fascination. It was still prime-time news three years after El Tejerazo, when Antonio Tejero strolled into the Congressional Palace, a pistol in hand, along with two hundred armed soldiers. Leopoldo Calvo Sotelo, on the verge of being elected Prime Minister, was a socialist, and the right-wing, devoted to Franco's memory, acted out its extreme displeasure by holding Parliament hostage at gunpoint.

The next day, the coup aborted, Leopoldo Calvo Sotelo was

confirmed as Spain's Prime Minister. The socialist could now shake hands with the monarch.

The phone. It was ringing.

"Digame."

Speak.

A muffled "Myriam" followed.

"Killian, is that you? I can scarcely hear you."

"Give me a minute."

She waited.

"Good, they're gone. Can you hear me now?"

She could. "Who is gone?"

"My keepers," he said, bitterly.

"Is the family so horrible?"

"I'm going mad."

He wasn't the only one.

"That bad is it?" she said.

"We had such a row."

"It doesn't sound good."

When he didn't respond, she said: "Are you still there?"

"Unfortunately, yes."

"You do seem miserable."

"Miserable would be an understatement."

A surge of emotion swept over her. She nodded in sympathy until she remembered he couldn't see her. It was herself she felt sorry for as much as Killian.

"If there were something I could do to make it better, I would."

"Well, now that you mention it, let's go out."

"Go out? When? You mean tonight?"

"It's Saturday. Who stays in on a Saturday?"

She did, for one.

"Can you give me a minute?"

Myria didn't give him a chance to say "yes" or "no." She put down the phone, or meant to. The receiver slid off the kitchen counter, where it dangled from its cord. She left it to hang and went into the dining room, stood there. The tele had gone blank. It often did. Interruptions in service were common occurrences.

It wasn't that she didn't want to see Killian. She didn't want him to see her, not then, when her hair hadn't been washed in a week, and she didn't know if she had a clean change of clothes. And then there was money. She was low on cash. Reason enough. She got back on the phone.

"Are you there?"

"Still here," Killian said.

"It's not a good night for me."

"I didn't hear what you said." He added that he couldn't stay on the phone much longer.

"I get it. I can't talk much longer either."

"So you'll come out."

"No, not tonight, I can't."

"Come out with me, Myriam. Say you will come out with me."

Did he ever give up?

"You really want to go out?"

"Is this ever getting tedious," he said.

"What can I say? I'm just not much fun these days."

He laughed. "You just don't seem the type."

"Excuse me?"

"Hard to get."

"Unlike you—" Swat! He was a pest and deserved to be treated like one. She deeply desired to see him splattered against a wall.

"Touché," he said, followed by: "Meet you outside your place in an hour."

There it was again: the outrageous dig apologized for by a show of manners, proof that he wasn't a complete jerk. Fine, if he'd pick her up, she'd go out with him. "An hour is too soon. Make it two."

"If you insist," he said, and sighed.

"Change your mind?"

"Never," he said.

"Then I'll see you in a couple of hours."

"Don't go yet."

"What now?"

"I forgot your address."

And there he was, Killian, at the bottom of the stoop. There he was: sinew-thin in tight black jeans. There he was: in a skin-hugging t-shirt. There he was: in heavy boots laced to his shins. There he was: dressed entirely in black.

Myria smiled by way of "hello" and he grinned, and said that they should get moving.

"Where to?" she asked

"I called Samantha," he responded.

Samantha! He had called Samantha, the belle of Colorado. Was it before or after he'd called her?

"Is she coming out with us?"

"She's having a party," he said.

"What's the occasion?"

"Her family wants to meet her American friends."

He might have warned her. Samantha was living in Santa Cruz, an elegant old-world address if there ever was one. Myria worried that she would make a poor impression, or rather, an impression of poverty. Espinosa had said as much, calling her trash. Killian must have been paying attention too. He had dressed down for her. It was touching in its own way. And yet Killian could wear what he liked; he was a guy, and his clothing didn't show the least sign of wear.

"I can't go to a party looking like this," she said, "not in Spain."

"Don't be ridiculous," he said. "Of course, you can."

"Spaniards are more formal about these things. They pay attention to appearances."

"Who really cares what they think." He looked her up and down. "Not you certainly."

Myria did care. A caring person, that's how she thought of herself. She cared passionately about Sheffield, her feelings fraught with adoration and apprehension. After three years, Sheffield must have understood that she genuinely loved him, but then he was a boatload of anxieties himself. He couldn't take all that caring. And yet here was Killian, who misread her entirely. Wrong as he was, she liked the pointed way he'd said: Who really cares what they think. Not you, certainly. She could be that person if she let herself.

Myria walked alongside Killian, a dozen interrupted questions on her tongue. Killian did all of the talking. And all he talked about was Samantha: she was from the Midwest, like he was; her family had money, like his did; she attended private school, as he had.

"You're perfect for each other," Myria said.

"I think she's engaged to some guy back home."

"You have your work cut out for you."

"Maybe you could put in a good word for me."

Myria promised that she would praise him to the skies. He laughed. He always laughed.

A glass—or rather two—of Cava later, Myria gave Samantha a kiss on the cheek, and thanked her for inviting her to the party. Samantha appeared mortified. She hadn't invited Myria to her party. Her discomfort intensified Myria's discomfort. She regretted coming. Neither spoke for a moment when Samantha hugged her. A fragrant, soft, feminine hug. But, it was so great to see her, Samantha was saying in her ear, and have another glass of champagne, and wasn't the house something else?

"Beautiful," Myria said.

Umber walls and leather settees in sienna, the warm Mediterranean décor as lovely as a setting sun.

"It's so sweet," Samantha said.

"Very," Myria said, not knowing what precisely she was agreeing too. She wished she hadn't gulped down her Cava. The bubbles were already going to her head.

"Killian and you," Samantha said, all twinkles and smiles.

"Oh, that," Myria said. "We're friends."

Samantha leaned in closer, and said: "Maybe I was wrong."

"Maybe you were wrong about what?"

"About Killian," Samantha said.

Myria was about to say something spiteful but instead put her mouth to the other girl's ear.

"Your pearls are divine," she said.

Samantha looked down at the strand of shiny nacre doubled around her neck. "These? They were a gift?"

"Nice gift," Myria said. "Did your fiancé give them to you?"

Samantha rolled one of the fat pearls between thumb and finger. "I guess you could put it that way."

"You don't sound very—" Excited was the word.

"It's just that—"

"Yes?"

"I don't miss him," Samantha said, as though surprised herself by the realization. "He calls every other day to see how I am, wanting to know if I'll be home for Christmas. How do I know? I just got here."

If only Myria could say the same about Sheffield. Samantha, she didn't pine, not even for a guy who wanted to marry her. She was like a milk-thistle, one that had gone to seed, and all the more beautiful for it, not caring if the wind scattered her in all directions.

While she fretted, Killian joined them, a flute of Cava in one hand and a cigarette in the other.

"Fabulous party," he said between sips and drags, alternating drinking and smoking in equal measure.

Samantha nodded agreeably and Myria did the same.

"You're looking very Tiffany's," he said, to Samantha obviously.

She took in his remark, her brow slightly creased, and glancing at Myria said that he must mean her pearls.

"The entire package," Killian said.

"So now I'm a package?" Samantha fussed with her pearls.

"He means you're a catch," Myria said.

"Gracious!"

"She knows perfectly well what I mean," Killian said, eyes stuck on Samantha.

"You're funny," Samantha said.

Myria began to think more Cava might be a good idea after all when they were called to attention by a butter knife tapped against a glass.

At the center of the room stood a man of a certain age, distinguished in appearance, the patriarch of the family, who welcomed the Americans. "To our friends!" he said, "a toast."

The Spaniards cheered.

"¡Arriba!" Glasses raised.

"¡Abajo!" Glasses lowered.

"¡Adentro!" Down the hatch.

"And let us toast tonight to a great Spaniard," the patriarch continued while the help rushed around to fill the guests' glasses. "To El Paquirri, a man much loved by his motherland, and very dear to me."

"What are we drinking to?" Killian asked.

"A bullfighter," said Samantha, and then hushed him with a vigorous shake of the head.

Servants hurried about with open bottles of champagne, filling one glass after another. The Spaniards raised their voices in chorus, the Americans doing their best to follow along.

"And now we drink to our health!"

"*¡Salud!*"

Samantha's host father beckoned her to his side. "Here we have our very own American princess."

Applause rose from the ranks. The "princess" blinked as if caught in popping paparazzi bulbs. Myria raised her Cava. Killian whistled. The Americans joined in.

The patriarch also clapped. "What is there left to say on this occasion? Only that dinner will be served soon."

Killian smiled at Myria. "I wouldn't be surprised to see Samantha's face on the front page of ABC."

Myria laughed and asked him if he ever read ABC, one of Spain's more conservative newspapers.

"On certain occasions," he responded, pointedly.

"Really?"

Killian gestured to a rococo frame on a nearby table and an autographed picture of Juan Carlos, King of Spain. "Monarchists," he said.

"People love royalty," she said, "even Americans."

Without missing a beat, he said: "Not the Irish."

"We treat the Kennedys like royalty."

"They are Bostonians," he shot back.

"They're still Irish and Catholic."

"What would you know of being Catholic?"

Myria answered: "More than you think."

Killian snorted. "What is the incarnation? When is the feast of the circumcision celebrated? Are you even baptized?"

Myria wasn't shocked at his indignation over religion so much as taken aback. Killian, for all his frivolous chatter, wasn't empty headed.

"As if you care," she said, to ward off further argument.

"Why wouldn't I?" he countered.

Time to change the subject. "I never asked you. Where did you go to college?"

"Yale," he said.

"I've heard of it."

"I haven't graduated yet," he said, his tone mournful.

"So why did you come to Spain?"

"You mean who made me come to Spain?"

The help had begun to usher guests to the back patio.

"Supper is being served," she said.

"I'm not hungry," he said.

"You're too thin. You need to eat more."

"Now you sound like a Jewish grandmother."

A servant offered to take her glass.

"Whatever makes you happy," she said. "I'm going to stuff myself."

✉✉✉

The back patio, enclosed by the high walls covered with climbing ivy, was made intimate by candle flicker. The linen draped tables sat four to six. Myria took whatever was passed her way: stews fleshy with veal and steak; ham sliced skin-thin; tortillas stuffed with onion and asparagus tips; fried sardines; bread pounded into morsels and mixed with vegetables; and a pumpkin-hued puree.

"You must try it," said the Spaniard who introduced himself as "Carlos," referring to the puree. "It is typical of Sevilla."

Or: "The pigs feed on acorns and that is what makes our *jamón* special.

And: "We eat fish most days."

To which Myria replied: "Yes, that has been my experience."

"Do you like our food?"

"Very much," she said.

Carlos filled her glass with red wine. "Rioja is best served with heavy meals."

Myria noticed his empty plate and asked if he wasn't hungry.

"We Spaniards do not eat so much after the sun goes down," he replied. "I might have the tortilla. It is a temptation I cannot resist even at this hour."

He encouraged her to eat. Myria fumbled a comment about him being a true gallant.

"You mean to say *caballero*," he said.

A Spanish girl to his right tickled the nape of his neck. He grabbed the mischievous hand and kissed it. She had made a dramatic entrance, wearing a floor-length red cape with boots to match, looking every bit like a wicked Little Red Riding Hood out for a night on the town. He said this and she responded with that. She laughed dismissively and he nodded affably. He tried to make a point about something while she fed him forkfuls of tortilla from her plate. Every now and again, the girl in red glanced at Myria, as if to ask: *Why are you staring?* It was rude of her, true, but how could she not stare?

Across the patio, at Samantha's side, Killian appeared to be enjoying himself.

"All I want is a hamburger." The grumbler, seated to her left, was apparently speaking to her, adding, "Don't you?"

Myria turned her attention from Killian to focus on her tablemate—the focal point of whom was his blond streaked, flat-top hair gelled firmly in place. "Try the tortilla," she suggested. "It's fantastic."

"You mean the quiche?"

"It's not quiche. It's Spanish tortilla."

He said something about Mexican food. Myria told him he was thinking of a burrito. He responded that would be an improvement.

"A burrito sounds great about now."

"In Spanish, burro means donkey."

"He-haw," he said.

Myria understood that he was no longer grousing about Spanish cuisine specifically; she was also on the menu. She was up for grabs. He was sampling her, head slightly cocked, staring at her face.

"I was kidding," he said. "Of course, I know what tortilla is. I've been to Spain before."

"Have you?"

"My father is Spanish."

"From Sevilla?"

"No."

"Where?"

"Madrid."

"Your Spanish must be excellent."

"My Spanish is excellent. My English is excellent. I grew up in the States. In Virginia."

"I've seen you at the Institute."

"Everyone knows who you are," he said.

"Everyone!" She doubted it.

"We call you the sad girl."

Myria reached for her glass of Rioja. "And why is that?"

"You always dress in black."

"I'm from New York. Everyone in New York dresses in black." She wasn't from the city but close enough. She didn't like the idea of her classmates talking about her, coming up with names like "sad girl."

Myria ran her spoon through the soup. The warm color made for cheerful eating, and she welcomed its heartiness with an open mouth.

"This is the best meal I've had in a long time," she said.

"Poor you."

Myria put down her spoon and interrupted the Spanish guy, asking if there were more Rioja. Barely taking his eyes off the girl in red, he reached for the bottle and filled her glass.

"*Los americanos,*" he said, not to Myria.

"*Quieres decir, las,*" said the girl.

"Gracias," Myria said.

"You know who she is?" her fellow Americano said. "Beatriz Rivera. She's from one of the richest families in Sevilla."

"Good to know," Myria said.

"Just saying."

"You haven't told me your name," Myria said.

"Port."

"Is Port a Spanish name?"

"It's a family name."

The way he stressed family had that *and not just any family* quality to it. He must be wealthy. Rich people gave their kids names like Port. Rich sounding names.

"Spain is great in some ways. The food though is tough to swallow."

"You mentioned that."

"A good, old fashioned hamburger," he went on, "with pickles, onions and tomato."

She had to admit that she liked pickles on her hamburger too.

"Samantha and I found a place where you can get a great hamburger," he said, "if you're able to pay for it."

"Do you and Samantha go out often?"

"Often enough," he said.

"I see," she said. "Are you dating?"

"It's not like that," Port said. "We get along."

"Samantha gets along with everyone."

"She's easy to be with," Port said.

"I've always enjoyed her company," Myria said.

Port asked about Killian.

"What about him?"

"There's something odd about that guy," he said.

"He's okay," she said, and could only imagine the things Port and Samantha said about Killian behind his back.

"I saw you come in with him," he said.

"He invited me."

"Are you two going out?"

"Are you kidding? He's a friend." And then ashamed, although she couldn't say why, "It was nice of him to invite me."

"Samantha didn't invite you?"

"No, Port, she didn't."

He grinned. "So you didn't come because of Samantha and you're not going out with Killian."

"Seems so," she said. "Of course, I like Samantha. There isn't one thing not to like about her."

"She's incredibly—"

"Isn't' she, though?"

Port asked her again if she was Killian's date. "You can tell me. I won't gossip. I promise."

"We're friends. He wanted me along."

"If I tell you something—"

"Don't," Myria objected before he could say another word. "Don't tell me anything."

"All I was going to say is that Killian is kind of weird."

"Isn't everyone," she answered.

CHAPTER TWELVE

FIESTA

The party went long, even the children keeping up with their parents until the guests started the multiple rounds of farewell kisses and hugs.

Samantha offered her cheek to each guest, her mouth frozen into a smile. Port had found an empty chair and entertained himself by flipping the pages of a magazine. Killian demanded more champagne from one of the servants.

"Time to go," Myria said to him.

"Myriam!" He put a hand on her shoulder. "Tell this, this person I want another drink."

"You've had enough," she said. "We don't want to overstay our welcome."

"Rubbish," he said.

Port put aside his reading. "I agree with Killian. It's too early to call it a night."

"Have you met Port?" Killian fairly shouted in her ear.

"I have," Myria said.

"Myria and me, we're best pals," Port said.

Killian shifted, listing against her. "Myriam tell Port to get us more champagne."

"I tell you what," Port said. "There's a great place around the corner. Let's grab Samantha and have a drink there."

"Samantha has other things to do," Myria said.

"She'll come," Port said. He went to navigate the crowd circling Samantha.

"So what's this about you and Port?" Killian adjusted his stance in an attempt to right himself.

"I haven't the least idea," she said. "He was at the table where we had dinner."

"You must have charmed him with your feminine wiles," Killian said.

"Apparently, you've mistaken me for someone else."

"You have your ways."

Myria frowned. "Oh, that's me all right." Before Killian could respond: "You're being silly."

"I like being silly," Killian said. "Outrageously silly. If only more people had a sense of humor."

Port turned up again and announced that Samantha would join them. "She just wants to change her clothes."

"There you go," Killian said. "Port always gets his way."

"Not true," Myria said. "No one gets his way all the time."

"Some do," Killian said. "Port hasn't told you he's filthy rich, has he?"

Port gave him a sour look.

"Go on," Killian persisted. "It's not as if it's some big secret."

"It's boring," Port said.

"His father does a lot of business in Spain," Killian said, "as in the millions."

"I told you it was boring," Port said.

Over Port's head, Myria caught sight of Samantha coming towards them. She wore a white sweater that skimmed her hips over black leggings. The pearls had been put away.

"Guess who?" she said, her hands over Port's eyes.

"Marilyn Monroe?" he said.

"Wrong," she said, in her upbeat manner.

Port laughed. Samantha slid her hands away. Killian touched a finger to Samantha's sleeve. "Cashmere," he said.

"Isn't it nice? Port gave it to me."

It seemed to Myria that Samantha received more presents than any girl she'd ever known. Pearls, cashmere—she wouldn't be surprised if Samantha showed up wearing a tiara, saying, "This? It was a gift."

"Let's get out of here," Killian said.

"Yes, let's." For once, Myria agreed with him.

The foursome ordered wine and pecked at the offerings of green olives, cheese, and blood sausage.

Port surveyed the crowded tavern while Killian chatted with Samantha. Myria, who wanted only to sit down, marveled how it was that Spaniards could keep on their feet, no matter how late the hour.

Killian held up his empty glass, and Myria, snatching it from him, said: "You are smashed."

"Not as much as I'd like to be," he replied.

"Drink some water," she said. "You'll thank me in the morning."

He sighed. "Do you ever let yourself have fun?"

"Never," she said.

"I want to explain something to you." Killian stopped there, either too distracted or disabled to explain.

"I'm waiting," she said.

He hiccupped. "I need a cigarette. Give me one."

"Sorry, I'm all out."

"I'll ask Port."

"You do that," she said.

"Forget Port. We should go ask that guy." Killian gestured across the room, hazy with the smoke of hand-rolled cigarettes, the smell pungent. "You see him?"

Myria asked him if he meant the one with his hair pulled back in a ponytail.

"Seek and you will find."

"Find what?"

"Probably some pretty good hash," Killian said.

Myria sighed, long and loud. She recalled that night when the girl with black lipstick stopped her and Amelia; that night, the girl hustled them, her partners in misdeeds chanting, "*plata*." The girl, she'd called it kief. Amelia had wanted nothing to do with them, or kief. You're tired, Amelia had said, tired people attract trouble.

"You're out of your mind," she said to Killian.

Killian laughed, giddy from all the drink. "Wouldn't that be great?"

"No," she said. "It wouldn't. Don't go asking for hash. It's dangerous. You could get arrested."

He assured her that the stuff was practically legal in Spain. "Everyone does it."

Myria remarked that she doubted very much that Port and Samantha would approve.

"Who cares," Killian said, and with a lurch was off.

"Where's he going?" Samantha asked.

"Bathroom," Myria said.

Samantha began to talk at her, an uninterrupted stream of effusive commentary: what a great time she'd had at the party, and wasn't the family kind to invite her friends, and how gorgeous the Spanish men were, and the women dressed like models, and how the fun ended too soon, and if she had her way she'd never go back to the States again.

So much glee, all of it exuded with a natural flush of the cheeks and a glittering smile. Myria wished, not for the first time in Samantha's company, that she could be as buoyant. Myria admired her, envied her, not because Samantha was well-off, beautiful, and intelligent. She'd met other blondes with money and far more chic. It wasn't Samantha's outward appearance that drew her in. It was her exuberance. Myria would have traded places with her in an instant just to know what it felt to be utterly in love with her own existence.

Killian edged between them. He opened his palm, revealing a fat spliff.

"Told you," he said.

"What's that?" Samantha asked.

Trouble, that's what, Myria wanted to say.

"Who will partake?" Killian looked at Myria.

To her surprise, Port reached into his pocket and produced a lighter, embossed in gold.

"Fire away," he said.

Hours later, Myria and Killian sat on the stoop of her residence, the night retreating, and with morning coming on, the sky laminate white.

"What day is it?" Killian put a hand to his forehead to shield his eyes from the glare.

"Sunday," Myria said. "I'm pretty sure it's Sunday."

"Oh, gawd."

"In fact," she said, "I'm sure of it."

"Well that would make sense," he said.

"I guess so," she said.

"I detest Sundays in Spain," he said.

"So do I," she said and broke into laughter.

Killian started to laugh too.

"It's like—"

"Purgatory," she said.

"You have no idea," he said, mournful.

"I have plenty of ideas," she said.

"It was an almost perfect night," he said.

"Yeah, it turned out okay," she responded.

"Except for Port."

"What about Port?"

"There's nothing wrong with Port except he won't let Samantha out of his sight."

"Who would?"

"Do you know how rich he is?"

"No, and I don't care," Myria said.

"His father works for Boeing," he said. "I mean, he's connected."

"You make it sound so sinister."

"Port is a fool," he said.

"I thought you liked him."

"He's bearable."

"He strikes me as a good guy," she said.

"I like Samantha more," he said.

"It's fairly obvious," she said.

"She's so—"

"What?"

"Just is," he said.

"That says it all."

Killian laughed. "Let's finish this one off," he said.

"What off?"

He took out a half-smoked spliff, the end charred, from the pocket of his t-shirt.

"You are unbelievable," she said.

"It gets better," he said, and digging into his pants pocket pulled out Port's lighter.

"Finders keepers," he said.

"You wouldn't do that," she said. "I mean not give it back to him."

"He won't miss it," Killian said.

"It's still his," she said. "You should give it back."

"Port has everything," he said.

"Not his lighter," Myria said.

"You want it?"

"No!"

"As you like," he said, and flipped the cover back, gave the wheel several turns until it ignited.

They passed the kief mixed with tobacco back and forth. Myria took light puffs, Killian inhaled heavily.

The streets widened and narrowed, came to a rapid boil under the morning sun. The crows were chanting something by Poe.

"But they were ravens," she said to the mute streetlamp. "Or rooks" to the pavement.

"I'm famished," Killian announced.

"The bar on the corner might be opened," she said.

Killian ground the spliff underfoot. Myria watched, entranced.

"Why don't we check out your place," he said.

Myria bolted to attention. "Not on your life," she said.

"But I want to see where you live," he pleaded.

"You can't," she responded, adamant.

"At least let me up to get water," he said. "My mouth feels like the Sahara."

"Killian, there are rules."

"Myria, why do you always say no?"

"I think I should be going now," she said.

"You are a tough one," he said.

"Go home, Killian," she said.

He sighed. "I'll call you later, okay."

"Whenever," she said.

"I'm going now," he said.

"You do that."

"Myria, I wanted to say—"

"Tell me you're going to be okay," she said. "Tell me it was a great night. Tell me you are going to get home safe and sound."

He shrugged.

"I don't want anything to happen to you," she said.

"Too late for that," he said.

"What do you mean?"

"Just the usual scolding for not being on time for Mass," he said.

"Not by me," she said.

"That's not what I meant."

"People go to Mass at this hour?" she asked, not quite following his train of thought.

"You can go to Mass at practically any hour."

"Why do it at all if you don't believe in the church?"

"Because I'm Irish," he said. "And that's what we do."

"I guess I just—"

"Don't you believe in God?"

"Never give it much thought." She felt a headache coming on.

He let his head drop against her shoulder. "Do you ever miss— where is it you're from?"

"Connecti-cult," she said.

"You must live in a big house," he said.

"Palatial," she said, "even the cat has its own wing."

"Cats don't have wings."

"They don't?"

Killian didn't answer. He'd dozed off, his head rolling from her shoulder onto her chest.

Myria would have to wake him sooner than later. He was oblivious, of that much she was certain. She wondered if being passed out like that brought him any peace.

The sun, like a general, was busy setting everything in order above, dismissing this cloud, then the next—or was it the wind? Before long, the sky attained its uniform hue.

"Killian," she said, and nudged him, at first gently, then with a push.

To her relief, he woke, stretched, rubbed his eyes, and drew a hand across his mouth. He asked if she had a smoke.

"No," she said. "The party's over."

"So soon," he said, groggy.

"I'm going to stand up now," she said.

"You think you can? Because I don't," he said.

"Yes, you can." She stood. "I'm going to my...to get some sleep."

"Don't go." He patted the cement step.

"I'm not the one who's going."

"Am I?" he asked.

"You are." She reached into the pocket of her jeans for her keys, grateful to find them there.

"I'm not sure how to get home."

"Do you have any money? We can get you a cab." She stepped onto the curb. The street was empty but for a few pied birds, and the trash scuttled along the sidewalk by the wind.

"Don't bother," he said. "I'll walk."

"Promise me you'll go straight home."

Killian was on his feet now and smiling down at her.

"We should do this again."

She wondered if he could manage the steps but he seemed to have pulled himself together.

"I mean soon," he said.

She kept an eye on him as he got himself down off the stoop, and in a meandering gait, set off in the direction of the river.

CHAPTER THIRTEEN

SMALL WORLD

For once, Myria was glad to have the residence to herself. The grimy walls looked shinier than she remembered, her dinner plate, barely picked at, still on the table. She sat, staring at her half-eaten supper, the bread roll, the slice of ham spilling out of it, like a tongue. Crusty old thing, it was smiling at her. She smiled back, hungry, and tore the sandwich in half, gnawing at it contentedly. A glass, reached for, slipped from her grasp to the tiled floor, where it shattered. Myria laughed at her clumsiness. Leaning over her knees, which seemed larger than she recalled, she began to pick up the fragments out of spilt water, and placed them on the table, arranging them like a child trying to put together a puzzle.

"Mother of God," a voice said in her ear.

Myria looked up from her mad assemblage to see Amelia.

"When did you get here?" she asked.

Amelia didn't answer.

"I've missed you," she said. "It wasn't nice of you to leave and not tell me." She put out a hand but Amelia melted away at her touch, vanishing into the shadows.

"Be like that," she muttered. The clock now attracted her attention, and with a shock, she saw it was well past eleven. A series of *what if's* assailed her: the dueña, what if she decided to come early; her housemates, what if they saw her like that; her sanity, what if she were losing it—because for a moment she really had believed Amelia was there.

Myria grabbed a napkin and used it to sweep the glass onto the plate, dumping the shards in the waste bin in the kitchen. With a broom, she swept the floor.

She pulled at the French doors to her room and the sun through the window caused a searing pain behind her eyes. It was only a few steps to her bed. Stepping over clothes, books, and towels, she reached the cot, too exhausted to deal with the shutters. Turning her back to the ferocious light, she silently prayed that sleep would come, quickly.

And there came a rap, rap, rapping, and a voice calling her name. She wasn't certain who or where.

The knocking continued, and it had to be at the doors to her room.

It was mercifully dark now.

"Come in, pasa."

"I was worried about you."

Amelia! She'd returned, finally, or Myria was still asleep, dreaming.

Myria sat up, mumbled that it was cold.

"Because you left open the windows."

"It was warm this morning."

"November in Sevilla is chilly at night."

Myria couldn't quite believe she wasn't dreaming.

"I suppose," she said. Her head clamored with the sounds of crashing cymbals.

"I will turn on the light."

"No, not that," Myria said.

Amelia bent down and picked up a towel or a shirt. Myria

couldn't tell.

"Do you throw everything on the floor?" Amelia started to collect other discarded items. "What a mess!"

"Just leave it," Myria said. "I'll clean up later."

"Close the shutters," Amelia said. "The cold will make you sick."

Myria already felt sick, her forehead pounding.

"You were gone," she said.

Amelia told her to move over. She sat on the cot. "Close the windows."

"I will," Myria said, "in a minute." The breeze no longer caused her to tremble. "I like the fresh air."

"You have taken enough fresh air," Amelia said, climbing over her and closing the shutters.

"What time is it?"

"I don't know," Amelia said.

"Did I miss supper?"

"You did."

Myria wanted to stretch out but there wasn't room with Amelia seated at the end of the cot.

"The dueña, you are not in her favor," Amelia said.

Myria remembered the broken glass. "It was an accident," she said.

"Wake up, Myria, wake up."

"I am awake."

"The dueña is upset because the telephone hasn't stopped for you all evening."

"For me?" she asked. "Who would call me?"

"An American," Amelia said. "He speaks terrible Spanish."

Myria let out an "uh-oh."

"He called so much."

"That much?"

"The dueña speaks not a word of English," Amelia said. "Well, she insists she does not know English. She speaks enough and understands more than she gives away."

"Did the calls stop?"

"When the dueña had me speak to the American."

"And what did the American say?"

"He kept asking for you, saying your name until I told him I understood.

"I see," Myria said. "Who was it?" But she already knew. It had to be Killian.

"A strange name," Amelia said.

"Killian?"

"Yes, that sounds right."

"Did he leave a message?"

"He told me that you should meet him at—"

"It doesn't matter," Myria said.

Amelia asked Myria how she was feeling. A little warmer now that the windows had been shut?

"It's just a headache."

"You smoked too much kief. Do you need water? An aspirin?"

Defensive, Myria denied it. Amelia laughed, her voice rising and falling, and rising again.

"Now you have tasted the fruits of Spain," Amelia said.

"Is that it?"

Amelia sighed. She rubbed Myria's hand. "It is poisoned fruit."

"Once was enough," Myria said. It was. She wouldn't touch the stuff again. She would stay clear of Killian and kief. She would study more. She wouldn't answer his phone calls.

"You will do a lot more kief if you keep seeing this boy. He is stronger than you, much stronger. He will lead you like a puppet on a string."

"It's not as if I can avoid him. We study together."

"So you like him?"

"I don't know him," Myria said.

"Is he handsome?"

"In a way," Myria said. "His eyes, they are incredibly blue."

"I met an American with blue eyes."

"You did?"

"Someone you know. A sailor."

Now Myria was surprised. "Neil? Where did you meet him?"

"Where you met him," Amelia said, letting go of Myria's hand.

"Did you meet him at the café by the river?" Myria asked, surprised. How could Amelia know who Neil was?

"He called me señorita and asked if he could buy me a beer."

"And you let him?" Myria imagined Neil taking one look at Amelia, her beauty washing over him in great waves of female allure. She wouldn't have to open her mouth. He fell for her instantly. Before they'd finished their first beer, he'd already made plans to spend the rest of his life with her. He'd give up the Navy, divorce his wife, abandon his kids.

The engine of these thoughts was the bitterness of losing Sheffield. Amelia would magnetize him. He would do everything to stick to her. Not Myria. She magnetized no one.

Amelia snapped her fingers at Myria. "You hear nothing I say."

Myria looked up. "Of course. What?"

"I told your sailor I do not drink beer. It is a taste I have never acquired."

"Is that where you've been all this time? With Neil?"

Amelia asked Myria if she thought her the type to go off with American sailors, as though it were the most ridiculous thing she'd ever heard. "No, *boba*, we spoke only for a short time. He was with his friends. Americans. Young boys, drunk and annoying."

"He's married, you know."

Amelia leaned forward. "I am teasing you. I never saw your sailor."

Myria was confused. "You never met him."

"In fact, no," Amelia said. "But the type I know."

"I thought you met him."

"Because you smoked too much keif," Amelia said. "If I told you I make sex with the king of Spain, you would think it true."

Myria just might.

"What if your sailor comes here once more?"

Myria couldn't fathom it. "Why would he do that? We met once, and besides he's married. And he has children."

Amelia smiled. "You are young. It could be you remind him of his daughter. And, like him, you are American."

"He's not coming back," Myria said.

"No, he is not coming for you," Amelia said, her tone leaving no room for doubt—or hope.

Amelia reached over and put her palm to her brow. "At least you don't have a fever."

Myria assured her that she wasn't ill, only tired. "I'm so glad to see you. No one could tell me where you'd gone," she said.

"Did they fill your head with fairy tales?"

Myria knew Amelia referred to her housemates.

"One or two," she said.

"They are silly girls," Amelia said

"I think so too."

"Silly girls," Amelia said, "that is true, not so different from you, Myria."

The comparison upset Myria. How could she be like Dolores? Without a mind of her own? Or Espinosa? Full of thorns. The other women nice enough but....

Myria began to tug nervously at the bedsheets. She didn't have one nice thing to say about the other women, only Amelia.

"Don't be angry with me." It was a plea. Take pity, please.

Amelia assured her she was not angry. "I only think you are foolish for smoking kief."

"It is foolish. Stupid." Myria said. "I won't do it again."

Amelia shrugged.

CHAPTER FOURTEEN

WHIMS

Myria pushed opened the doors to the Institute to find Killian waving a cigarette about. Port and Samantha stood by. The four of them had fallen into the habit of having coffee after classes, frequenting the same café across the plaza.

"Myriam!" Killian called out sonorous as a songbird. "We've been waiting for you."

"I couldn't escape," she answered. "The prof is half-mad, went on a diatribe about how Lope de Vega's *Fuenteovejuna* had been co-opted by Marxists. He kept us for fifteen minutes past the bell, saying that Spain is not better off, the situation is very bad. I'm not sure what all that had to do with the play we were reading. It was written in the 17th century. Marxism hadn't been invented yet."

Port and Samantha exchanged glances. Taking his cigarette from his mouth, Killian remarked that it takes a fascist to hate a Marxist.

"Is there a difference?" Port challenged.

Killian: "I would say so."

Port: "Two sides of the same coin."

Killian: "History begs to differ."

Samantha: "I've never understood Marxism, not really."

Myria: "Ask Killian. He'll explain it to you."

Killian: "I'm not that political."

Myria: "What he means to say is he's not a Marxist."

Killian: "You're right about that."

Port: "Can we get some coffee now?"

Samantha enthusiastically agreed.

They started down the street, where slant rays of sun shone through palm trees. Samantha fell into step with Myria while Killian and Port went on ahead.

"What a nice day," Samantha said. She edged her way into conversations, picking the obvious topics such as the weather before delving deeper.

"It couldn't be lovelier," Myria said.

"I've noticed something," Samantha said.

"Have you?"

"You seem so much happier."

"Happy as a clam," Myria said, "that's me."

"Are you and—"

"Samantha, please!"

"Now come on. I know for a fact you've been out with Killian."

"I've been out with you too," Myria said. "And Port."

"Not alone."

Yes, she'd been out alone with Killian as Samantha put it—out clubbing, getting acquainted with the seedier side of Sevilla; all those bars. She had dozens of hangovers to remember them by.

"Killian and I are friends," Myria said. "How many times do I need to tell you?"

Apparently, she needed to repeat it again because Samantha laughed.

"Ask me what I think," Samantha said.

"Maybe later, okay," Myria pleaded.

The waiter swiped some crumbs off the bar with a dish rag after which he lined up the cups of espresso. He knew their names by now and they knew his. Jorge greeted them with his usual *"Buenos días."* He showed remarkable patience, particularly with Killian, who spoke Spanish as little as possible, and Jorge, being a quick study of character, turned it into a joke, saying in English: "No sugar for you, only for the ladies" or "Very sorry, no toast and butter today."

Myria noticed a guy hovering nearby, smiling at Killian. She nudged him, and he turned to look, crying out, delighted: "Mohamed!"

Mohamed bowed his head slightly. "Friend, I told you I would come."

Killian put an arm around him. "You made my day." He introduced him to the others. Mohamed greeted them each in turn.

Myria liked him right away—his gentle manner, his eyes bright green like Amelia's; his hair, furrows of tight black curls, reminded her of her father.

Port made room for the newcomer and Samantha asked if he wanted a coffee. Mohamed hesitated and Port said: "You are our guest."

"Isn't Port generous?" Killian laughed.

Jorge's expression was tense as he served the newcomer, and then, without a word, removed himself to the furthest end of the bar.

"Skipping school today," Killian said to Mohamed.

"Do you go to school?" Samantha asked.

Myria watched Mohamed carefully, wondering if Samantha's blond haloed presence would cast its usual spell. He didn't ogle and instead answered with studied politeness, his English clear and strong.

"I am at university here in Sevilla."

"Mohamed is studying linguistics," Killian said.

"Linguistics," Port echoed.

"Yes, I am in my second year," Mohamed said.

"I never met a linguist before," Samantha said. "What do linguists do?"

"They study language," Killian said.

"I'd like to hear more about your studies," Myria said.

Mohamed lifted his cup with both hands, drank, and then set it down. He moved with a gracefulness Myria found unusual.

"I speak Arabic, French, and Spanish," he said. "I will become a professor."

"One day," Killian cut in, "Mohamed is going to come to the States. I've already told him he must."

"To see America is something I want very much," Mohamed said.

"It's a long haul from Marrakesh," Port said, "expensive too."

Myria stirred her coffee with a tiny silver spoon, embarrassed by Port, his lack of tact.

"My home is Fes," Mohamed responded.

"Like the hat?" Port asked.

"No, like the city," Myria said.

"You know Fes?" Mohamed asked.

"I've heard of it," she said, but then she knew about as much about Morocco as she did Colorado. She wasn't even sure where in Morocco Fes was located.

"You would like it there," Mohamed said. "It is the third largest city in my country."

"So big?" Myria asked.

"It sounds wonderful," Samantha said.

"Ask your friend," Mohamed said, referring apparently to Port. "He has been to Morocco."

"I barely remember it," Port said. "My father dragged us there on business."

"Did you see Fes?"

Port thought a moment. "No, don't think so. I was a—well, I don't remember much." He added: "Nice hotel, though."

"Port has been everywhere," Samantha said.

"Yes, everywhere," Port said.

"This is my first trip out of the States," Samantha said. "I just love it here. I never want to go back."

"You hear that, Mohamed," Port said. "She never wants to go back home."

Mohamed responded: "I can understand why. Spain is beautiful. Morocco is also beautiful."

"It must be extraordinary," Myria said.

"You must come then," Mohamed said.

"We should all go," Killian said.

"I could take you," Mohamed said.

"I've been," Port said, unenthused.

"Don't listen to him," Killian said. "We're going. It's settled."

Myria glanced at Mohamed. He seemed pleased.

"Yes, we're going," Killian repeated.

"I'm so excited," Samantha said. "When do we leave?"

Mohamed said they could go whenever they wished. Myria sensed he was being accommodating.

"We don't want you to miss class," she said.

"When's the next break?" Killian asked.

"I must go now," Mohamed said, apologetic, "but it will be soon."

"We're counting on it," Killian said.

Mohamed asked how much for the coffee. Killian told him not to worry.

"Port will take care of it."

Port smirked. "Port takes care of everything."

"Don't worry about it," Myria said to Mohamed.

"It was my great happiness to meet you," Mohamed said.

"It makes us happy too," Samantha said.

"We will talk later," Killian said.

Mohamed slapped him on the back. "You are a true friend." He finished up his coffee and excused himself.

Myria scarcely listened while Killian and Samantha talked excitedly about a possible Moroccan adventure. Port asked her why so silent.

"Am I?"

"You need another espresso," he said. "It will wake you up."

"I just can't seem to get going today."

"Barhopping much?"

"Not this again," she said. "Talk to Samantha much?"

"It's just—"

"What's just?"

"Just you and you know who, that's what."

Avoidance was her best option. "It looks as if we're going to Morocco?"

"Lead the way."

"Killian will, without a doubt," she said. "He's been here for a month and is already restless."

"Restless is to put it mildly," Port said, "crazy is more like it."

"Of course, Port will come," Killian said over Samantha's head. "And you too, Myriam."

"I can't wait," Samantha said.

Port asked Jorge for the bill. Samantha rushed off to be home in time for the mid-day meal. Killian asked Myria if she was going as well, to which she said "yes," and he informed her he was coming along because he needed a walk.

Colorful Sevilla: the terra-cotta roofs, the white limestone houses, splashing fountains brilliant in the sun, the shade trees twittering with birds.

"Where did you meet Mohamed?" Myria asked.

"I guess you could say he found me."

"What do you mean? He found you?"

Killian explained. He had been wandering the old city one afternoon and Mohamed approached him.

"He told me he wanted to practice his English."

"Just like that?"

"Well, he introduced himself first."

Myria thought a moment and then: "Do you ever feel as if you are wearing a sign that says I'm an American in huge letters on it—the way people just assume."

"What is wrong with that?" Killian smiled. "Where is your national pride?"

His questions surprised Myria. She had never given much thought to her national pride. It never came up in the States. She told Killian that in Spain people just assumed things about her. It made her uncomfortable.

"Not me." Killian said. "I shudder to think of being anything but American. I wouldn't want anything else on my passport but citizen of the United States. Imagine what it must be like to be Mohamed? It must be miserable to travel on a Moroccan passport."

They'd reached the bridge that led across the Guadalquivir, the river flowing quickly, and above it, the frenzied cries of swooping gulls.

"It would be nice to get out here for a while." she said. "Go somewhere else."

"Glad to hear it. I didn't want to go to Morocco by myself."

"You suppose Mohamed will take us?" she asked.

"He said he would."

"When do you think?"

"There's the break coming up."

"There's always a break," she said. "It's amazing how many long weekends we have."

Killian laughed. "You wouldn't be amazed if you were

Catholic."

Myria responded that he might be right but if anyone was a heretic he was. He wasn't paying attention, his eyes on the café.

"Have a beer with me."

"One beer," she said.

"Good girl," he said.

They settled in at a table closest to the bridge. A waiter came, put a plate of potato chips in front of them, and they ordered two Sun Eagles, a Spanish label.

"Tell me more about Mohamed," she said.

"It's not as if we spend a lot of time together," Killian said. "For one thing, I just met him. Besides, he speaks English well enough as it is."

"He speaks English pretty well, I'd say."

"And drinks like a fish," Killian said. "He can talk you blue in the face after a few drinks."

"Can he?"

"He's good company, though."

"I thought so too."

"What makes you say that?"

"He just has a nice way about him," Myria said.

"I've been on him about going to Morocco," Killian said. "It would be fantastic."

Myria could only imagine. Killian was stubborn, obsessive, pesky—and a whole lot of other words that meant *I get what I want*. She also went along with him; it was easier than arguing.

"Where is he living?" she asked.

"He has cousins here."

"I suppose there are plenty of Arabs in Andalucía."

Killian was swift to correct her. "He's not Arab, he's a Moor."

The waiter arrived with the beer. Myria uttered "*gracias*."

Killian raised his glass. "Here's to Morocco."

Myria drank up before asking: "Is it expensive there?"

"That's the beauty of it," Killian said. "It's dirt cheap."

First round finished, he asked her if she wanted another beer.

"No more for me."

"Why not," he said. "You have all afternoon to sleep."

"Believe it or not, I need to study."

"Study! Whatever for?"

"Insane of me, I know, but I actually have to work."

"Aren't you done with college?"

College. She couldn't hear the word without being reminded of Sheffield. Where he was, what he was doing? She had no idea.

"It might seem ludicrous," she said, "but I hope to get something out of my time here. Something I can use to get a job."

Killian flung his arms to the sky, stretching and coming to rest with his head on the back of the chair, eyes closed. "Work. The mere horror of it!"

"It's an evil many of us can't avoid."

"Girls don't need to work. They can just marry some rich guy."

"How progressive of you," she said, irritated.

He lifted his head, scrutinizing her. "So who was he?"

Myria bit down on a chip. She might as well tell him. If she didn't, he'd keep pecking away at her. "Just a guy."

"But not any guy?"

She stuck another chip in her mouth, the salty wafer dissolving on her tongue. "He was just a guy I went out with in college."

"You can do better than that," he said, prodding her.

"Are you sure you want all the details."

"As long as they are gory," he said.

"I figured as much," she said, and ran her finger around the rim of her empty glass.

"Did he dump you?"

"In a manner of speaking," Myria said. She didn't say: He shredded me to pieces. She didn't say: I was a nervous wreck afterwards. She didn't say: There are so many days I just want to lie down and cry.

"What was his name?" Killian asked.

"Sheffield."

He let out a loud "uh-ha." "Did you like him?"

"Like him? We went out for three years."

"Three years!"

"I know!"

"We even lived together for," she paused, "maybe it was a year."

"Without being married," he said, aghast.

"You sound so shocked. People do live together without being married."

"Not where I come from. Where I come from we call that shacking up."

Jerk! A remark like that didn't deserve a response. She bit down on another chip.

"Is he rich?"

"Why, do you want to marry him?" Myria snapped.

Killian leaned back again, making a joke that—what's his name? Sheffield—didn't sound at all like her type.

"Let's have another beer," he said.

She gazed out onto the river: the current a reddish brown, the ravenous birds, the slow moving ferries. "Fine," she said.

"Good girl."

If he called her "good girl" one more time, she might strangle him. She was no one's "girl," not anymore.

CHAPTER FIFTEEN

LOST

She had never felt her heart beat so quickly, a percussive rhythm, hard enough she could hear it. She reached for Samantha's hand, the pressure startling the drowsing blonde. How she slept, Myria didn't know. But why would Samantha be anything but calm? She was from Colorado, the Rockies, and steep mountain passes were nothing new to her. Port looked over at Myria, rolled down the car window; a gust of cold air swept in. The three of them were crammed into the back of a black sedan, the engine idling, the high-beams on, the light extending a few feet at most. Nothing could outstretch that darkness.

In the front of the car, Killian and Mohamed, heads together, studied a map in silence. Occasionally, Mohamed turned around and smiled. They were lost, but not to worry. They were lost in the Rif Mountains, but not to worry. They didn't have a clue how to get where they were going, but not to worry.

Nothing about the day prepared Myria for being stranded on a sharp curve of road well after sundown. She had breakfast with her housemates, announced that she was headed for Morocco. It made her feel superior. For once, she was the one going somewhere—and not merely to a small town or to a friend's for the weekend. She was headed to an exotic place, a foreign country.

"Morocco! You haven't any notion of what you'll find there."

"It's a strange country, not at all like Spain."

"Be careful."

"You must be very careful."

"I'd have to be dragged to Morocco."

"A depressing place. Poor."

"Desperately poor."

"You may not survive it."

"Quiet!" Amelia intervened. "Why do you like to scare her? Of course, she will survive it. People go to Morocco all the time."

Amelia paused, her green eyes on Myria. "Just don't let your friend get you into trouble."

"What friend?" Espinosa asked. "She has a friend?"

"A novio," Dolores said.

Myria answered no, not a novio. "I'm going with some people I met at the Institute."

"Americans, I imagine," Espinosa said.

"One is Moroccan."

Espinosa looked askance. "You are foolish to trust the Moroccans."

"They act very nice but watch out," Dolores said.

"You can't trust a Moroccan," Espinosa insisted. "You said as much, Amelia."

Amelia frowned at her. "That wasn't the friend I was talking about."

"Who then?" Dolores asked.

"Myria knows who," Amelia replied.

Myria assured Amelia she had nothing to worry about, and went to get her things together.

They loaded their luggage into the trunk of the car Port rented. Myria noticed that Mohamed traveled without any baggage. She'd packed for hot weather, trading in her usual black attire for colorful sleeveless shifts and sandals, beachwear she had picked up at a local flea market.

Killian insisted on driving and got no argument from Port. He told Mohamed to sit in front with him.

"Buckle up, children." Killian said, turning the key in the ignition. Myria had never seen him in such high spirits.

"To the best road trip ever," Samantha said.

"This will be one for the papers," Port said.

"You will see," Mohamed said. "There is no country under the great blue sky like Morocco."

Several hours went past traveling along a tranquil road, where olive groves sprang from the clay of the red soil, rolling terrain, through white-washed villages.

Without warning Killian pulled the car over and got out. He had brought along a bottle of champagne.

Eager to stretch her legs, Myria got out of the car. When Killian passed the bottle to her, she said, "Might as well." Soon they were all sitting on the hood. Samantha remarked that the weather was positively steamy compared to Sevilla. Port answered that was because they were traveling south. Mohamed listened appreciatively but offered no comment.

"A toast!" Killian popped the cork, slugged at the bottle, and then passed it to Myria.

"*Arriba*," she said.

"Down the hatch," Killian said, boisterous.

She took a swallow and handed the bottle to Samantha.

"To our adventure."

Samantha drank and gave the bottle to Mohamed. He let Port have it. "Guests drink first."

"But Mohamed," Samantha cried. "You are our guest."

"It's okay," he responded. "All is well."

"Then give it to me," Killian said.

"Wait your turn." Port drank and made a face. "The stuff is warm."

"An all time low for you I imagine," Killian said, "forced to drink warm champagne."

"If you can take it, I can," Port said and took another drink.

They finished off the Cava, left the bottle on the side of the road, and resumed their places in the car. At the wheel, Killian kept up a lively stream of chatter while the rest stared out the window. Before reaching Algeciras, he cracked open another bottle.

"We'll never get this through customs," he said, "so drink."

"You can never drink too much champagne," Samantha said.

They passed the second bottle, Mohamed again gently declining, and Port complaining that there was nothing more disgusting than champagne that hadn't been properly chilled.

"Gawd," Myria said, shading her eyes from the bright afternoon light, forgetting that she was already wearing sunglasses. "I think I'm drunk."

"Isn't it great?" Samantha burped.

"Pull it together," Port said. "We've got to get across the border, and we don't want any trouble."

Instead of feeling insulted at the notion she might be anything less than "together," Myria found his presence of mind comforting.

"Right you are."

With the rolling Guadalquivir Valley behind them, the drive wound through villages scattered along the western coast; blue seas slipped in and out of view. At the maritime hub of Algeciras, they boarded a ferry, sailed through the straits to land at Ceuta.

According to the guidebooks, visitors could see the Spanish mainland from Ceuta but equally as important, the Rock of Gibraltar. As if in collusion, a band of clouds veiled the view of the famous island. Through the haze, Myria discerned only a glimmering outline narrowing as it gained in elevation to form a sharp pinnacle.

"Imagine the number of people who have wanted a piece of that pile of stones," Killian said.

"You never really hear about it, do you?" Samantha said.

"You do if you read history," Port said. "England, Spain, and Morocco have been fighting over it for centuries." He looked at Mohamed. "Isn't that right?"

Diplomatically, Mohamed gave no response.

Still in Spain, they had yet to pass customs. Mohamed told them it was a short drive on the outskirts of the city.

"Not yet," Killian said. "Let's find some place to eat. I'm famished."

"I'm famished too," Samantha said.

After some back and forth, they agreed to venture out of the ferry terminal for lunch, driving around the small city in circles until Killian pulled over and shut off the ignition.

"Do all places in Spain look the same?" Killian laughed. "You'd think we were still in Sevilla."

A cathedral, painted canary yellow, with twin spires, was the object of his comments.

"But we're not in Sevilla," Myria said, exhilarated. "It's entirely new."

"New or not, I need food," Port said.

They filed into the nearest restaurant. Port pronounced it "shabby."

"You mean colorful," Myria said, her response swallowed up by the loud music, some folkloric sounding tune.

"Five beers," Killian shouted to the barman. "And menus."

They ordered mortadella, with peppers and olives, served on Spanish bread. The five travelers ate without talking; the beer refreshingly cold, which meant no complaint from Port. Killian finished off Mohamed's beer.

Piling back into the car, Samantha was heard to ask: "Where are we going again?"

"Morocco," Port said.

"I think she knows that," Myria said.

"Chaouen," Mohamed said. "You never have seen a place like

it anywhere."

"It's supposed to be fabulous," Killian said.

Mohamed clapped him on the shoulder. "You will be astounded."

At the border, Moroccan officials, rifles slung across their chests, stopped the car, none too pleased at the sight of them. In French, they were ordered to get out; their vehicle, passports, and visas examined with suspicion. One of the officers pointed at Mohamed, took him aside, and went over his documents. Myria didn't like seeing him singled out. He'd done nothing wrong.

"Do you think we should say something," she asked Port.

"Wait," he said. "You don't want to mess with these guys."

"It doesn't seem fair," she said.

"Myria, don't interfere."

The officer at last satisfied that Mohamed's papers were in order, sent him back to join the others.

"*Maroc, Maroc,*" Mohamed intoned, as he slid into the front passenger seat.

Myria reached over and ran her hand lightly through his thick curls. "You are home now." He nodded without turning to look at her. She leaned back in her seat, her mind wandering. Sometimes, she imagined that she had woken up in her dreams. Only later, she would realize that she hadn't woken at all.

Killian turned off the car, and the road vanished. Night swiftly closed off the world around; without light, Myria's eyes told her next to nothing, and for the first time she experienced space as pure emptiness. She longed anxiously to be anywhere but suspended in all that darkness.

"We're going to have to turn around," Killian said at last.

Myria's stomach lurched. Turn around? Turn around!

"I hope you know what you're doing," she said.

Port pushed open the car door. "Are you kidding?"

For a moment, Myria wondered if he'd abandoned them. At least, there would be a witness if they plunged over the cliff.

He got back in the car "You don't have much room," he said to Killian.

Samantha yawned. "What time is it?"

Time to die. A miserable thought, Myria knew, but fear had taken hold, and wouldn't let her focus on anything but the horrible possibility of a violent death.

The motor started up with a cranky growl. Again, the sheen of the high beams. Killian adjusted the mirror. "The taillights must be out. I can't see a thing back there."

"I will get out and check," Mohamed said.

Myria could now see somewhat better, her gaze fixed on the lanky Moroccan. He took a step or two, staring out into the void, seemingly at ease, no stranger to the place.

When he got back in the car, he told Killian he didn't have more than a few meters, but he could get the vehicle turned around if he cut sharply to the right.

Killian nodded.

"Who has a smoke?" he asked.

Port lit a cigarette and handed it to him. "Anyone else want one?"

"Me," said Myria, morbid.

He passed her the pack and matches. She lit up.

The cigarette hanging from his lips, Killian put the car into drive and did as Mohamed recommended, cutting the wheel sharply to the right, then backing up slowly, cut the wheel again, until they were facing a sheer wall of mountain.

A flash of light was followed by a screech; a car coming in the other direction stopped short.

The driver screamed out his window.

"Mohamed?" Killian dragged heavily on his cigarette.

"A moment." Again, the Moroccan got out of the car, walked up to the other driver. Whatever he said must have calmed him because the driver put his car in reverse, backing up the mountain at an astonishing speed.

"All right," Mohamed called.

Killian smoked a moment before stubbing the cigarette out in the ashtray.

Myria wished fervently she would black out. Killian, one arm over the seat, smiled at her, and then hit the gas.

"Stop!" Mohamed cried. He told Killian to cut the wheel again to the right. Forward then back, forward then back; with each turn of the wheel, Myria imagined them toppling over the precipice.

With enough room for the other car to pass, Mohamed waved on the vehicle. When he was settled once more in the passenger's seat, Killian put the car in drive again, following two red taillights down the mountain. A half an hour later, they turned onto another road, and shortly after that, the terrain less steep, they continued on until Mohamed informed Killian that they were nearing their destination: Chaouen.

"There is no other place like it," Mohamed said. "You will find it amazing."

Myria asked Port for another cigarette. She smoked in silence, Mohamed's words repeating in her ears:

You will find it amazing.

CHAPTER SIXTEEN

THE BLUE CITY

Myria and Samantha sat, facing each other, on the twin beds in their hotel room.

"I can scarcely believe," Myria said, "we made it." She reached for Samantha. Samantha clasped her fingers, their folded hands forming a bridge over a strip of jeweled carpet.

"Exciting, isn't it?" Samantha unwound her fingers, and looked about the room: the walls painted a regal shade of blue, the hour-glass shaped window. "It couldn't be more perfect."

"Mohamed was right," Myria said. "It is spectacular."

Samantha nodded and then said she was going to find the bathroom.

"Do you know where it is?"

"Not sure," Myria said. "Down the hall, I expect."

They opened the door to find Killian on the other side. "And where are you two going?"

"Ladies room," Samantha said and slipped past him.

"She's in for a surprise." Killian laughed.

"I'm sure she'll tell me all the details," Myria said.

"Too bad we couldn't share a room," Killian said.

Was he flirting or just being annoying?

"You have Port and Mohamed to keep you company."

"Port is in a state of shock," Killian said. "I don't think he's used to sharing a bathroom."

"Welcome to Morocco," Myria said. "I hope he isn't complaining too much. I don't want him to make Mohamed feel uncomfortable."

"As if he cares," Killian said.

"He should care. Mohamed is doing us a favor."

"Port is a snob," Killian said, "but he's useful in a pinch."

Myria frowned. She didn't want to think of herself as someone who used people "in a pinch," a manipulator.

"I take it all back. He's probably not accustomed to budget hotels."

"Port will adjust." He stepped through the threshold and looked around. "It will do," he said.

"Don't you love all the colors?"

Samantha had by now returned. "Love what?"

"The décor," Killian responded.

"It's so blue," Samantha said.

"And pink, red, orange," Myria added, referring to the bedspreads.

"Dizzying," Killian said.

"Fantastic," Myria said. "Although, isn't it interesting." She stared thoughtfully at the carpet, its complex geometric patterning. "There aren't any pictures, just puzzles."

Killian made some reference to the prohibition against graven images.

Myria continued: "In Spain, there are so many religious figures, statues—everywhere you step, another Virgin, weeping."

"Not always weeping," Killian said.

Samantha was going through her bag. "What's next?" she asked.

"Dinner," Killian said.

"I'm famished."

"Me too," Myria said. She watched Samantha pull a woolly

sweater over her head.

"I should have brought warmer clothes," Myria said.

"You can pick something up when the markets open," Killian said. "Right now, let's get something to eat.

Chaouen glowed. The streets white as sheets pulled over the stones, tumbling steps, walkways that twisted up one alley, down another, lacking any definite direction or sharp angles; a village that to Myria seemed to have been molded by a thousand busy hands, and then washed in blue pastels.

The melee was brought to sudden order as the five travelers found themselves in a square plaza laid out in ceramic tiles. There wasn't any argument about where to eat since there was only one restaurant open for business. Regardless of the snap in the air, they decided to sit outside.

"We have the place to ourselves," Port observed.

"Yes, where are all the tourists?" Killian said, being ironic.

"In summer months, you can't budge from your hotel," Mohamed said, "so many people come to Chaouen."

A man swathed in a kaftan brought them tea, taking a moment to exchange of few words with Mohamed in an Arabic. Not for the first time that day, Myria was grateful to have him along. He was their friend, guide, translator—all in one delightful person. Mohamed would do anything for them. She was certain she could trust him with her life.

Myria reached for her cup, breathing in the scent of mint, and liking that it was so warm and sweet, sustaining somehow.

Skewers of roasted meats arrived: a platter of saffron rice mixed with vegetables, a bowl of slivered almonds, and flat bread.

"No wine, I suppose," Killian lamented.

Mohamed offered a smile of regret.

"No booze for you," Myria said. "Try the rice. It's delicious."

Port pronounced the dish oily but it didn't stop him from stuffing his mouth. Samantha also ate with gusto. Killian sampled only the meat. Mohamed watched in silence as they gorged themselves.

"You must eat with us," Myria said to him. "Please eat, or I will feel like a complete pig." She pushed the platter of half-eaten pilaf in his direction.

Killian snorted and Myria gave him a caustic look. "Please," she repeated to the Moroccan. "There's plenty for everyone.

Mohamed helped himself to the rice, and now it was Myria's turn to watch, as he took his food with two fingers, using the flatbread to spoon up whatever his hands couldn't hold.

"I feel so at home here," Myria said.

"Well, listen to you," Port said.

Over the rim of her teacup, Myria asked: "What's that supposed to mean?"

"Only that you seem content, dear," Killian said. "Not like you at all."

Samantha glanced at Port, who winked at her. Myria wanted to stuff a kebob in the girl's mouth, pour her tea over Port's head. So Killian called her "dear?" It struck her more as brotherly the way he'd put it. They were friends. Nothing more.

"Mohamed, ask the waiter if they take travelers checks," Port said.

He was up and out of his seat and went into the restaurant.

"They better," Killian said.

"We need to change money," Myria said. She hoped that Killian was right when he said that Morocco was dirt cheap. Her funds were fast draining away. She didn't look forward to having to call her mother to wire more cash when she returned to Sevilla.

Killian gazed at her thoughtfully. "Tomorrow the banks will open."

Samantha exclaimed that if she drank any more tea she would float off. "I think I'm ready for bed."

"It has been a long day," Port said.

Mohamed returned to the table. "No problem," he said, referring to the travelers checks.

"After all that driving, I need a walk," Killian said.

"Myria will go with you," Samantha said. She slung an arm around Port's neck, her voice breathy: "Take me home."

"Home? Haven't you noticed, Dorothy? You're not in Kansas anymore."

As the two were playing at Wizard of Oz, Killian talked in a hushed voice to Mohamed, who nodded vigorously, answering one question after another, his usually calm expression terse.

The waiter came with the bill. Port reached for it without a word and handed it to Mohamed, leaving it to him to sort it out. Mohamed told Port the sum and he pulled out his wallet. "This should do," he said. Satisfied, the waiter went back into the restaurant.

"See you back at the hotel," Killian said, waving the others off.

Myria sipped her tea, saw her friends walk across the meticulously tiled plaza. She wanted more tea, barrels of it, some excuse to stay put, in that tranquil spot, at perfect ease, knowing from the restless way Killian tapped his foot that he was already on the search, and for what, she didn't need to ask.

"You are out of your mind."

Killian's mouth was moving, and she heard every word, and each one set off alarm bells in her head. She hadn't come this far to wind up in a Moroccan jail, she told him.

"Relax." Killian said, utterly unperturbed.

He was brilliant. He was wealthy. He was handsome. He was charmed. He was an American. No harm had ever come to him and no harm would. Or so he believed, incapable of considering the consequences of his actions.

"I'm not doing this," she said.

"Of course, you are," he said. "It will be fun."

"You don't even know where you are," she said.

"As a matter-of-fact, I do."

He gushed now, over their great luck, because didn't she understand that the best place to buy hash was in Chaouen?

"Stupid me," she said. His recklessness dismayed her.

"You will see," he said. "There's nothing to it. Mohamed told me as much."

"And yet," she said, "he went back to the hotel"

"A favor," Killian said. "I didn't want to tell Port and Samantha."

"Why not?"

"Because then I'd have to share."

"Samantha is fast asleep by now. And Port—"

"Port isn't my keeper." Killian pushed back his chair and stood.

Morose, Myria considered her options: either she could try to find her way back to the hotel alone or she could go with Killian. The way back to the hotel, she couldn't remember it in that maze of a village.

Killian grabbed her hand across the table. "You only live once, Myria."

"How comforting," she said, wrestling free her hand.

Killian talked as they left the plaza and turned down the street, at one point stopping, his expression confused.

"Are we lost?" she asked.

"Uh, maybe," he said. "Let me think."

"We can try again tomorrow," she said. Perhaps he would come to his senses by then.

"I'm not giving up," he said. They were off again, climbing and descending, each step taking them that much farther from the hotel.

Turning a corner, they nearly ran into a man coming in the other direction. Myria and Killian were easy to spot as foreigners. Their dress was so different from their fellow night wanderer, his face partially concealed by a beige djellaba. Myria expected him to hurry past but he stopped. When he pulled back his hood, his face was as identifiable as a passport photo. He was American, not young—at least not anymore, his skin cratered by lines and acne scars. He was also stoned. Myria could tell by his pupils, large and yet, as if retreating from the light of a naked bulb hanging from the nearest doorway, his lids at half-mast.

"Far out," he said, by way of greeting.

Killian asked who he was.

"I go by many names," he said, enigmatic as a sphinx. "You can call me your H-man."

"Delighted," Killian said. "So where do we get hash around here?"

We! We! Myria wanted to scream: Not me. Him!

"Do you have any?" Killian asked.

"Nah," H-man said. "But there are people." He looked at Myria: "Hey, little girl, you like the Rif?"

"I couldn't tell you," she said. "We just got here."

"You got a name?" he asked.

"Go ask Alice, I think she'll know."

H-man cracked up. "You're pretty funny."

"I'm not," Myria said.

H-man laughed again. "Cool with me."

"Leave her alone," Killian said.

"Hey, I'm not hassling her," H-man said.

"Better not," Killian said. "About your friends?"

"Details, details, details," H-man said.

"And they are?" Killian asked.

"Some for me, some for my friends."

Killian glanced at Myria. He appeared to be losing confidence in H-man. But then: "Are you for real?"

"I'm here," H-man said, "at your service."

"Lead the way," Killian said.

They climbed a flight of stairs and entered a candle-lit room strewn with carpets and pillows.

"Wait here," H-man said.

He disappeared behind a thick, beaded curtain and returned with a Moroccan. They spoke Arabic, glancing every so often at Killian. Every cell in Myria's body was screaming "run."

"How much?" H-man said.

"Enough," Killian said.

"You need to be more specific," H-man said, with unexpected clarity.

"Hash first." Killian.

A woman peered out from the curtain and the Moroccan yelled at her in Arabic. She was gone, instantly, the Moroccan also disappearing behind the jangling beaded hanging.

"You are something else," Myria said to Killian. It was no compliment.

"Just wait," Killian said. "You'll thank me later."

"She will," H-man said, huddling in a corner.

Out came dark-brown bricks wrapped in cellophane. The Moroccan sat cross-legged on the carpet and leaned over to inspect a ceramic plate at his side. It was stacked with domino-sized squares, saffron in color. He took a piece and worked it between his palms, putting some aside, and using the rest to fill the narrow clay bowl of a pipe fashioned with a hardwood stem the length of his arm. After he got the pipe going, he passed it to Killian.

"Told you," H-man said from the shadows. "The shit couldn't be better."

"It's not bad," Killian said and took another toke. He passed the pipe to Myria. She dragged on it lightly, and the pipe went back to the Moroccan. The hash went around the room until the bowl was empty, a haze of sweet-smelling smoke filling the room. Killian took a match to the bowl causing the resin to sizzle.

"How much?" Killian asked.

"Depends on you," H-man said. "My guess is you're a recreational user."

"A gram will do," Killian said.

"Figured as much" H-man said. "Usually, this wouldn't be worth my friend's time but summer's a long way away. That's when you really see the—" H-man rubbed thumb and forefinger together: the international sign for "money."

"I guess we lucked out," Myria said.

"How you feeling, Alice?" H-man smiled at her.

She couldn't say how she felt, if she felt anything at all. Her thoughts separate from her somehow, the candles lengthening, brightening, and the designs in the carpet beginning to wander. Myria traced the lines with her finger, certain that there was a secret there—and if she followed the signs long enough the universe would crack wide open.

Killian held out the empty pipe. "More."

H-Man and the Moroccan exchanged words in Arabic. The Moroccan didn't seem displeased. "At your pleasure," he said, in very fine English.

Now there was pleasant conversation. Now, everyone was friends. Now, there was no sense of illegal doings.

"A gram costs," the Moroccan paused, "fifty dollars."

"Fine by me." He pulled his wallet from his pocket. American dollars fluttered onto the floor. "This should do."

The Moroccan eyed the cash. "I am satisfied."

Killian passed the pipe to Myria. "We are too."

H-man offered to take them back to their hotel.

"No!" Myria left the carpet to wander on its own. "We'll be fine."

The hash went into Killian's pocket. He looked over at H-man. "Later," he said.

Myria thanked the Moroccan several times. He didn't look at

her once.

"See you sometime, Alice," H-man said.

"Not likely."

The Moroccan nodded without smiling. She could feel his disapproval.

"So now where?" Killian stared up at the lamps illuminating blue washed buildings. He patted his pocket.

"Back to the hotel," Myria said. A nervous laugh welled up inside her but she choked it down before it bubbled over. "I'm tired. I need to sleep."

"Let me try to think," Killian said.

"Didn't you say you knew where we were?"

"Let's go this way," he said. "Down."

"Maybe we can ask for directions." Directions to where? She'd forgotten the name of the hotel.

"From whom?" Killian said. The streets were plainly empty, the wind chiming. A feral calico dashed in and out of the shadows.

"Are we lost?"

By then, the calico had sauntered back into the street. It was rubbing up against her ankles. Here, kitty, kitty. Maybe the cat could take them to their lodgings.

Killian grasped her elbow. "We are but who cares?"

Someone or something breathed on her. She put out a hand, to push away whatever it was huffing over her. The breathing wouldn't cease, it grew heavier, louder. Stranded on the extreme edge between sleep and waking, sudden fear caused her to lurch into consciousness with a shout.

"Are you okay?"

There was Samantha, dressed for the day. She hovered over Myria.

"Dreaming," she mumbled.

"It must have been some dream," Samantha said, and went to open the shutters, the sun flashing through the window.

"You snore, did you know that?" Samantha was now combing her hair.

"That must have been it," Myria said, groggy.

"What?" Samantha was now pulling her blond tresses into a ponytail, fastening them with a sparkly clip.

"The noise in my ears."

"You're lucky I'm a sound sleeper." Samantha was now inspecting herself in a compact mirror.

"I'm sorry," Myria said, embarrassed that she snored. Fat men snored. Old women snored. Not girls.

"You should hear my brother. He sounds like a bullhorn when he gets going." Gazing intently at her reflection, Samantha now applied a coat of frosted pink to her lips.

"You have a brother?" Myria, eyes closed, wished for a pair of blinders. The bright day cut like a saw through her. She rolled over, away from the light.

"Five of them." Samantha tilted her head back, raising the mirror just so. "I'm the only girl."

"Uh-huh."

"You also talk in your sleep."

Myria heard the snap of the powder compact as it closed.

Last night: it was all bits and pieces, still beyond her sleepy grasp to assemble into a complete scene.

"Why do you wear makeup?" Myria said. "You are a natural beauty."

"Where I come from, there is no such thing." She settled herself on the edge of Myria's bed, leaning forward, staring into her face.

"Sorry but you look ragged," she said.

"Don't be sorry," Myria answered. "I feel ragged."

"You and Killian have a nice time?"

Myria rubbed her temple. "We walked around a bit. Not much to do here at night."

"That's not what I'm asking."

"You've already asked me that a dozen times."

"Okay, okay," Samantha said. "I won't ask anymore."

"There's nothing to tell, really. We went for a walk. Oh, there was a cat."

Now it all came back, the entire night, scrolling before her like a film reel, every bit of what took place painfully real.

Liar, she was a liar. Samantha had a right to know the truth. What if H-man were an informant? What if the police were to knock on their door? What then?

"Where is the bathroom again?" Myria asked.

"Down the hall, dear," Samantha said.

Myria threw off the bedspread. She was still wearing yesterday's shift, the brisk air causing her extremities to tingle.

"We're going shopping today," she declared. "It's so cold. Do you think they sell sweaters here?"

Samantha told her not to worry. "I brought two."

"You are an angel," Myria said before she stumbled down the hall to the latrine.

⊠⊠⊠

One by one, they assembled in the hotel lobby. Myria avoided Killian by greeting Mohamed with a ringing, *"Bon jour!"*

Mohamed looked remarkably refreshed. He hadn't changed his clothes in days. Still, it was if being back in his native country cleansed him, restored his spirits. He was, to Myria, exquisitely aware, the way he anticipated their needs, demands. He was always tactful, but never calculating, exuding warmth and kindness. Proud of Morocco, he most certainly was, but his manner showed no hint of arrogance. Being from the United States, with its rugged individualism, not one of them fully absorbed how deep-rooted his hospitality: all were family once friends—that much Myria sensed.

Before anyone said another word, Mohamed announced that they would find a good cup of coffee nearby. "Better than you will find in Sevilla."

"Why is that?" Port asked.

"Because you haven't lived until you've had our spiced coffee." Mohamed said.

"Spiced with what?" Killian smiled at Myria. She continued to ignore him.

"Cassia, sesame and cumin, sometimes pepper," Mohamed said.

"Cassia sounds wonderful," Samantha said. "What is it?"

Mohamed explained that it was a spice much loved among Moroccans.

"He means, cinnamon," Port said in that *been around the world two hundred times* tone of his.

The spice in the coffee warmed Myria, made her tongue tingle. She tore her croissant in two, dunked half into the exhilarating mixture, and stuffed the crusty bread in her mouth.

Killian ordered another coffee.

"One for me too," Samantha said.

"It's truly beautiful here," Myria said to Mohamed, her mouth half-full.

"A historic city," Mohamed said.

"Then let's have a look around," Port said.

"I haven't finished my breakfast," Killian said. He picked at a slice of bread spread thick with fermented butter. "Is there any fruit?"

Mohamed spoke to the waiter. A plate of dried apricots soon appeared. Killian took several and passed the plate to Myria. "They're sweet."

"Like Myria," Samantha said, mischievous.

"It would take more than a few apricots to make Myria sweet," Killian said. She assumed he was mocking her, again, until he added: "Which is why she is so special."

"That's me. Special," she said, smiling at Samantha while silently cursing her. What would it take to get it through her pretty, little head that Killian was a friend? There was nothing more between them. There never would be.

"When do the banks open?" Killian asked, abruptly. "I'm flat out of cash."

"I guess this means I'm picking up the tab," Port said, "as usual."

Myria told him she would pay him back, every cent.

Port shrugged. "It's not my money."

Killian finished off his coffee. "But it will be one day."

They passed the day making a haphazard tour of the city. The Rif Mountains, its snowy peaks rearing skyward like the horns of a giant ram. Chaouen had been built at the base of a slope down which ran rushing waterfalls. Women, their long robes hiked to their knees, washed laundry in the river, slapping the soaking clothes against the stones. Children splashed in the water nearby.

Mohamed taught Myra that *souk* meant market and *medina*, old city, as they walked along. Vendors offered up a colorful and chaotic display: powdery dyes of all shades transformed burlap sacks into objects of wonder; there were wheels of bread, dried fruits, spices, and nuts for sale; hand-woven textiles. Above their heads, tangles of green vines formed canopies and provided shade.

Killian couldn't have been more pleased, an expression of delight had replaced his usual pout. He snatched a few moments with Myria to ask her how she was doing.

"Sleep well?"

"Like a rock," she said.

"Me too," he said.

"You know..."

He went to reach into his pocket.

And she'd been having such a pleasant time. She had almost forgotten the night before, or rather preferred to think it never happened. It was a false hope. Now, wherever they went, they might be stopped by the police. She didn't know how much hash was enough to get them in trouble. She assumed it wouldn't take much.

"You should throw that stuff in the river," Myria pleaded, begging him to be rational for once.

"Why would I do that?"

"Because I don't like the idea of walking around with..." What was the word? "Contraband."

Killian stroked her cheek. "No one knows. And no one cares."

"Promise me you won't tell anyone," she said, her pulse accelerating as he ran his finger across her lips.

"Only Mohamed knows," he said.

"Don't take advantage of him," she said, pushing his hand away.

"Whatever do you mean?"

"You know exactly what I mean."

Killian sighed. "We're going to have to do something about it sometime."

"But not now," she insisted.

"Tonight," he suggested.

"Where? On the street? At a café?

Killian pondered. "The hotel."

"Brilliant," she said, sarcastic. "I'll meet you in the bathroom."

"That's not a bad idea." He laughed. "The place stinks to high heaven."

"True," she said.

"Okay then."

Myria walked away. She feigned interest in a ceramic. The

vendor's eyes fixed on her as she held it up to the light. He took it from her, speaking in Arabic. She let him talk at her, smiling, then shaking her head, until Mohamed showed up at her side.

"Do you want it?" he asked.

"Not really," she said.

"Let's go." And with a word in Arabic to the disappointed vendor, they moved on.

"I like it here so much," she said to Mohamed.

"You will like Fes even better," he responded.

"You make it easy to leave then," Myria said, although, if she had her way, she would never leave that city, its seraphim blue houses and white streets.

Over dinner, Port declared that he missed Spain if only for the wine. Killian, for once, was silent. Samantha tried to get his attention by waving a kebob in front of him. He took it from her, sliding the meat off the skewer.

"How long is the drive to Fes?" Myria asked.

"Not far," Mohamed said. "I am anxious for you to meet my family."

"You seem so fond of them," she said.

"It has been too long."

Myria gave him an affectionate smile. "Will they mind the company?"

"They will treat you as one of us," he said, returning her smile.

"Who would have imagined that Morocco could be so welcoming," she declared.

"That's because you've never been to Paris," Port said.

"In what way is Paris better than Morocco?"

"Pernod, for starters," Port said.

Killian countered that he bet Port had never tasted Pernod in his life.

"I think it went out with World War II," he said.

"I declare," Samantha said, "the way you two talk." She looked wide-eyed at Myria. "Do you know what Pernod is?"

"It's a drink," she said. "I've read about it."

"What makes it special?"

"Ask Port," Myria said.

"We have Pernod in Morocco," Mohamed said.

"Do you?" Port said, as if nothing could be more ridiculous.

"Why wouldn't they," Killian said, licking his fingers. "They were colonized by the French."

Mohamed added, rather sadly, that in some ways they still were.

"You're not as bad off as Algeria," Killian responded.

"Now that's some consolation," Port said.

Myria flopped on her bed, propped herself up on one elbow. After the heavy meal, she felt like a fatted calf. She watched while Samantha went through her stash, laying out pendants cast in shiniest silver and inlaid with polished glass.

"I like that one the best," Myria said when Samantha held up a bright yellow gemstone.

"The reds are pretty too," Samantha said.

"They are."

"But these are fantastic." She held up a pair of ceramic beaded-earrings that hung to her shoulders.

"Very exotic," Myria said.

And there was more: bangles, necklaces, a jeweled box, an array of scarves, and a velvet bag filled with antique coins.

"It cost almost nothing," Samantha said, amazed at her good luck.

"Imagine that."

Samantha asked if she could see what Myria had bought.

"There wasn't enough time," she said. Enough money for baubles, rather.

Samantha looked at her. Myria smiled. Her arm had begun to

ache, so she sat up.

"You didn't buy anything!"

"I'm not much of a shopper," Myria said. "Besides, I don't wear jewelry."

Samantha reached for a blue silk scarf. "Here, this is for you."

It was a pretty bit of workmanship, the dye the exact color of the city's blue houses.

"You want to give it to me?" Myria said.

"I want you to have it," Samantha said.

Before Myria could protest, the scarf had been draped around her shoulders, its silk smooth against her neck.

Samantha stepped back, head cocked, as if studying a portrait. "It's a good color for you." And after a pause, said: "You should wear more color."

Myria took the scarf between her hands. "It's lovely." She looked up at Samantha. "And so are you."

A knock sent Samantha to the door. "Who is it?"

"A friend." It was Killian.

Samantha undid the door latch.

"Well, look at this," he said. "I think you bought the store."

Myria would have liked to crawl under the bed, somewhere out of sight. She knew Killian wasn't there to admire the jewelry.

"I couldn't resist," Samantha said.

"Who could?"

"Not me, that's for sure."

Killian glanced at Myria, who now had wound the scarf tightly around one hand.

"You aren't going to bed are you?"

"I am," Samantha said, a little too quickly. "I'm all done in."

"I'm all done in, too," Myria said.

Killian went to open his mouth. Myria shook her head, vehemently.

"Okay," he said. "I'll see you in the morning."

"Yes, you will," Myria said, relieved. Killian! He never seemed to know when to quit but maybe he was learning.

Still, he lingered, leaning against the doorway, with an up-to-no good smirk on his face, and those scandalously blue eyes of his.

"Myriam, give me a minute," he said.

Samantha was occupied with a pair of hoops, her head nearly resting on her shoulder as she fished for the hole in her earlobe. She glanced at Myria, all jewels and smiles.

"What for?" Myria wouldn't make it easy for him. Bastard! He was blackmailing her.

"I wanted to say good night to you."

"Ah, you can say it right here."

"No, I really can't," he insisted.

Myria was certain that Samantha's hopelessly romantic imagination was off and running. There would be no way to stop it if she went with Killian. The worst of it was that he seemed to be in on the joke—that they were a couple—and more than happy to use it to get what he wanted: a partner in crime.

"Don't mind me," Samantha said. She'd managed to insert both earrings and was turning her head, right then left, to see how they looked in profile.

"It'll just take a minute," Killian said to Myria.

She unwound the silk from her hand, set it aside.

To Samantha, Myria said: "Isn't he mysterious."

Samantha unhooked the earrings. "You know what? I'm going to put all this away and go straight to bed."

The door closed behind them, Myria hissed at Killian. "You are out of your mind. Crazy! A crazy, crazy person."

"Don't you love it?" His face had taken on a jaundiced color in the anemic light of the hallway.

All appeal to sense having failed, she said: "What do we do with it?" By "it," she meant the hash.

"Come on," he said. "I'll show you."

She followed him down a short flight of stairs to a window at the end of the corridor. The window opened without any effort.

He leaned his head out. "Look at that. It's incredible."

Myria put her hands on the sill and saw what he was talking about: it was as if there weren't enough space in the sky for the radiance swirling above them.

"It's gorgeous," she said.

He turned, his back now to the open window, and pulled a joint and lighter from his pocket.

"I could come back here," he said.

"It'd be nice to stay longer," she said.

The joint was burning now. Killian filled his lungs, holding the vapors in, and then exhaled the smoke out the window.

"Your turn," he said.

Myria took a drag. She figured if she helped him smoke the hash, the faster they would be rid of it. She didn't feel anything at first. She pulled a strand of tobacco from her tongue and passed the joint back to Killian.

"You need to learn how to roll a better joint," she said.

"Do I?" He toked heavily on the spliff. "It was the best I could do without rolling paper." He coughed and took another hit. "You try making a joint out of a cigarette."

"Sorry," she said. "It's better this way." It was her turn again. She smoked, fixated on the starry night.

"What way?"

"No pipes or paper." she said. "It's like any other cigarette."

"Exactly," he said.

"Exactly," she said. A warm sensation had come over her, relaxing from head to toe.

Killian took the joint from her. "I wish I'd made another," he said, plaintively.

"No more?"

"Not of this one," he said and flicked the spliff out the window.

After a long silence, she said: "We're here and everyone else is there."

Killian laughed. "It's more like we're there and everyone else is somewhere else."

"No, really," she said. "It's just us, in this place, and our friends, family are all far away, and that's kind of great. Don't you think?"

"You're stoned," he whispered in her ear.

"I am not," she said, "just a little, maybe."

"It's cold," he said. "I'm going to close the window."

"Right," she said. She couldn't feel the cold.

The window shut, stars vanishing. Myria slid to the floor, her back melting into the wall.

Killian sat beside her.

"I wonder," he said.

"About?"

"Things," he said, "about you."

"What about me?"

"If you're still stuck on what's his name."

"I wouldn't know," she said.

After a long silence, he stood, reached for her hand, pulling her to her feet. "I'll take you back to your room."

"Don't worry," she said. "I can get there on my own."

"You're sure?"

"As sure as anything," she said. "See you tomorrow."

She made her way down the green hall, up the stairs, to stand in front of the door to her room behind which she hoped Samantha was sound asleep.

CHAPTER SEVENTEEN

ROAD BLOCKS

Myria was up before Samantha, peering through the shutters, the sun rising between the two high peaks for which the city was named. Chaouen, meaning: "look at the horns." She opened the shutters a bit wider, breathed in the cool air to clear her head.

It was a travel day. They had a four-hour trip ahead of them before they would reach Fes. Mohamed encouraged them to avoid the bus route, even if it was faster. Another route was decided on, one that would take them deep into the mountains. "There," he said, "they would see the beauty of the land."

She was in no hurry to get on the road. But that's how it was when traveling; always on the move, never time enough to explore, to seek out places secreted away from tourists, the ones that only those who lived there saw. A day in the blue city was not enough. She'd liked to spend a week or more. What she couldn't predict was that one day, years later, she would return. It wouldn't be the same, but then neither would she.

In the latrine, where there was no shower, she did her best to wash up. She ran a comb through her hair, wrestling free the tangles and knots. Without a mirror, she had become invisible to herself—and it was lovely not to care how she looked. With it came freedom from all the insecurity that plagued her over the years: the other children making fun of her almond-shaped green eyes, and messy hair, and the bump in the nose that she'd inherited from her mother; or the pale brown moles on her right cheek, which marked her as her father's daughter. She couldn't see any of it. What a relief to think that she could be as she was, without any cosmetics.

Before she dressed, she sniffed at the sweater Samantha lent her. It reeked of tobacco and hashish. There was nothing to do about it, except purchase some oils that would mask the odor. She might have enough money.

Samantha had gotten out of bed by the time she returned to their room.

"I hope you don't mind," Myria said, "if I borrow your sweater one more day. I think it will be warmer in Fes."

"Keep if for as long as you need," Samantha said. She stretched, let out a delicate "coo" and asked if there were any hot water.

"Not a drop I'm afraid."

Samantha shrugged. "Oh well, I've hiked the Rockies for weeks without a bath."

It occurred to Myria that she didn't cut Samantha enough slack. She withheld her real opinions and it made her false when the other girl was completely transparent. She was blond and bubbly, but she wasn't some fainting daisy. She was strong and ready to tackle any adventure.

"I'd like to visit Colorado one day," Myria said.

"You should," Samantha said. She wrapped herself in a terry-cloth robe and grabbed for her toilet bag. "It's not Morocco, though."

Myria rolled the phrase over in her mind. It's not Morocco, no, and maybe there was no other country like it.

Careening vehicles came at them from the other direction. When she wasn't closing her eyes or gripping the seat, Myria marveled that many of them were Mercedes, relics from another era, each one loaded with far more passengers than she thought imaginable, each one traveling at break-neck speed. Port drove defensively. They snaked their way east, the road plunging down the Bab-Berret pass.

Scrub lands gave way to alpine greenery, barren steppes, and flowery shrubs along the roadside came and went from view with the tumble of the mountain. Adobe style houses, pitched on dried-up riverbeds, clung precariously to gravel hillsides.

Farther down the eastern ridge of the Rif, oak forests grew denser, the road more rutted as they neared the town of Issaguen. By then, the road had nearly fallen apart, potholes everywhere.

"How much farther to Fes?" Port asked Mohamed.

"It's not so far," he said, "a few hours."

"Can we get gas here?"

"And something to eat," Samantha said. "I need food."

If Issaguen had seen better days, it would be hard to tell. The village was a dismal sight with a café or two open for business but not much else.

"Is anybody home?" Killian being funny.

Mohamed responded that few tourists traveled that way.

Myria gazed over Samantha's shoulder at the roadside, where robed men milled about, donkeys ambled by, and gutted sheep, blood dripping, hung on hooks.

"We're off the map now," Port said.

"Fabulous," Killian said. "We can brag to all our friends we've seen one of the most destitute towns in all of North Africa."

For more times than she could count, she wished Killian wouldn't speak that way in front of Mohamed, even if he was only joking. The Moroccan assured them that the food in Issaguen would be better than in the tourist towns.

"You will have a real Moroccan meal here," he said.

"It's up to you guys," Port said. "Café one or café two?"

They pulled up alongside a restaurant. A man sat at the entrance, working a strand of wooden prayer beads in one hand.

Killian was the first out of the car. Tall, his blue eyes hidden by expensive sunglasses, and dressed in jeans and sandals, he was certainly a tourist—and yet, because he took everything in stride, he was more than someone simply passing through. He couldn't get enough, enjoying every dodgy crook and cranny, his complaints a kind of habit.

The restaurant owner tucked his prayer beads in the pocket of his robes when he saw them coming. Mohamed greeted him in Arabic. They were ushered into a small room, dark and stuffy, bereft of a single window. They took over a table closest to the door.

There wasn't any reason for ordering. Everyone who came into the place was served the same meal: mint tea, saffron rice with mutton, and bread.

"Not bad, really," Port said.

"And it will cost nothing," Killian said.

"The tea," Samantha said, "it's so sweet and..."

"Minty?" Myria said.

Samantha smiled. "That too."

"I really do like it here," Killian said—a rare concession of approval on his part. Mohamed beamed.

"So do I," Myria said. She worked her tongue against a scrap of gristle that had caught in her teeth.

Port pushed his plate away. "I didn't see a gas station."

"We will find one further on," Mohamed said.

"How much gas do we have?" Killian asked.

"About half a tank," Port said.

"No problem," Mohamed said, "more than enough to get to Fes."

Port resumed his place at the wheel, Mohamed at his side. Killian, content to be a passenger, sat to the far left, Myria in between him and Samantha. They were less than thirty minutes outside of Issaguen when Port announced: "Road stop."

"Where?" Killian asked.

"Just ahead," Port said.

"Damn it," Killian said.

Myria craned her neck to see. Men in army fatigues and black berets waved one vehicle after another to the side of the road.

Port put on the brakes. Killian casually reached into his shirt pocket and took out what was left of the hash. He broke it in two, gave half to Myria, and said: "Eat it."

She didn't bother to protest. The soldier's guns were enough persuasion. She chewed. The hash wouldn't dissolve.

"Is there any water?"

Killian's jaw was tense, unmoving. He must have swallowed his portion whole. "We don't have any."

"Shit," Myria said.

"Just swallow," Killian said.

Samantha reached over and rubbed Myria's head. "It'll be okay."

"Right," Myria said and swallowed hard, the hash sticking in her esophagus. She tried again; it was like trying to swallow dirt—but, with one of the soldiers waving his rifle in their direction, she managed it.

Port rolled down the window. The soldier addressed him in French.

"He's telling us to get out," Mohamed said. "We have to do what he says."

They scrambled out of the car and walked several feet to a narrow ditch. The roadside was now crowded with men, women, children—and a bleating goat. The officer spat at Mohamed's feet. Myria couldn't bear it, the way that he was singled out for abuse.

"I don't understand," she said in a low voice to Killian. "Why do they go after him like that?"

"Because he's a poor Moroccan," Killian said.

"How miserable for him," Myria said.

"And you're a poor American," Killian said.

"It's a wonder you'd even talk to me," she said, in a prickly voice.

"I like talking to you," he said.

"How could you?" she said. "I'm practically white trash."

"You're not so bad," he said. "You got yourself a rich boyfriend."

Sheffield. Again! She didn't enjoy being reminded of him, especially in the way Killian did—to cause her embarrassment. Why, she couldn't fathom. "Well, here's the thing," she said, "I didn't get him."

"I'm glad," Killian said.

"For my pain?" she asked.

"Because you're better than he is," Killian said.

Myria would never understand him. But then, she never understood Sheffield either, not really. Neurotic was the word that came to mind. At the moment, she was in the throes of more than neurosis. On the verge of panicking, she didn't think she could stand much more. The soldiers swarming about; the way they continued to harass Mohamed.

"It's one thing to be poor," she said, "but it shouldn't be a crime."

"I wouldn't know," Killian said.

"Lucky you," she said.

They watched as a soldier went to inspect the car: ashtray, seats, dashboard, and side pockets. He stepped away from the car. He snapped his fingers in Mohamed's direction. The Moroccan asked Port for the key to the trunk. Every bag was opened, contents emptied in a heap in the dust. The soldier, the butt of his rifle resting on the ground, bent on one knee over Samantha's belongings. He held up a scarf and sniffed it—to see if it smelled of hash, Myria assumed. The sweater she wore stank of it. Frightened, she looked up, seeking escape in the fold and thrust of the upper Rif, wanting desperately to hide in one of its enormous pleats.

The soldier, scarf still in hand, began to banter with Mohamed, his manner amused. Mohamed answered in a respectful tone. Myria could make out a few words: *Américains, Espagne, Fes*. The scarf dropped to the ground as the officer got back to his feet.

"He wants to see your documents," Mohamed said.

Port reached for his wallet and pulled out his license. It occurred to Myria that he was the only one with an international driver's license, and that it was probably a good thing that the rental car was in his name.

The officer, explained Mohamed, was interested only in passports and visas.

Scowling, the officer examined the blue covers with the American eagle emblazoned in gold. He flipped through the passports, checking the photos against faces. Samantha glanced at Myria, to see how she was holding up, probably. Not so good, Myria wanted to say; instead, she tried to repress any sign of fear that might give her away. Killian sighed, bored. He muttered something about their whole day being wasted.

"We're Americans."

"Outrageous," Port said.

"I mean really," Killian said, "this sort of thing would never happen in the States."

"No, it wouldn't," Port said.

"Could you two just shut up," Myria said, choking down more terror than hash at the moment.

The guard handed Port their passports, and patting Mohamed on the shoulder moved on.

"Well, that was fun," Killian said.

Mohamed was already gathering up their clothes. Myria and Samantha also got to work, throwing their belongings into suitcases without much thought of what belonged to whom. Mohamed held up Killian's duffle, and Myria snatched it from him.

"How about some help here," she said to Killian.

Port picked up a pair of jeans and dusted them off. "Glad I didn't bother to bring any formal wear," he said.

Killian burst into laughter. "A tux—now that would have made an impression."

A series of sputters and roars could be heard ahead. A silver Mercedes at the head of the line drove off.

"Time to go," Mohamed said.

What hadn't been packed got tossed into the trunk.

"We can sort it out later," Killian said, "when we get to Fes."

"You will see," Mohamed said, "it is even better than Chaouen."

Port got behind the wheel. "To that, I say, let's get the fuck out of here."

"They didn't even try to shake us down," Killian remarked.

"Small favors," Port responded.

"No kidding," Killian said.

"At least that's over with," Port said.

"And just when things were getting interesting," Killian said.

"Please," Myria said. "If you think this interesting, I wonder how you'd feel about the inside of a Moroccan jail."

Mohamed turned to her. "I am sorry for the trouble."

"Don't say that," Myria said. "It's not your fault. You have done everything for us."

"Moroccans, we are not bad people," he said.

Saddened that she'd hurt his feelings, she said: "I never once thought they were."

Samantha leaned across the seat. She offered Mohamed one of her glittering smiles. "It wouldn't even occur to us." She sat back and remarked to no one in particular: "I'm having a great time."

Throughout the trip, Mohamed had spoken little, except when asked for something, or to offer help in some way. Killian had described Mohamed to Myria as a talker, a drinker, and a guy who liked a good time. Once they'd crossed the border into Morocco, she noticed a change in him. When in the streets, he guided them to cafes, through markets, showed them the best sights. He made every effort to make certain they had everything they needed. At meals, though, he would have gone hungry if not encouraged to eat. He laughed only if they did. He was quick to offer apologies for inconveniences big and small. He never failed to put them first, and by doing so, it prevented him from behaving as if he was one of them.

So she was glad to see him become less guarded as they neared Fes. He smoked cigarettes with Killian and Port. He spotted a gas station and they got out, stretched their legs, while Mohamed took care of the car.

Back on the road, he explained that Fes was the oldest of Morocco's imperial cities—the others, Marrakech and Meknes. He talked about his family and how long it had been since he'd seen his mother. He said he was her entire life. His decision to study in Spain had been very difficult for her.

The road never stopped doubling back on itself, an incessant series of tight switchbacks. If they weren't descending, Myria would have sworn they were traveling in circles. They looped north, and then west, the road hugging the fortified walls that had protected the city for centuries from invaders.

Mohamed became even more animated now that they were in striking distance of their destination. Fes was a city within cities, a labyrinth, connected by hour-glass-shaped gates.

"In Morocco, the old is new, the new centuries old." Mohamed said, excited. He went on, keeping up a stream of enthusiastic talk, trading jokes with Port and Killian. He laughed easily. Finally, he was able to be himself. He was almost home.

CHAPTER EIGHTEEN

FES TO MARRAKESH

They entered Fes el-Jdid with crazed hoots. Samantha congratulated Port on his driving. He smiled at her in the rearview mirror.

"One heck of a trip," he said.

"It was a blast," Killian said, no hint of his usual sarcasm, particularly the sarcasm he seemed to reserve for Port. He had a genuinely good time, and not even the rough spots had tamped down his spirits.

"Now I will take you to my family," Mohamed said in a proud, happy voice. "You will meet my father, my mother, and my sisters."

Myria couldn't even imagine. If she showed up at her doorstep with four strangers in tow, her parents would be completely freaked out.

"Who has a smoke?" Port asked.

"I want one too," Samantha said.

Killian lit cigarettes, five in all, one by one, then crumbled the empty pack and dropped it on the floorboard.

Some discussion ensued about the car. Mohamed mentioned a lot where someone would look after it. They would pay, of course, but it didn't matter. They had made it to Fes.

Without bothering to put their disheveled clothes in order, they grabbed a toothbrush, or a shirt, and stuffed them into one of the duffle bags.

Mohamed's father greeted his son by taking his shoulders firmly in both hands and kissing the top of his head. His mother stood by, her cheeks wet with tears. Their affection openly displayed, bestowed without reservation upon the young Moroccan, who appeared on the doorstep with his friends, a ragged quartet of foreigners.

Following Mohamed's example, Killian removed his sandals.

"When in Morocco," he said.

"You take off your shoes," Port said.

"I will if you will," Samantha said.

Killian dropped his dirty sandals next to the door on his way in.

Mohamed's mother had dried her tears. Myria saw her glance in her direction. Cautious, she managed a smile. After a word with her son, she vanished into a back room.

Port and Killian did what Americans do: they shook hands with Mohamed's father.

"I'm not sure what to call him?" Samantha was referring to Mohamed's father.

"Not sure either," Myria said. It didn't seem the right moment to interrupt Mohamed and ask, "Hey, by the way, what is your dad's name?"

Mohamed turned to them. "Why are you standing in the door that way? Come in. Come in."

Myria placed her shoes next to Killian's. And there they were, through the threshold, and clearly not knowing what to do.

"This is my papa," Mohamed said.

He translated as Myria and Samantha engaged in pleasantries. "How nice to meet you." "You have a lovely home." "Thank you for having us." "We hope it's okay we are here."

Papa looked at his son, who translated their every word into the throaty melodies of his native Arabic.

"My father is pleased to have you as his guests," Mohamed said.

Myria looked about the living room. No sofas, tables, or chairs. The rough stone floor had been covered in Moroccan style carpets, one laid over the other, and large pillows lined the beige walls.

Mohamed said his mother would return soon with tea and pastries. They could wash up in the bathroom. The latrine at the hotel in Chaouen was positively modern by comparison. It had a toilet and a working sink. Myria took one look at the hole cut out of the concrete floor, the bucket of water nearby, and couldn't help but find it grim.

"If you don't mind," Killian said pushing past her. "I haven't taken a piss all day."

Myria remembered Samantha telling her that she'd hiked the Rockies for weeks without a bath. When her time came, she pulled down her underwear, wishing as never before that there was toilet paper. She eyed the water bucket and dipped a hand in, splashing off, and then shook her hands dry.

The tea and almond cookies, arranged on the largest silver platter Myria had ever seen, was set on the carpet in the center of the room. They gathered around. Myria asked Mohamed if they could meet his sisters. She heard them, from the back of the apartment, taking to each other.

"Maybe tomorrow," he said.

His father called out. The sisters' chatter ceased.

"I'd like that very much," she said.

After that, she noticed he spoke almost exclusively to Killian and Port.

There were customs. Myria was only beginning to understand. She would do her best to observe them but she had arrived unprepared. Would it have been so different in the States? She was too tired at the moment to think more about it. She ate an almond cookie, pronounced it "delicious," and drank her tea.

Mohamed's mother returned to clear away the dishes. Papa stood and patted his son's shoulder.

"Good evening," he said, in English.

A chorus of bedtime blessings went up in the room, accompanied by several more "thanks" and "your hospitality is most appreciated."

Mohamed brought out blankets.

"What a day," Killian said.

"The stories we will have to tell," Samantha said.

Myria was trying to decide which corner of the room to claim as hers. With a blanket under one arm, she decided it didn't matter, and flopped on the closest pillow.

Killian said he wanted a smoke.

"We're out of cigarettes," Port said. He was already flat on his back.

Killian paused. "We could go out to buy some."

Before Mohamed said a word, Myria intervened. He'd be up in a flash, ready to take Killian anywhere he wanted to go. Mohamed had done enough for them for one day.

"No one is going anywhere," she said.

"All right then," Port said. "Lights out."

Killian sighed. "How boring."

"Someone put a leash on him," Port said.

"It would have to be a very long leash," Samantha said.

"There's no leash long enough," Killian said. He nudged Myria with his toe.

"Keep your feet to yourself." If she weren't so drained, she would have continued to scold him. As it was, she didn't have the energy. Her lids sank over her eyes; her body sank deep into the carpet. She needed to sleep, forget everything—even her name.

⊠⊠⊠

Fes was a city built out of some design that exceeded her com-prehension. If she liked or disliked it, what did it matter? The city transcended her, both in time and space, and she was nothing to it.

Mohamed would ask: "Do you like Fes so far?"

"It's amazing," she would say, and how stupid it made her feel to say so. Amazing was a silly word. Amazing couldn't begin to describe Fes. She would have to do better.

The moment they'd entered the medina, the old city, she became confused, ungrounded. Her legs moved under her, but so did the streets. She would reach the end of an alley, or climb a set of rough-hewn steps, turn back to see where she'd come from, and couldn't be certain if she'd come that way at all. Navigating it would have been impossible without Mohamed.

Every shop was open for business. The shopkeepers didn't wait for them to enter. They came at them, urged them inside. If they refused the invitation, Myria could hear anger, or was it disappointment? Whatever she heard, she imagined that she'd personally insulted the person.

"Don't worry," Mohamed would say.

"I'm not."

Whatever was touched was already sold. It was only a matter of agreeing on a price. Bartering took some getting used to, as usually it meant paying more than less. Without much money to spend Myria kept her hands to herself.

Samantha pointed to one shop and the five of them went in. The owner brought out tea. Killian and Port drank up. Mohamed followed Samantha into the back of the store. When she joined them, she had three new scarves to add to her collection.

"I'm going to mail these back home as presents," she said.

It's good quality," Mohamed observed.

The shop owner launched into commentary that only the

Moroccan understood. Myria imagined that he expected them to
purchase more than a few scarves. He had a family to feed. He
had a business to run. He had money to make. It was the same
everywhere, wasn't it? Ideally, they would leave arms laden with
reams of dyed fabrics.

She would leave Fes with only her impressions as a souvenir: the
sense of traveling back in time; the sight of ramparts, tunnels, and
stone corridors; the smell of burning incense. Water, she could
hear it, rushing, but where? She tried to hone her ear. She couldn't
pick out one distinct sound. The stones were vibrating with the
footfall of hundreds of feet, hoofs, and carts. And then, as if in a
relay of voices, she heard it: *"Allah Akbar."*

"The call to prayer." Mohamed said.

"What does it mean?" Myria asked.

"Allah is the almighty," he responded.

It was the first time she noticed the call to prayer since she'd
arrived in Morocco. Either she was distracted, or half-asleep, but
in the Rif, the call was like a rumble from above, thunder. Only in
the Fes did it take on a more tangible reality. She learned to listen
for it and to recognize it when she heard it.

Later, Killian asked her if being in a Moslem country made her
feel strange.

"Because?"

"You're Jewish"

"Should I?" she said. "I don't think Mohamed would care."

"Mohamed will never tell you how he really feels."

"Are you calling him a hypocrite?"

Killian said: "Of course not."

"It sounds that way," she said.

"I meant he's too considerate. He wouldn't want to insult you
to your face."

She smiled, her housemates coming to mind, Espinosa in
particular, who never held back. Whatever she thought, she said.

"I don't think Mohamed is capable of insulting anyone," Myria said.

"Maybe," Killian said.

"I sometimes wonder if there isn't more anti-Jewish sentiment at home than in Morocco."

Killian shook his head. "Jews have it okay here in Morocco, but I wouldn't say they are better off."

"Well, we don't really know, do we?" she said.

He looked past her, staring at some sight—or commotion—in the distance. "I would wager a few things, and one of them is that we're all better off in the States."

"So why leave then?"

He shrugged. "I didn't give it a lot of thought."

Neither had she.

Seated on cushions, the dishes came and went, served in large ceramic plates from which everyone ate, using their fingers, mopping up the spiced juices with bread. The slim cups for tea never went empty. They were treated to pastries. They tried everything. They couldn't refuse to sample whatever was served— and they wouldn't. It was more than a meal: it was a banquet. A feast.

Papa had allowed his daughters to eat among them. They sat, smiled, nodded, and sipped tea. Much of the time they were up and about, helping their mother.

Myria kept tugging at the hem of her dress, aware that her knees were showing. She didn't dare sit cross-legged, although it would have been more comfortable, but leaned sideways against a pillow for support.

Afterwards, they lied about, stuffed and lethargic.

It appeared that Mohamed hadn't told his parents he'd be leaving the next day with his friends. His father didn't take the news well, shaking his head and sighing audibly. His mother sobbed, bent over, repeating her son's name. Her grief was distressing to witness. Mohamed glanced at his friends.

"She is always like this when I go," he said.

"We understand," Myria said, in an attempt to be consoling.

"I feel horrible," Samantha said.

Myria gave her a wide-eyed warning. "They can hear you."

Samantha cupped a hand to her mouth. "I think they blame us," she said.

"He has to get on the road sometime," Myria said.

"So do we, come to think of it," Port said.

"I'd rather you didn't remind me," Killian said, and yawned.

Neither Killian nor Port paid much attention to the sad scene unfolding a few feet away. Maybe their disinterest in the family's sorrow was best; it spared Mohamed from having his mother gawked at by the Americans—the very same Americans who would spirit her only son away come morning.

Mohamed's father gestured to his firstborn to follow him. Taking his mother by the elbow, Mohamed excused himself, and guided her to the back of the apartment, out of sight, although not out of earshot. Her frightful keening could still be heard.

"Such a shame," Samantha said.

"What makes you say that?" Myria asked.

"They seemed to like us," Samantha said. "At least, I thought so."

"Not much we can do about it," Port said.

"Nope," Killian said.

"His parents don't want us to take him along, that's obvious," Myria said. "Maybe we should go without him."

"It's up to Mohamed," Port said.

"The worst thing we could do is leave him here," Killian said. "He'd think we'd dumped him."

"I suppose that wouldn't be very nice," Samantha said, "after all he's done for us."

"It's not as if he's gotten nothing out of it," Killian said.

"A free ride to Fes, for one thing," Port said.

"A bit of adventure," Killian added.

"Being with you is adventure enough," Myria said.

Killian was flat on his back, staring at the ceiling, the fissures and brown patches of exposed concrete where the plaster had fallen away. "Why thank you, Myriam."

Only the direction had been decided on: they'd head south. They'd done little to prepare. What was there to do? They wore the same clothes they had on when they'd arrived. They'd slept in them, toured the Medina in them, and would sleep in them again. Trips to the bathroom were infrequent and turned each one into an emergency. Killian vowed that he wouldn't eat another thing until he'd moved his bowels.

"I haven't taken a proper shit in days," he declared the next morning.

Samantha cracked up. Port gave Killian a *we're all in the same boat* look. Myria cringed. Bathrooms and what she did in them were matters of extreme privacy to her. It would take a great bout of constipation to get her to announce to her friends she hadn't "taken a proper shit."

Mohamed did what he could to address Killian's complaints. "You must drink more mint tea. It aids the digestion. Why do you think Moroccans drink tea? It is good for the health. You drink it and have no problems."

Killian groaned. "The tea is pure sugar. Too much sugar is bad for you."

"Sugar is not bad for you," Mohamed said. "Why do you think Moroccans use so much sugar in our tea? You feel good, stay healthful."

"If that were true—" Killian let out an abject sigh.

"I can bring you tea," Mohamed offered. An offer was only

as good as one's actions in Morocco. He went straight to the kitchen. Myria could hear him exchanging words with his mother, apparently explaining the situation to her. She seemed to have calmed down since the night before. She served them spice cakes for breakfast. She'd poured out the tea. When they finished eating, she had returned to take away the dishes. But if Mohamed said that Killian needed more tea, his hard-worked mother would never refuse. If the silver tea set had been cleaned, polished and stored, it would be taken out again. Water would have to be boiled. The tea would have to steep. Only then, would tea be served, and not by Mohamed. In his home, the women did the work. The mother, his sisters: they were his dueñas. Myria's own mother had a job. She was a college professor. She didn't have time to clean, cook, or put supper together. It wouldn't have occurred to Myria to say to her: "Can you get me a cup of tea?"

Samantha said she wouldn't mind another glass of tea when Mohamed's mother brought out the serving tray, on which rested the domed pot with its swan-like spout, an item of rare luxury in their friend's modest home.

Again, they gathered in a circle. The glasses, inserted into silver holders, were filled.

Myria asked Mohamed how to say "thank you" in Arabic.

"No need for thank you."

"But I want to know how to say it," Myria insisted.

"*Shukran bezzef,*" he said.

When Mohamed's mother turned to go, she called out the phrase, no doubt mangling it, to the woman. Mohamed's mother turned around. What did Myria want?

Port blew on his tea. "Now you've gone and done it."

"Mohamed," Myria said, "please give your mother our thanks."

Over his shoulder, Mohamed said a few words to his mother. She smiled at Myria before returning to the kitchen. What would she do while they drank tea? Would she stare out the window?

Was there a window? The outer room had none. Sometimes, the front door would be left ajar; when closed, they were completely shut in. There had to be some kind of ventilation or the house would be filled with smoke. Stench from the latrine would make the place smell foul. There were ways to combat bad smells by lighting incense. Mohamed referred to it as "amber."

She caught Killian staring at her.

"A *dirham* for your thoughts?"

"Nothing much," she said.

"Feeling better?" Mohamed asked Killian.

"Not exactly fabulous," Killian said.

"Fabulous is good, yes?" Mohamed asked.

"Such a New York thing to say," Port remarked.

Mohamed didn't quite get Port's meaning from the expression on his face.

"Port is making fun of Killian for acting like a New Yorker," Samantha explained.

"I never hear anyone say 'fabulous' in New York," Myria said.

"It means good, right?" Mohamed asked.

"More like wonderful," Port said.

"Much better than good," Myria said.

Killian laughed garrulously.

Mohamed must have thought him crazy. Myria set down her cup. "Sometimes you just have to laugh," she said.

Samantha agreed. "No help for it."

"It's the sugar," Port said.

"More sugar for Killian," Mohamed said.

Killian—tears of mirth streaming from his eyes—shook his head. He brushed at his cheeks and, with tenuous composure, said: "I'll pass."

At night, after lights out, the four of them discussed in hushed voices where they should go next. South. Along the western coast or through the interior? The coast didn't spark much interest.

Perhaps, if the weather were blazing hot, they would be inclined to head to the beach. Myria hadn't taken off Samantha's sweater since she'd arrived, the stone city making for cool days and even colder nights. Another possible obstacle was the coast itself: wherever there were beaches, there would be tourism. Even if the Moroccan coastline wasn't crowded at that time of year, they'd heard stories of what had happened to the Spanish beaches along the Mediterranean: chock-a-block with condos and discos. At all costs, they wanted to avoid the ravages of tourism. It was decided: the interior sounded more appealing. The route would take them through the High Atlas. To their ears, the mountain range suggested a certain rugged romance. Destination: Marrakesh.

"Faster road goes east," Mohamed said when they told him. "Most go that way. It will take you through Rabat and on to Casablanca."

"By faster road, you mean highway," Port said. He had a copy of Frommers in his lap and was attempting to read it in the dim light.

"Casablanca doesn't interest me that much," Killian said. "I can skip it."

"I've seen the movie," Port said.

"Me too," Myria said. "It's played weekly on the tele in the pension where I live."

"You poor thing," Port said.

"Of all the gin joints, in all the towns, in all the world, she walks into mine," Killian quoted.

"You sure know your Casablanca," Samantha said.

"Who doesn't?" Port said.

"Did they even film Casablanca in Morocco?" Myria asked.

"I doubt it," Killian said.

"Not likely," Port said.

"You mean there is no Rick's café?" Samantha said.

"Sorry, darlin', no gin joints for you," Port said.

Mohamed's lips parted but he closed his mouth without a word.

"We agree," Killian said, "Skip Casablanca."

"I'm with you," Port said. "Marrakesh won't be too hot this time of year."

"Marrakesh must be raging hot in the summer," Killian said.

"If we're going that far south, now is the time," Port said. "It will be nice and cool."

"Good point," Samantha said. "The mountains will be pretty."

"How long does it take going through the Atlas Mountains?" Port asked.

"From Fes, it will take a full day," Mohamed said.

"Not a problem," Myria said. "We want to see the countryside."

"The real Morocco," Samantha said.

"Real Morocco," Mohamed intoned.

The "real" Morocco. Myria could see their friend was perplexed. Wasn't everything in Morocco real to Mohamed? He'd never been to the States. He didn't know that the northeast corridor was a grim stretch of highway running up and down the coastline. Strip malls, rest-stops, and chain restaurants, the gaudy oases of commerce lined up along the massive thoroughfare. He hadn't experienced the crushing traffic of the "beltway" that held Washington commuters hostage day in and out. He would no doubt see something of his own Fes in Manhattan, high rises built of solid brownstone. But what would he think of the houses that clotted the suburbs with their thin veneer of aluminum siding? He didn't know that very few things in the States were built to last decades much less centuries.

"Can you get us there?" Port asked Mohamed, "to Marrakesh?"

"I know it well," he said. "My uncle lives in the High Atlas."

"Splendid," Killian said.

"Fabulous," Samantha said.

Scrambling skyward, snow-capped peaks caught the rays of the great round sun. Beneath the opulence, the road was little more than a rutted byway that dipped without stopping, as if the mountain wanted to spit them out onto the flatlands that were home to Marrakesh.

Killian suggested they stop the car to buy snacks from the vendors who set out their wares on blankets along the roadside.

"We're out of cigarettes," he said, an added incentive for Port to pull over.

"Asni is a town not far from here," Mohamed said. "We can rest there."

"Why not stop here?" Killian, persistent as usual.

Port stopped the car. A man propped against a date palm lifted his head, watched them cross the road.

Mohamed made what sounded like pleasant conversation with the vendor. He gestured to the bottled water, bundles of cigarettes tied up with string, and piles of cookies spread out under the man's feet.

"Let's get a dozen of those," Killian said, excited at the sight of the Moroccan pastry.

"You ever eat *majoun*?" Mohamed asked him.

"It looks delicious," Samantha said.

"Delicious," Mohamed said, "and strong. The majoun is special. It is nuts and spices, and cannabis. In English, majoun is what you say, love potion."

"Make that two dozen," Killian said.

All Myria could think was: *Here we go again.*

"Is it okay?" she asked Mohamed.

"It is," he said.

"How much?" Port asked.

When Mohamed told Port how much, he shook his head, muttered something about "extortion."

"Let's get water, too," Samantha said.

"I'm not sure about the water," Myria said. The plastic bottles bore dents and other signs of wear, and the contents filmy.

"If you haven't gotten dysentery yet, you probably won't," Killian said.

"There's always typhoid," she said.

Mohamed rattled off a few words in Arabic. The man's voice rose in agitation. Killian had already helped himself to the majoun.

"Not much different from a granola bar," he said, laughed, and reached for another.

"I'm starving," Samantha said. "Let's get a bunch."

Port pulled out his wallet. He handed Mohamed several dirham notes. Mohamed told him they owed the man more.

"Fine," Port said.

They walked away with two liters of water, twenty or so cigarettes, and majoun cookies.

As they drove away, Killian broke into song: "And we're gonna get high as a kite tonight."

"One of these days," Myria said. "You will be the death of me."

"Lighten up," he said, and passed the majoun around.

"You know," Samantha said, chewing, "they do taste like granola bars."

They wended their way down the mountain road. An hour or so later, minaret towers could be seen in the distance. Beyond the walls of Marrakesh, was the desert. The proximity of a great expanse of wind-swept dunes gave the location all the mystique of a settlement built at the extreme edge of the known world.

Unlike Fes, the municipal overseers of Marrakesh had not loped off entire sections of the city to cars. They could drive wherever, park wherever there was a space. After the relentless day of travel, all they wanted was to get out of the car. It had become a rapidly deteriorating ecosystem, cluttered with debris, dusty inside and out. They parked in an alley.

The hotel had the advantage of being located within walking distance of the main square. They did as they'd done before: grabbed only the necessities out of the trunk, stuffed them into a duffle, and went inside. Mohamed approached the hotel clerk. Killian stood by, for once silent. Port inspected a vintage poster of Marrakesh that took up half a wall. Myria looked at Samantha and Samantha at Myria, and the two of them laughed.

"Am I a mess?" Samantha asked.

"Not at all. Fabulous as always," Myria said. It was true. Without makeup, her hair a mass of blond tangles, she looked like a lioness.

"You are a liar," Samantha said.

"No, I mean it."

Mohamed reported that two rooms had been booked.

"Do they have bathrooms?" Myria asked.

"One on each floor," Mohamed said.

"Not private?" She was still hopeful. She was desperate for a shower.

"For that you'd have to pay more," Killian said.

"Damn," Myria said.

"You're a tough girl," Killian said. "You can take it."

"There is a shower," Mohamed said.

Having lost interest in the poster, Port was close enough to have overheard him. "Sure there is," he said.

Jemaa el-Fnaa, the great square, drew hundreds. The snake charmers charmed, oven smoke rose from food stalls, morose chimps, kept like dogs on leashes, scratched at fleas; parrots screeched from under hooded cages. The air reeked, incense burners glowed. Street musicians kept up a lively cacophony; reed instruments piercing the noise with bird-like sounds; the Bendir players drumming as if in a trance.

Eye contact. It was to be avoided. Myria saw a woman, obviously Anglo-something, scream as a snake charmer placed a spotted cobra around her neck. She had made eye contact.

The exotic-starved eye. The eye that sought the freakish, the alien, the unknown. Those were the eyes of the tourists. They stared. And if it was rude, it couldn't be helped. They had come to see a spectacle. A great spectacle. And they'd found it, in the great square, the kinetic energy, the press of bodies, the eye always roving, and if it settled on some person or object, it was an invitation. Invitation to enter the carnival, to merge with it, and find that other eyes were just as alert—more perhaps, and watching.

What did they really understand? The troubles, the same that afflicted Spain, had led to years of police crackdowns in Morocco. The police kept watch everywhere in Marrakesh. From the moment they stepped out of the hotel, they were followed.

If the hotel manager had tipped off the cops, the five of them didn't know. Myria couldn't quite comprehend why, yet again, their Moroccan friend was surrounded by gun-toting militia. He was another face in the crowd. But, wherever there were police, it was Mohamed who caught their attention. The history of French and Spanish invasions, both countries hanging onto territories that would divide the country—its language, customs, and laws—didn't make for a vigorously independent and democratic Morocco. The leftists wanted secular reform; the right, Islamic reform; the government hunted both groups down, and civilians were caught in the middle. These spare facts ran through Myria's head like a ticker-tape machine, each stub a reminder of what was at stake for Mohamed.

Port and Killian immediately attempted to intervene on their friend's behalf. A policeman, not much older than they were, shouted at them in Arabic. The pair stepped back.

It looked for a moment as if they were going to cart Mohamed off.

"We can't let that happen," Myria said, frightened for him.

"Port, do something," Samantha implored.

Mohamed kept his head down, answering question after question.

"What a bunch of assholes," Killian said.

"Agreed," Port said.

"I think this is more about us than him," Myria said.

Killian seemed about to explode. "This is harassment, plain and simple."

"Freak out all you want," Port said, "it won't do him any good."

"No wonder his parents didn't want him to come with us," Samantha said.

"You might be right," Myria said. "We should have left him in Fes. At least, he'd be safe there."

More police had arrived, some in plainclothes, others armed with rifles. Now and again, they looked over at them. Scowled. Bullied Mohamed. One seemed to enjoy poking him in the chest.

A policeman sauntered over to Killian and asked him something in French.

"Speak English," he responded.

The policeman pointed at Mohamed. *"Votre ami?"*

Killian answered: "Ami, yes, yes."

The policeman considered. Killian repeated: "Ami."

"What is your business here?" the officer asked, this time in English.

"Travel," Killian said.

A *sure, sure it is* smile made the officer seem all the more threatening. "Hashish? You like to smoke?"

"I don't get it," Killian said. "Smoke what?"

Angrily: "Smoke. Do you like to smoke?" The officer pressed two fingers to his lips, huffing on an imaginary joint.

Killian, indignant: "Whatever do you mean?"

"Your Berber friend there—he shows you how to find cannabis. You know cannabis?"

"You're mistaken," Killian said.

Unconvinced, the officer continued: "How do you come to here?"

"We drove," Port said. "I'll show you my papers."

"Your papers? From where do you drive?"

"Fes," Samantha said.

The policeman smiled salaciously at her. Pretty blond girl. She made him hard, down there. Such a pretty thing. The other one, darker in appearance and wearing a dirty sweater, shrank from him. Scared. He could smell it on her.

Myria was anxious. But it was nothing compared to how angry she felt. Fuck him. Fuck him. She could have screamed it.

"Americans." A statement, not a question. The policemen had already pegged them. His questions were a game of cat and mouse. Would he snare them? Were they worth his trouble? Scruffy. What a sorry bunch. They didn't look like they had a *dirham* to their names.

"Americans, yes." Killian said.

"Why your friend?"

"We're friendly people," Port said.

"A little too much," the policeman said.

"Have you ever been to America?" Samantha asked.

The policeman looked at her as if she were crazy. Pretty blond girl. Crazy. He'd like to make her crazy.

"Can we talk to our friend?" Myria asked.

The policeman ignored her. "You have more friends? Many friends? He asked, speaking to Killian and Port.

"Only Mohamed," Killian said.

"Maybe a very bad boy," the policeman conjectured.

"Absolutely not!" Killian declared.

The policeman smiled again, officious and smug. "You believe it?"

"We do!" Samantha cried.

"Just let him go," Port said. "He's harmless."

The policeman didn't like that sort of talk. He got in Port's face. "You want him?"

Port flinched. Hesitated. Got himself together. "*Ami, ami*," he said.

The game must have started to bore the policeman. A waste of time.

"You have hotel?" he asked.

"Yes," Port said.

"Go back there. Tomorrow, we will see."

The sun was going down over the city, cloud plumes the color of faded carnations.

Abruptly, the officers walked off.

Myria insisted they do as the police said: "Go back to the hotel."

"But we've come all this way!" Killian called them cowards. "Why come if we aren't going to explore?" He wasn't finished. "It's absurd to go back to the hotel when there is so much to see. You can't be serious."

"I'm tired," Myria said.

"Me too," Samantha said.

"Tomorrow, we can see the souks," Port said.

"Right," Samantha said. "I've seen enough for tonight."

Shaken as he was, Mohamed said: "It's no problem. You want to stay here. We can stay."

"No," Myria said, firmly. "Back to the hotel."

"After that bit of fun," Killian said, "I need a drink."

"No problem," Mohamed said. "You can drink here."

"Is there a bar around here?"

Mohamed didn't respond.

Samantha said: "A bar? You really want to go to a bar?"

"There's bars aplenty in Spain," Port said.

"Spain is a long way away," Killian said.

"How about we do what the nice policeman ordered us to do."

Myria wanted only to get out of there. The festivities in the square could go on all night. She didn't care.

Outnumbered, Killian sighed.

They passed an uneventful night, in their fleabag hotel, listening to the drumming coming from the square. Before turning in, Myria went to the window, looked at the sky, unadorned but for a crescent moon, melon in hue. She pulled down the shade and crawled into bed.

"Are you okay?" Samantha was already under the covers.

"Fine," Myria said.

"It was nicer in the Rif," Samantha remarked. "No police."

"You were pretty much a hero," Myria said.

"What do you mean?"

"You didn't seem at all scared by the police."

"I wasn't," Samantha said. "Not really."

"You don't let much get to you, do you?"

"He wouldn't have arrested us," Samantha said. "On what charges?"

"That's the thing," Myria said. "I don't think they need a reason."

Samantha turned on her back, an arm slung under her head. "I guess anything is possible."

The yellow rose of Colorado. Beautiful Samantha, who looked like china but was made of granite.

"Did you see the way that cop looked at you?"

"Not my type," Samantha said.

"Me neither."

"He was a creep."

"The police scare me," Myria said, "especially when they wave machine guns in your face."

Samantha murmured something about being too sleepy to talk. Myria worried about whether they would get out of Marrakesh in one piece.

Hard not to grow apprehensive at the sound of footsteps from behind, or to become suspicious if a passerby stopped and stared, or resist the temptation to balk when turning down a blind alley.

The medina had all the excitement and color of a circus tent, its canopies bristling orange, pink, and red.

Myria used her precious spending money on a duffle made of leather. Only later, did she realize that it stank of rotting animal.

The others were weary. Mohamed did his best to rouse their flagging spirits. The majoun had given them a hangover, and he had to prod them, like cattle, through the medina.

"I've had enough," Myria said at one point. She'd seen little, but the night before remained vivid. She didn't want a repeat. She wanted to get out of Marrakesh before the sun went down.

"Me too," Port said. "I've seen all the Moroccan carpets I want to see for a lifetime.

"That, and the fact that this whole place could go up in flames at any second," she said.

"You don't like it here?" Mohamed asked.

"It's overwhelming."

Bewildered, Mohamed said: "Most Americans like to spend money here."

"There are many beautiful things," she said.

Samantha held up two tunics. "White for you and blue for me," she said.

"That's sweet of you," Myria said. "But I don't want you to buy me a shirt."

"I already did," Samantha said.

"You're crazy," Myria said. "You know that. You didn't have to."

"It's the perfect shirt for you—hair color, eyes, everything.

A collar jeweled with red stitching, tasseled sleeves, and embroidered hem. "I'll pay you back."

"Forget that! Just promise me you will wear it."

Myria did like the shirt. It felt cottony and new.

Port pointed to a food stall. "Time for lunch."

"Eat!" Killian launched into yet another complaint. "It's all anyone goes on about. Food! I'm not at all hungry, not at all. I couldn't take a single bite."

"You're not hungry because you've stuffed yourself on majoun," Port clucked.

"Listen to you." Killian wouldn't take much clucking from Port. "You've stuffed yourself as much as I, and not just on majoun. I didn't want to mention it but you are looking a little portly."

Port gave it right back to him. "Kill-joy, you are such an ass."

"Kill-joy is it? Poor Portly, you actually believe you are clever."

"It doesn't take much of an intellect to state the obvious. You are a miserable person. I feel sorry for your kind. Really, when you think about it, who wouldn't feel sorry for you?"

Now it was Killian's turn to volley. Instead, he remarked in a feathery voice that Samantha had shopped her way through Morocco.

Samantha shook her head, pointing out that she had reined in her spending because there was only so much she could haul back to Spain.

Port repeated that he was hungry and Mohamed told him he knew of a better place for lunch than the souk. "Less expensive," he added.

Mohamed's uncle lived in a mud-hut village in the High Atlas. The village took up the hillside, the one road into town narrowing to a footpath at the top. They left the car at the bottom of the hill and set out for Uncle's house: Port in his white boating hat, Killian dragging on a cigarette, Myria in her rumpled shift. Mohamed smiled and waved at people. Some called out. He answered.

A group of young children circled Samantha. Curiosity brought out the giggles. They laughed. A child tugged at one of her hands, another child at the other hand; more laughter from the children,

Samantha laughing too.

"Everyone loves Samantha," Killian said to Myria.

"What's not to love?" Myria said.

"Between you and me, I thought her a dimwitted blonde at first," Killian said loudly, and smiled with obvious wickedness when Samantha turned and frowned at him.

"I said, at first," Killian called out.

"I'm not the only pretty face here," Samantha said.

Killian glanced at Myria. "She'll do."

"I was talking about you," Samantha said.

"Vanity, vanity," Myria said to the both of them. "All is vanity."

Myria watched as Samantha stopped to talk to a little boy with great, brown eyes. He pointed to Mohamed. Samantha laughed and kept going.

Uncle's house seemed cut out of the mountain slope, rigged with a wooden door held aloft on a knotty frame; inside, there was a small room behind which the rest of the house was curtained off.

Behind the curtains, hands appeared with trays of mint tea, the meat-laden stew named *tangine* after the earthenware pots in which the dish was cooked, and crockery piled high with spiced nuts and figs.

The women never made an appearance, although Myria could hear their bantering.

Only once did Myria catch uncle's eye. Instinctively, she lowered hers.

Nephew and uncle talked. Killian smoked. Port picked over the nuts. Samantha enjoyed the last of the tangine, licking her fingers.

Myria wondered if they would spend the night. She liked it there, in that hidden space, unknown to the rest of the world. It made her feel safe.

CHAPTER NINETEEN

MORTIFICATION

Myria returned to the residence to find her housemates gathered round the table.

"A phantom!" cried Epinosa.

"Look at her!" Dolores exclaimed. "You are as dirty as a Berber."

"I missed you." Amelia rose from the table, greeted her the Spanish way—two kisses, one on each cheek.

"The dueña was about to rent out your room," Espinosa said. "You were gone so long."

"I wasn't gone so long," Myria said.

"Was it as bad as everyone says it is?"

"It was incredible," Myria said. She set down her duffle.

"You smell of camel," Dolores said.

"She smells of adventure," Amelia said. "Romance."

"I had a wonderful time," Myria said.

"Tell us," Maria Celeste demanded.

"I can't," Myria said. "You have to see for yourself."

Espinosa smirked. "Our poor *pesetas* don't stretch so far."

Myria didn't have the inclination or energy to argue with her. She had driven hundreds of miles on tricky roads. She waited for hours at the border. She endured unwarranted searches of her personal items. She stood by while the Moroccan officials grilled Mohamed. She waited yet more for the ferry. After boarding, she bought some peanuts and stood on the deck, throwing the shells overboard, watching the choppy seas devour them.

"Is there any food?" Fried smelts, potatoes, day old bread. Anything would do.

"You are hungry?" Amelia buttered a roll and passed it to her across the table.

Myria smiled by way of thanks. She licked the butter off the bread, to the horror of Espinosa and Dolores.

"She eats like a savage," Espinosa said.

"An animal," Dolores added.

"I'm dying of hunger," Myria responded, not at all worried that she had offended the two women.

"Have my *bacalao*." Maria Celeste pushed her plate of salted cod in Myria's direction.

Myria examined the fish, suspicious that it might contain bones, tiny and sharp as thorns. Fish could be a nightmare in that way; more than once a bone had caught in her esophagus.

Her housemates gaped while she pulled the bacalao apart with her hands. Myria sensed their eyes on her, their bewilderment. Perhaps they'd never had a bone stuck in their throats, or they were used to a mouthful of spines. Satisfied that she'd hunted down and removed all and any cartilage, she picked up a sliver of moist white flesh, then another, and ate.

The snap of a match being struck caused Myria to look up. Espinosa lit a cigarette, held the match aloft, and blew out the flame. She handed the cigarette off to Dolores, who used it to light her own.

From the kitchen, Myria heard the clanging of pots. The dueña would soon come to take away the dishes. She always made a great din, a clamor that signaled to the women lunch was over now.

"The dueña will be surprised to see you," Espinosa said to Myria and then, "Someone give her a napkin."

Myria licked her fingers. "I'm fine."

Amelia laughed with obvious pleasure. "You are like a child. It is very funny to see."

"Child is not the word I would use," Espinosa said. "Pig, yes."

Dolores stubbed her cigarette out on her plate. "I thought Americans civilized."

Myria rubbed her hands together. "In Morocco, it's the custom to eat with your hands."

"You are a Berber now?" Espinosa laughed.

"Perhaps she is," Amelia said.

"I might be," Myria said.

"You are not," Dolores said. "You have gone a little crazy, though, that is very clear."

The dueña cut short the discussion by barreling into the room. She stood, hands on hips, and heaved a great sigh.

"Dueña," Amelia said, "Myria has come back."

"I can see that," the widow replied, less than enthusiastic. The dueña got to work, scraping leftover cod, orange peels, olive pits, and crushed cigarettes into a gray bus tub.

Before she hauled her load back to the kitchen, she scolded Myria, saying: "When you went away you left your room a mess."

The women smiled at one another. Myria replied that she was so very sorry.

"I will clean it up, I promise, dueña," she said.

"You see how dear you are to her," Espinosa said, after the dueña had gone.

Myria held Espinosa in her gaze. "I do think she is fond of me."

"As we all are," Amelia said.

In an anxious voice, Dolores said: "Put on the tele or we will miss Cristina."

"I cannot believe she has not told the novio yet," Patricia said.

"She cannot keep a secret like that from him forever," Maria Celeste said.

"He is blinded by her sweetness and beauty," Espinosa said. "He sees her as an innocent, a virgin. But one day, he will discover the truth."

"And she will be on the street again," Dolores said, deeply saddened at the prospect of her beloved character forced to endure more hardship.

"I would not tell him," Patricia said. "Who would?"

Good question, Myria opined to herself.

In the bathroom, Myria hurriedly stripped herself of her dress, the fibers of which had become part of her skin, along with the dust, smoke, and toils of her travels.

The shower came on with an irritable spurt. Exhausted, she on the shower floor, her face between her knees, staring at blue tiles.

She stayed put, losing track of time. When someone knocked on the door, she ignored it. Another knock. The door opened.

"Myria!" Amelia drew the curtain back. "What is this?" Amelia reached in and turned off the dripping showerhead. "Did you fall asleep?"

She had fallen asleep. Something about the water, the way it dripped, like a metronome: drip, drop, drip…

"You want to drown?" Amelia.

She rubbed at her eyes with her fists. "Drown? How?" she asked.

"Sometimes it happens."

"There's not enough water in Spain," Myria said.

"It is lucky for you," Amelia said.

Myria shrugged.

"We must get you on your feet."

"Why can't I just stay here?" She was serious. The shower stall seemed as good a place as any at the moment.

"You will get sick," Amelia cautioned.

"Will I?"

"You will catch a cold."

"You think?" Myria asked.

"You must get up."

"Must I really?" It would take a crane to lift her up. She was done in, too tired to move.

"Yes, you must," Amelia said, insistent.

Myria sighed.

Amelia frowned.

"I'm fine," Myria said.

"You want to sleep here?"

Myria wrapped her arms around her legs, resting her head against her knees. "I haven't taken a bath since I left." She looked up at Amelia. "You know, I don't think I've ever gone that long without a bath."

"Out!" Amelia ordered.

Myria couldn't stand up. "I don't have a towel."

"Where is your robe?"

"I don't know."

"Stay here," her friend said. "I have a clean robe in my room."

"You needn't bother."

"Do you plan to walk naked into the dining room?" Amelia shook her head vigorously. "You can't."

"I don't think anyone cares," Myria said. "We are all women here."

"And that is the problem," Amelia said. "You must cover yourself."

"I don't care," Myria said. "I don't."

"Ach! You are behaving so strangely," Amelia said. "Stay here. I will bring you a robe."

Amelia closed the door behind her. Myria curled up on the shower floor.

✉✉✉

Wrapped in Amelia's robe, she walked past her housemates. Unsteady on her feet, hands dangling. She was a marionette, jerky in her movements, her head wobbly. Amelia nudged Myria from behind, past the women watching Cristina on the tele.

The dueña was busy rinsing dishes in the sink. Myria stopped short. Amelia gave her another push, propelling Myria through the kitchen, reaching around her and opening the door to her bedroom.

"Here, in here," Amelia instructed. "You will feel better now in your own room."

"I need to lie down." She splayed out on the cot.

A perfumed hand stroked her hair. "Why do you do this to yourself?"

"I wish I knew." It was her voice responding. Myria was certain because she could feel her lips moving.

"You must sleep."

"I am a terrible person."

"Ach, for the love of God, you are not."

Myria sat up. "I am. I am."

"Enough. Lie down."

Myria slumped back on the cot, an arm hanging off the side. She put a hand to her forehead. She should be nicer to her friend, not so drunk. Nothing takes to booze like self-pity and beat up pride. Swallowed up she was with hurt and loneliness.

"I am sad."

"You are sad because of that boy," Amelia said, adding, "the crazy one." She went on. "Do you love him? Love! A useless word. We say we love our parents, the family cat, the sunset, memories of our childhood, the money we spent on ourselves. All these things—these common things—we say we love them."

Myria didn't think them so common. Who didn't love money? Everyone was greedy for love. As for the rest, she could say with utter honesty that she loved cats, and sunsets. Sunsets were beautiful.

"I don't love him," she protested. "I don't think anyone could."

Amelia shrugged. "If Eve could love a snake, then there it is."

Myria closed her eyes, praying the room would stop gyrating.

"Ah, but you are sleepy," Amelia said. She took Myria's hand from her forehead and cradled it in her own. "I will go."

"Oh, don't! Tell me about Eve and the snake." Myria knew all about Eve and the snake. "How could she love him?" Good question. "Did she love him?" Dear God!

"It's just that…" Myria tasted the salt of her tears in her mouth, the bitter salt of losing Sheffield only to fling herself at Killian.

"Snakes are more loveable than we imagine. Such charmers," Amelia responded, laughing.

"You are right. Love is like some terrible joke."

"Love comes and goes," Amelia said. "Complete devotion is different."

Myria supposed Amelia was right. She rolled onto her side, so the other woman would have to take her hand away. She couldn't bear to be touched. She worried the tears would start all over. She didn't want to cry.

"What happened to Eve?"

"She found that she likes snakes," Amelia said. "So she is the mother of all our errors. It's all we talk about. Silly woman, she allowed a snake to take her virginity. Stupid woman, we tell ourselves, to let herself be deceived. Never do we talk about how Eve made love with the snake. What it was to be so full of passion."

"Because she was completely ashamed of herself," Myria said, nodding in agreement with her own statement when Amelia abruptly climbed over her, a thrust of the hips opening up just enough space for two—a sudden twin-ship she found comforting.

"Much better."

Amelia felt liquid from head to toe, a body at peace, effortless as a sleeping fish. Myria began to relax. Her head hurt less. Her stomach might be better.

Amelia smiled. "How do you bear it? This bed is worse than the floor."

They spoke softly now. Amelia was right, the cot wasn't comfortable. Dark, wasn't it? It must be getting late. What time was it? Who knew?

"Are you better?" Amelia asked. They had changed positions. Amelia rubbed her feet. Myria stared at the kitchen light through the glass doors.

"My head hurts less."

Amelia said. "Now you will sleep."

"Something stupid happened," Myria said.

"You need not say anything," Amelia responded. "I already knew what happened when I first saw your face." She sighed. "It is that boy, that crazy boy. I told you he was dangerous?"

"I was stupid."

"Stop," Amelia said. "You are not Eve."

"No?"

"It is impossible. Of all women, Eve experiences sex in ways we can scarcely imagine. We try. We fail."

"I feel as if I've failed."

"Ach, you must stop this," Amelia chided. "You have punished yourself enough. Believe me when I say, you are no Eve."

Myria put both hands on the inside of her thighs. She rubbed agitatedly at the soft flesh between her legs. During long days at the beach, half of it spent sitting in the muddy flats chasing after hermit crabs, she'd returned home covered in muck. In the shower, struggling out of her bathing suit, she tried to wash it all away but getting clean proved surprisingly difficult. For days, she swore there were seaweed, shell fragments, and silt in her crotch—a grimy feeling.

She began to sob.

Myria should have known. This was her constant recrimination to herself. She should have seen it coming. She shouldn't have put herself in that position. She should have stayed back at Mohamed's uncle's home, and not let Killian drag her with him. She recalled him saying he needed air, in that insistent, high-pitched voice, almost child-like in intensity, as if to deny him would result in an outburst of uncontrolled frustration and rage. Samantha had merely yawned in response. Port stared at the wall, lit with undulating shadows from the lamps, and smoked a cigarette in silence. Mohamed and Uncle carried on in their native tongue. Tea came and went. Uncle gestured to his nephew, who disappeared and returned with woolen blankets.

Uncle picked up one of the lamps by its handle and gestured for his nephew to follow him.

"I will pay my respects to my aunt," Mohamed said and slipped behind the curtain.

They wouldn't see him again until morning. The reasons were obvious enough: his family couldn't allow him to bed down on the floor with two girls. They were welcome to spend the night. Mohamed was not welcome to spend it in the same room with them.

Port and Samantha looked at each other.

"Sometimes I miss the Ritz." Port sighed.

"The Ritz!" Samantha exclaimed, followed by a burst of tee-hee's. "You're about as far away from the Ritz as you can get."

"Truer words," Port said.

Samantha laid out a blanket, then another, claiming her space on the floor.

"Where I come from," she said, "we don't get to the Ritz too often."

"Give me a break," Killian said. "I see Ritz written all over you."

"What do you mean by that?"

"Money," Killian said. "You exude money."

"But what Port is talking about is a whole other world. You should know." Samantha lied down. "Lord in Heaven! I might as well be sleeping on a rock."

Myria let drop her bedding in a heap, wondering if she should fold the blanket in two or spread it out on the rough floor.

Killian tapped her on the shoulder. "Come on. Let's get some air. I'm suffocating."

"I'm not going anywhere," Port said.

"You weren't invited," Killian said.

"If I weren't so beat," Samantha said, "I'd go."

Hugging a blanket to his chest, Port surveyed the room. "Go where?"

"Why should you care?" Killian said in a tiff.

"We're miles off the map, no idea where, and the last thing I want to do is go looking for you when you get lost."

"I don't imagine anyone could get lost," Samantha said. "The village is tiny. It's smaller than Cheouen."

"Don't be such a bore," Killian said.

"*Au contraire*," Port said.

"You two," Samantha said. "You're giving me a headache." She reclined, blanket drawn to her neck, and suggested to Port that he mind his own business. "Myria isn't afraid to go, are you? With Killian, I mean. Maybe Port is right. Someone should go with Killian. I'm so tired I can't move a muscle."

She sat up and to Killian said: "You wanted Myria from the first, right?"

"As a matter of fact...."

On her knees, wrestling with a corner of fabric, Myria wished

Samantha would shut up. In better light, her face would have given away her embarrassment. Was there anything more obvious than false discretion? If, what Samantha said, came anywhere near being discreet? Did her friend expect she would have rollicking sex with Killian in the streets of…

Where were they? Somewhere in the High Atlas.

Killian prodded her not so gently with his foot. "Let's go for a walk." He was doing it again, that thing he did, a combination of insisting and begging.

Myria fussed with her bedding. She glanced over at Samantha, wrapped in festive colors, lovely as giftwrap. Samantha gave her an encouraging nod. There was a word in Spanish for women like her: *alcahueta*. Samantha was perfectly willing to pimp her off on Killian, not for money but to satisfy her curiosity. Ever since Killian had set his fantastically blue eyes on Samantha, she couldn't hide her fascination, or revulsion. Myria remembered her, in the café near the Institute, declaiming: *East or West, never heard anyone talk that way, and said so to Killian, then felt real bad because he got red in the face, and insisted that if he sounded different it was because he was Irish. But he's still American! No one in Colorado talks like that. I don't think it's because he's Irish. It's some kind of….*

The issue wasn't simply that Killian wasn't her type; there was more to Samantha's persistent matchmaking. If she succeeded, the girl would be absolved of any hurt she may have caused Killian. Samantha was also on a mission to rescue him. Because, if there was one thing Myria had figured out when it came to Samantha, she couldn't date, much less be close friends with a guy who was "different." But then, Samantha knew so few boys who were different. She had to be completely certain because not knowing was to invite all sorts of complications into her life. Fine it was to have Killian around far from home where she didn't have to answer to her parents, church, and friends.

If only Killian had a girlfriend, it would solve so many problems for Samantha. She had to find him a girlfriend. She figured he and Myria got along. Well, they didn't get along, not really. It could work, though, the two of them together, boyfriend and girlfriend. Myria was lonely. Killian was different. They would be good for each other.

Myria couldn't imagine herself with Killian, certain when it came to attraction she left Killian cold. Samantha's obsessive matchmaking wouldn't drive him into her arms.

Killian prodded her again with his foot.

Get lost. Bother someone else. Samantha. Go bother her.

"Let's go," he said, sounding not at all like a guy wanting to get a girl alone. Antsy was all, in his usual state of hyper-restiveness. There was only so much confinement he could stand. The evening had been long and tiresome for him. He'd picked at the food, groaned audibly when more tea was served, often interrupted Mohamed to interpret for him, and repeatedly demanded a cigarette from Port. Several times, he stepped outside without excusing himself. Uncle graciously ignored his restless guest.

"There's nothing out there," she said.

"Everything is out there."

"I'm not going."

"Come on!" Killian persisted.

"Killian, give it up," she heard Port say from his corner and then ordered Samantha to turn off the damn lamps, to which Samantha swiftly responded that Port do it because Samantha had finally gotten comfy and wasn't moving for the life of her.

"Myria, go with Killian or we will never get any sleep," Samantha said.

Myria asked her if she wouldn't like to come. "It will wake you up."

"No, too beat. Besides, I'd just be a third wheel." Samantha yawned breathily.

Myria grumbled at her from across the room. "I'm beat too."

His patience exhausted, Killian took action. He grasped at Myria's elbow in an effort to haul her to her feet.

"Excuse me!" she fairly squeaked.

He let go. "If you won't come, I'll go by myself."

Myria sighed. Killian was bluffing. He wouldn't step out that door without her. But did she want to hear him complaining through the night, and probably well into the next day? He would go on about how utterly bored he had been. There would be no sleep, much less peace, until he got what he wanted.

She stood up and said: "Fine, let's go."

Myria followed Killian outside. She sniffed the air, gathering scents: juniper, wool, stagnant water. Killian smelled of cigarettes and body odors. She stank—a wet dog smell.

Killian lit a cigarette. She asked where they were going.

"The car," he said.

"We'll never find it in the dark."

"It's just down the road, Myriam," Killian said. "I stashed some majoun in the car. I want to get it."

"Okay, whatever."

When they reached the car, Killian got his majoun. He broke off a piece for Myria. She told him she wasn't hungry.

Killian laughed. "Don't you feel as if you've been high for days? It's fabulous."

"I do," she said.

"I could stay here and never go back," he said.

"It is beautiful," she said.

"Never go home," he said.

"Wouldn't you miss your family?"

"Not really."

"What about your friends?"

"Probably," he said. Killian was looking at her, and she up at him. Six-feet tall straight up and down, and lithe enough to levitate, he was striking; so tall, so thin—and his eyes, their cutting blue brightness, incantatory sparkle. "I'd miss you, Myriam," he said. It sounded as if he thought of her leaving many times, and each time hurt more.

"Oh, me too," Myria said, surprised. He spoke constantly, Killian, filling the air with volumes of commentary that it hadn't occurred to her there were essentials that went unspoken. Or that she might be one of those essentials. Her mind swept along: odd of him to let himself be vulnerable, not at all like him, almost unbelievable, really. Samantha. Had she said anything to him—as in, Myria was sad and miserable, desperately lonely?

"Have you been talking to Samantha?"

"I talk to Samantha all the time."

"About me?"

"Come to think of it...." He looked away, up at the sky riveted with twinkles. "You and I speak every day or night."

"Do you and Samantha talk about me?" She repeated "about me."

"Samantha? If I had a chance with Samantha, I wouldn't spend it talking about you."

The cut went just deep enough to stir envy. Myria didn't need reminding that Samantha was the brighter candle of the two, spreading her blond-haired, cheery light everywhere she went and over everybody. Myria liked standing in Samantha's light, sometimes, not very often.

"I was joking, Myria."

"Don't worry about me. Samantha is beautiful and sweet. It's amazing when you think about it. She may be the sweetest person I've ever met, and pretty." Myria's voice trailed off as she said: "Oh, so pretty..."

"Do you know what I like about Samantha?"

"You don't have to tell me. She's a knockout."

"To state the obvious," Killian said. "The world is full of pretty blondes. Samantha would be nothing but one more, except she doesn't work at it. There's nothing affected about her."

Myria agreed. Samantha wasn't vain, or horribly spoiled. She possessed other flaws: meddling, toe-treading, gossiping.

Killian finished the majoun and said: "It's all the same to her. Take me or leave me, that's Samantha."

"She doesn't have to try hard if that's what you mean."

"Samantha doesn't try at all." Point made, Killian tipped back his head and oooed about the swirly sky—its ghost planets, raiding comets, and milky streams.

"What's a ghost planet?"

"Ghost planets are sighted all the time."

"You're serious."

"Of course, I'm serious."

"It's cold," she said. "Let's get in the car."

At the moment, the car provided a backrest for Killian, who had spread himself over the side-panel, and was using the roof as a headrest. Off on some majoun cloud, he said he had never felt better in his life.

"It's freezing." Myria grasped his hands and pulled. He lifted his head, pulling her to him in a game of tug-of-war. She lost—landing against him. She looped her arms around his neck and bent over him, like a willow branch; she wondered if he would kiss her and kissed him instead-a swift brush of the lips--and more hugs, and then a tug at her skirt, a hand sliding down her panties, off to touch her moist reticule, inner silks, folds and knobs, recondite tubing; after which a spidery probing, and the swiftest fear as Killian put a finger up her vagina. She wished for a simple kiss and got a speculum prying, an impersonal finger-fuck.

Myria wriggled free, stumbled up the hill. The road, pale brown in the moonlight, the houses dark heaps in the shadows.

"Where are you going?" Killian caught up.

She snapped. "Asshole!"

"Me? But why?"

Angered, frustrated. "You are such a jerk, such a jerk, a jerk!"

"Well, thank you for that," Killian said. "Myriam, what's to get upset about?"

"You use me! You use me!" By then, she was in a fit.

"Gracious!"

If only bullets of shame and blame would fire out of her mouth; she would never have to see him again.

Killian pawed at her shoulder. She shook him off.

"Tell me! I can't have you angry with me for the next few thousand miles we have to go before making it to Spain."

Angry? Myria despised him.

And then, in a bleak sort of way, Killian said: "And to think— before tonight, I never kissed anyone."

CHAPTER TWENTY

WASH, WASH, WASH

Myria was up and dressed the next morning. She let out a breezy "good day" to her housemates when entering the dining room. The women managed lethargic welcomes in response, and went quiet. Myria remained on her feet, spooning sugar into coffee. The sweet, acidic brew stung her tongue. Amelia asked if she wouldn't sit down. She couldn't sit down. She had to remain standing. If she sat, she was afraid she wouldn't get up again. She'd collapse into one of the chairs, her rump sealing to the shallow wells of the worn upholstery.

Her housemates, their spirits dampened by the early hour, comprised so many limp occupants assembled around the table. They nibbled crusty rolls, asked in drowsy voices for someone to pass the thermos of coffee. Patricia gave a long stretch before she lit a cigarette, after which she slumped back in her seat. Only Amelia, put together meticulously as always, appeared rested and alert.

"But it is early yet, no?" Amelia said.

"I don't want to be late for class." Myria smeared half a toasted roll with marmalade; the marmalade was watery and made her breakfast even less appetizing.

She had woken with a raging hangover. Drinking too much

brought only anxiety and misery. She was one of those drinkers—the kind that, instead of becoming boisterous, grew morose. Try as she might, she couldn't shake it off. Coffee would do nothing to help her nerves, causing more jitters, but enough of the strong Spanish brew would keep her on her feet.

With a mouthful of toast, she pondered one of those obvious if small details that living in Spain impressed on her: In the States, marmalade could be cut with a knife, it was so thick, and the coffee, watery, while in Spain, the jam served at the residence was liquidy and the coffee was robust.

"You have been later," Amelia said, a lilt of amusement in her voice.

"Late or not," Myria said, "I have to get to class."

"You have a busy day," Amelia said. "What a shame. I was hoping to talk to you."

"I'd like that," Myria said, "but…"

"I know," Amelia said. "You're a busy girl."

"She is no busier than the rest of us," Espinosa groused.

"So much work to do," Patricia said.

"How nice it would be if we could take vacations?" Espinosa snapped her fingers. "Just like that."

"Vacations!" Dolores exclaimed. "Who has time?"

"Or money," Espinosa said. She looked up at Myria from under sleep-heavy eyelids.

Myria heard Patricia yawn again. Dolores told her to cover her mouth.

"You will make us all yawn," she said.

"Yawning is contagious," Esperanza affirmed. "All creatures yawn. It's a medical fact."

Patricia reached for her coffee cup.

"It has been theorized," Esperanza continued, "that yawning triggers a sympathetic response in the nervous system."

"Translation, please," Dolores said.

"Well, it is not so easy," Esperanza said. "People who are sensitive to the behavior around them will often mirror that behavior. Contagious yawning is a form of empathy."

"Espinosa must be immune," Amelia said and winked at Myria.

"And here I thought it meant someone was just being very, very boring." Espinosa snorted.

Amelia rounded her lips, drew in her breath and then exhaled, patting her mouth, letting out a percussive, almost musical sound.

"What a coquet you are," Espinosa said.

"Never with you," Amelia said, smiled sweetly, and blew a kiss across the table.

Espinosa batted the invisible kiss away with an impatient wave of her hand.

Myria left the two women to their sniping. She had zero interest in entering the fray. She felt lousy. With unsteady hands, she poured herself another cup of coffee, forgoing sugar and milk. She hoped a potent dose of caffeine would ease the pounding in her head—another reminder of having nearly drunk herself blind. She couldn't piece yesterday together, and perhaps it was for the best. If she let herself, she knew it would all come back, in a flood of images, a movie reel of the mind she didn't want to watch. She didn't have to relive it, not the he-said, she-said, or the he-did, she-did; she thought she could summon every word, emotion, sensation if she allowed herself. She could stand there all day, ruminating, sifting through recollections, trying to comprehend what had taken place. But how could she? She couldn't think of Killian much less utter his name. If she did, her stomach revolted, sending up harsh bile that tightened her chest and scorched the back of her throat.

She noticed that she had spilled coffee down the front of her shirt. Her cup trembled like a vessel in rough seas in her hands.

Amelia looked on, and it was only when Myria raised her eyes that she caught the other woman studying her, not in a rude way but concerned.

Setting down her coffee on the table the best she could without her hands shaking, Myria forced a smile. "I'm a mess." She glanced at the wet stain on her blouse. "It's not so bad after all," she said to Amelia. Her friend asked her if she'd bought the shirt in Morocco.

"I did."

"Very nice," Amelia said. "But you should have washed it first."

Espinosa laughed. "She is washing it now with her coffee."

"You must try to wash the stain now," Amelia said to Myria.

"They sell those clothes as new but they are not," Espinosa said. "You don't know where they've been, or who wore them before. It's why you must wash, wash, wash."

Myria looked down at her blouse, a white tunic with blue stitching at the collar and cuffs. She couldn't remember where she'd bought it. Then she remembered Samantha had given it to her. *This will look so pretty on you.*

She searched the table for a clean napkin and dabbed at her shirt, which did next to nothing but kept her quivering hands busy.

Espinosa remarked unenthusiastically that she must be off and pushed back her chair. A chorus of scraping wood followed as the other women got up from the table. Amelia remained seated, composed and determined not to be rushed through her breakfast.

"Are you leaving too?" Amelia asked Myria, in that clear, calm voice of hers.

"I should go too," Myria said. "And you?"

"Would you like me to walk with you?" Amelia smiled.

"Very much so." Myria smiled back, hoped her expression was equally as sunny. She wanted all to be well between them. But there it was: the sensation of reeling toward some misery she'd rather not relive at the moment.

"I will gather my things," Amelia said.

Myria nodded, still busily wiping her damp shirt with her hands.

"You are not well, not at all," Amelia said as soon as the front door to the residence closed behind them.

"It's just tiredness," Myria said, "from traveling."

"Generally, when we return from holidays, we are refreshed."

"Normally," Myria said, despondent.

Amelia remarked that they would have to take the stairs.

"Is the elevator out of order again?"

"It never worked," Amelia said.

Myria sighed at the thought of all those stairs, but didn't protest. She was too tired to complain.

They walked through the darkened lobby and out into the street. In every direction, at every turn, the clear skies above brightened the city, with no shadow or gray cover that might mar its radiant eminence.

"Such beautiful weather," Amelia murmured, and was quick to put on her sunglasses.

"You look stunning," Myria said.

"Always with the compliment," Amelia said, and when Myria didn't respond, went on, "I have no need of compliments. People care too much what others think of them. Let them think what they will."

"Always the best course of action," Myria said, wondering if the remark were meant specifically for her.

In her uncannily perceptive way, Amelia said, "You have very thin skin. But, yes, I was talking about you." She stepped up her pace, her heels clacking against the pavement. "You take every word to heart."

"So what now? You are angry with me?"

Amelia laughed. "This is what I am talking about! I could never

feel anything but affection for you. But you distrust me. You do it
to everyone. I told you this before. You prefer the shadow to the
daylight."

"I trust you."

"Last night, you told me something dreadful happened. Am I
wrong?"

It was precisely this line of questioning that Myria wished to
fend off.

They merged with the crowd of pedestrians crossing the bridge.
Amelia remarked that Myria didn't have to confide in her, not if
she didn't want to.

"It's not you," Myria said.

"Of course not," Amelia said.

"But you are angry with me."

"Not with you, my dear, Myriam, never with you. It is something
you need to believe."

Myria couldn't focus. The sun was so strong on the river, a hot
glare, as it if the currents would combust into flames—and Myria's
sorry head along with it.

"You must never let that boy hurt you again," Amelia said.

The director stood at the Institute door, rotating the chain of
skeleton keys, as one would recite a rosary, contemplative and
unaware of Myria coming up the steps behind her.

"Señora Blandura, I'd like to speak to you."

The señora let slack the key chain. She turned with an abruptness
that startled Myria. The woman's sallow complexion, the chain
swinging now at her side, her apparent unwillingness to greet
Myria with anything more than the dim look she leveled at her.
Not welcoming, no. Señora Blandura asked what she wanted.

"To speak to you," Myria said.

"About?"

"It's personal," she said.

The chain began to jangle as the older woman resumed looking for the front-door key. Señora Blandura found it at last and, as she pushed her way into the Institute, she told Myria to follow her down the hall to her office. There, Myria waited, as again, Señora Blandura rifled through the keys.

Myria stood. Waited.

"Come in," the director said, opening the office door with a shove of her shoulder. She deposited her tote bag on the floor and lowered herself with a sigh into a wooden chair behind a cluttered desk.

"What is it?" The señora reached for a pen. Myria supposed she wanted to have it in hand to jot down whatever she had to say.

"I was thinking…" Myria began before the director cut her off, again with a curt command to "spit it out. I don't have all day."

"Transfer," Myria said. "I want to transfer."

The señora put down the pen. She asked what Myria meant, exactly.

"I want to transfer," Myria repeated.

The señora frowned. "The break wasn't long enough for you?"

Myria managed a feeble: "It's not that." Except it really was that.

"At the Institute, we believe in allowing students ample time for study and travel. We anticipate that young people will want to go off and explore. We've arranged to make that possible by allowing for a seven day break in the fall and spring, as well as the bridge holidays in celebration of Catholic observances, which also have a cultural function, and allow our students to gain greater appreciation of Spain's religious heritage. Of course, there is the Christmas break."

Myria didn't respond, so the señora continued: "If you were to transfer now, you would have to make up the semester elsewhere. All of your work here would amount to very little." The señora, who had been speaking very fast, took a moment to catch her breath. "At the very least I would need from you a reasonable explanation."

The words fell on Myria like hatchet strokes to the head. She had no ready response, only a very bad headache, a sick feeling in her stomach—and a terrible sense of wrongdoing, or guilt, or shame. Whatever she felt, she couldn't explain herself to the calloused-faced woman who sat before her.

The señora leaned back in her chair just a bit, opened a drawer, and pulled out a small bottle of lotion. She dabbed a bit on her hands and began to rub the creamy white substance into her palms and through her fingers. This went on, with repeated applications, while Myria continued to stand across the desk.

Engrossed in moisturizing, the señora appeared to have forgotten entirely about Myria, which was far from the case.

From the moment she had approached her, the señora had grasped right away that the girl standing across her desk, whose casual clothes never impressed her, and whom she never would have thought about twice in any other circumstances, was deeply unhappy. Unlike the typical rich, spoiled students she so often dealt with, those who found Sevilla provincial and wanted to get away out of boredom, she knew that this girl, who looked as if she didn't have two cents to rub together, wasn't suffering from restlessness.

By the dark shadows under her eyes and the quiver in her voice, she was—just the señora's wretched luck—in trouble. Either she had reason to complain about another student, her housing, or the Institute itself. Whatever the complaint, it would reflect badly on her, the director, if she didn't manage the situation efficiently.

Continuing to rub her hands, the señora's restrained demeanor gave way to obvious displeasure. Deep rivets in her brow, flared nostrils, lopsided frown. The señora's day had scarcely begun and already this girl brought her trouble. With her left hand, she worked the fingertips of her right, sometimes pulling and sometimes twisting, as though trying to undo a series of knots.

This girl! Didn't she realize the position she put the director in? If she left, how would she fill her spot? Already, the Institute was overstaffed. There were fifty less students this fall than the year before. The señora blamed the low numbers on the socialists. Socialism—the word sickened her—was on the rise. Whether from politicians, economists, reporters, socialism was all over the news, along with E.T.A. Conservatives, sounding the alarms, warned of the country sliding into barbarism. There seemed to be no way of stoppering national dissatisfaction. Union organizers protested. Anti-American sentiment swelled. The señora felt directly imperiled. Her job depended on a steady influx of wealthy American students. How were the instructors to be paid? Not that there weren't one or two she'd like to sack if she had the power to do so. Only the Board had the authority to fire the instructors. The older generation of instructors—those who remembered well the early years of Franco—kept their personal views to themselves and stuck to the curriculum. Some detested the socialists just as much as she, and only last week, the director had congratulated Antonio Degulado for steering the students in the right direction. Every time she passed by his classroom, the door always open because of the stifling heat, she could hear his deep, booming voice as he went on about how socialist intellectuals had hijacked Golden Age literature. She needed a dozen more like him, although in truth, a dozen more would probably be twelve too many. It would be best for everyone to stick to the curriculum without polemics.

The señora eyed the girl with suspicion. Setting the lotion aside, she began to shuffle papers on the desk.

Without looking up, the señora said: "The last time a girl—" The señora caught herself. "...the last time a student approached me as you are now it was because she had gotten herself in trouble."

The question came as another blow, one that cut deeper than all the others. But gasping, gulping, groaning—any sign of distress, even a twitch of the eye, would give Myria away.

She couldn't speak. The cat had Myria's tongue in its mouth and kept tugging at it.

"Are you in trouble? If you are you should let me know immediately. Do you need a lawyer? A doctor? Both?"

Myria shook her head and that made the pounding worse. The coffee didn't seem to be working. And she had to pee—really pee. She did what she could to stay on her feet, even resorting to the schoolgirl trick of shifting her weight from side to side. When that didn't work, she crossed one leg over the other. She couldn't go on. Now she wanted only to reach the bathroom before it was too late.

Instead of giving the director an answer, Myria told her between gritted teeth that she needed to use the *retrete*, the toilet.

"Then go!"

Myria bolted out of the office.

Coming from the bathroom, Myria caught sight of Killian at the other end of the corridor. His presence jolted her out of the hangdog despair. Instead of despair, she felt anger—deep down anger, in-her-gut anger. She had a strong urge to spew until he was slimy from head to foot, dripping with her emotional sewage. Just vomit on him. He deserved it.

Myria wondered if he saw her. He hadn't looked in her direction, and that too bothered her. He didn't have the awareness—yes, that was the word—to notice her as she noticed him. He lacked any awareness of her, despite the way she stared him down, with the long hall between them, and through the crowd of milling-about students. His height made him easy to spot. He stood out. Same as ever: tall, gaunt, but handsome. At the moment, his shoulders were pressed to the wall behind him, arms folded, one leg crossed over the other. Facing him, a book clutched to her bosom, was a brunette with severe bangs. Myria recognized the brunette from her Golden Age literature course, or maybe Advanced Spanish Composition.

Reminded of her classes, Myria felt ill again. She'd applied herself the best she could. The professors seemed to like her well enough. At first, that was. And her Spanish improved. She understood more even if it took great effort to speak at times. Her writing had improved. An essay on a play about a revolt in a small Spanish village earned her some praise. The instructors didn't give grades. It was pass or fail. But the Golden Age literature professor had written *muy agudo* in the margins of her paper. Sharp. She'd written a sharp paper. She glanced again in Killian's direction.

Now, none of it mattered. Because of him, of what had happened, all that work gave her no sense of accomplishment— not anymore. But what had happened? Why didn't it matter?

Well, her studies never mattered to him. She remembered the way Killian made fun of her every time she mentioned how hard she studied. The joke that never grew old for him: what she needed to get ahead in life was corral a rich husband. He said it to her that afternoon while they were sitting at the café near the river before they had gone to Morocco.

She remembered his smirking and her squirming. A worm on a hook, that was Myria dangling with all her fears, sorrows, regrets, self-loathing in front of him. What she should have done …because what the fuck! Except, if she really thought about it, she would have remembered his kindness as well; the way he had pressed and pressed until the whole sad story of Sheffield tumbled out of her. He had made that dismissive remark, letting her know she was better off without Sheffield. Kind of him. His gentle, sweet side reaching out to her when she needed him most. Killian had his moments. Thoughtfulness, decency, vulnerability, tenderness—there was that side to him too. But now, exhausted and on edge, Myria swallowed hard.

Her jaw began to ache. Biting down didn't spare her any pain; it merely acted as a sort of gag, prevented Myria from erupting into screams.

Myria shifted so she could better see Killian. Nothing was different about him. Same as he ever was. No different. Did he find the brunette to his liking? She glanced from him to the girl.

A guy brushed against the transfixed Myria. "Hey? What's happening?"

Distracted, she responded: "Not much."

"Haven't seen you around," he said.

Myria tried to remember his name.

"I've been traveling," she managed.

"Cool," came the response. "Where to?"

"Morocco."

He gave a slow whistle of appreciation. "African adventures," he said. "I bet it was a wild time."

"Wild time," she repeated, her tone flat.

"I bet," he said and then asked if she remembered him.

She studied him for a moment. "No," she said. "I'm sorry."

He didn't seem at all offended. "I didn't think so. You always have your head down."

"Do I?"

"We're both in Golden Age," he said. "You always dress in black. You sit in the back."

Killian said the same thing when they'd met—about her clothes. She winced.

"Do you keep a seating chart?" Snap!

He winced.

She had embarrassed him. She was an idiot. Here was this nice—whoever he was—chatting her up and she cut him.

"I think I've seen you," she said, trying to make it up to him.

"Did you?" he said. "I seem to remember that you never say

anything in class."

"Probably not," she said.

"What's that about?"

"I think the professor is a jerk."

He grinned, not at her but over her shoulder. "Killian, man, where you been at?"

Myria looked up, around, and saw Killian not more than a whisper's length from her.

"Globe-trotting," Killian said, as if nothing could be more delightful.

Myria's unnamed friend also laughed. She noticed the girl with the severe bangs hanging back, bored with the conversation by the expression of her pretty face.

"Around the world in…" The guy smiled at the brunette.

Killian fixed his eyes on Myria. She was instantly caught in those extraordinary blues of his, and then looked down at her feet, finding them less unsettling.

"A Moroccan holiday," Killian said in a triumphant voice. "It was a blast. How about you?"

"I travel some, but not as far as Morocco."

"You should really go. It's fabulous, absolutely fabulous. Myria came too. She can tell you about it," Killian said. "Do you know each other?"

"We're getting better acquainted." He held out his hand to Myria. "Lance."

Myria took Lance's hand. He squeezed gently.

"You don't know Myria?" Killian asked.

"No," Myria intoned, speaking to her feet.

"We see each other around," said Lance.

"Do you?" Killian laughed.

Myria's eyes flew to Killian. He winked and then, to Lance, said: "We had a great time in Morocco. Ask Myria. It was the adventure of a lifetime."

"So Myria said." Lance had released Myria's hand.

The brunette with the severe bangs let out an audible yawn.

"Hey, I've seen you around," Lance said to the pretty brunette.

The bell rang.

"I've seen you too," the other girl said, obviously pleased to have been sighted. Together, they walked off, leaving Myria and Killian to one another.

"Good guy, Lance," Killian said, "boring but not a bad guy at all."

Myria struggled to hold her tongue.

"You're quiet," Killian said, his voice soft. Myria gave Killian a cold look and walked swiftly down the hall. She came to a halt outside the closed door of her Golden Age class. Killian was coming down the hall after her. She pushed the door open and left him standing in the hall.

CHAPTER

TWENTY-ONE

LANCE

The professor, dressed in a tailored black suit, his white hair slicked back, held aloft a lit cigarette. Whenever he felt he had made a point, he drew heavily on his smoke and then tipped ash onto a ceramic plate. He detested the Socialists and regularly accused them of ruining Spain. It wasn't unusual for froth to accumulate at the corners of his mouth while he railed against leftists.

"If you believe what you see on television, there is misery in every corner." He waved his cigarette about. "I would suggest an opposing narrative, one based in reality, and not utopianism." He stopped waving, smoked, and repeated "reality" several more times.

Lance had taken the seat next to her. He leaned over and whispered: "What a fuckin' asshole, like Hitler."

True. Degulado came off as a jerk. Hadn't she told him as much? Hitler was another story; it was a bit excessive to compare Degulado to Hitler.

"Fucking Hitler."

Myria smiled to show Lance that, yes, she got it. She might have added an expletive of her own if her head didn't feel twice its normal size. Smiling was painful enough. She imagined Degulado would have enjoyed the idea that, with the repeated hammer falls of his mighty rhetoric, he was taking a blunt object to her skull.

Lance muttered another four-letter word under his breath. He seethed in the seat next to her.

Degulado wasn't a run of the mill creep. He was repulsive. The spittle, the incessant smoking, was tough to ignore. Despite the frothing, Degulado was charismatic. He was a force. A man whose mind had been dowsed in the fires of the best literature Spain offered and who decided he'd take a match to every book, not to turn it to ash, but to make it erupt, in flames, so that, in a spectacle of fire and brimstone, with the incendiary vehemence of an against-the-world politics, his message might carry over. As a professor, he knew he had a captive audience. But how to captivate the sleepy, bored, uninformed? How to set an earthquake rumbling under their comfortably ensconced derrieres? He would recruit them with his strident talk, his well-rehearsed furor.

Not one sleepy soul in those rows of seats polished to the hue of church pews cared to be roused to his particular drumbeat. He was ranting to the wrong choir.

No matter. On went Degulado: he glowered, leaned against the broad desk behind him, drew heavily on a cigarette, lecturing, spittle erupting at the corners of his mouth, exhaling heavily, the air around him castle-wall gray, ash falling on his suit, hacking convulsively between cigarettes, grabbing a white handkerchief from his coat pocket, stuffing the dirty cloth back into his pocket, running his hands through his gelled white hair, lighting another cigarette, scowling, smoking.

Myria heard renewed rumblings to her right. Lance had tipped his chair back as far as it would go without falling over. "What crap," he said, loud, very loud. "Go tell it to the Hitler youth."

Degulado fell abruptly silent. He scanned the room to settle his attention on the precariously balanced Lance.

Myria cringed. Holy Shit! She expected a vehement rebuttal. Spittle flying, the brilliant professor would sweep down on the poor kid and crush him. She glanced at Lance, his arms dangling at his sides, not at all intimidated. Degulado would make pulp of him when he was finished.

The professor didn't go on the attack. A strange transformation had come over him: smiling wide, both hands rested on the desk, shoulders pulled back.

"You seem out of sorts, young man," Degulado said, in English.

A student in the front row cleared his throat. Others turned around in their seats to see what Lance would do.

Lance leaned forward, his chair coming to rest on all four legs on solid ground. "Fascists are always verbose."

"Would you be kind enough to repeat what you said?" Degulado asked.

"I said," Lance raised his voice, "fascists are always verbose."

The professor pushed off the desk. He went to the board and searched the tray for a piece of chalk.

Hand poised to write on the dusty black panel, Degulado ordered: "Once more."

Lance's voice rang out: "*Los fascistas siempre son verbosos.*"

Degulado's hand swept across the board, copying Lance, word for word, first in Spanish and then in English.

Los fascistas siempre son verbosos

Fascists are always verbose.

The professor stood back and studied the board a moment.

Imaginary pins dropped.

"What do we notice about this statement?" Degulado was still speaking in English.

Silence.

Degulado reached for his cigarettes. "I recognize this, albeit in its bastardized form."

His face smug, Lance tipped his chair back again.

"It should read," Degulado said, "revolutions are always verbose. Shouldn't it, sir?" The professor lit another cigarette, inhaled to satisfaction. "My good friend must know this because my good friend—" Degulado looked briefly in Lance's direction—"must be on familiar terms with Leon Trotsky."

Lance parried. "We're the best of friends."

Degulado snorted. "But have you read *The History of the Russian Revolution*?" He persisted. "In three volumes?"

Lance rallied. "In Volume II, Trotsky states that revolutions are always verbose."

"And the Bolsheviks did not escape from this law," Degulado responded, trenchantly.

"What he said could equally be applied to the Fascists," Lance replied, agitated. "Had Trotsky risen to power, the Russians would have been spared Stalin. The revolution would have been saved."

"Possibly," Degulado responded, his composure unruffled. "I am concerned only with these words you have stolen and twisted."

"Okay, maybe I twisted them a little," Lance confessed, his smile a wicked smile.

"A great deal of twisting," Degulado said. "My concern is if your classmates understand the import."

"I'm no expert on imports and exports," Lance quipped.

Myria had watched the exchange in awe. Degulado was not the average blowhard. He knew things. Lance was not the typical student.

Trotsky? Trotsky!

Degulado said: "Very humorous reply. We can talk economic determinism after class. Here, we are concerned with semantics. I would like to hear from you what this means—and not your slogan, but what these words, without the benefit of the author, revolutions are always verbose mean."

"It's simple," Myria blurted. Where had that come from? Too late to reconsider. She had Degulado's eye on her now.

"Tell us! Enlighten us," Degulado said, challenging her.

"It's about—" Myria halted. She knew this. She did. "It's when people are all talk and no action."

"Precisely," Degulado said.

"Pretty much," Lance added.

"So what is the lesson?" Degulado stubbed out his cigarette.

Lance responded: "You have to be as good as your words."

"Interesting," Degulado said. "Trotsky would have replaced words with arms. Don't you agree, sir?"

"Like Cervantes," came Lance's rebuttal.

"Ah yes," Degulado said. "You have an excellent point there. We can trace a direct path from the famous discourse in the *Quixote* between arms and letters to the revolution, except for one important detail."

Another student—unknown to Myria—held up his hand. "Cervantes was a soldier. He believed in action."

"Very true," Degulado said.

"He believed in justice for the people," Lance said, sternly correcting his classmate.

"He believed in justice of a kind specific to the era in which Cervantes lived. The Marxist dogma does not hold," Degulado said.

Lance shook his head in disagreement.

"He's right," Myria said.

Before Lance could jump in, Degulado told him to wait his turn. "Go on," he said to Myria.

"Yeah, go on," Lance said, smolder in his voice.

"Cervantes wrote the *Quixote* to show that Spain had fallen into a state that made it vulnerable to ridicule. He wanted to appeal to the people to dispose of a weak king," Myria said, adding: "If Cervantes had his way, the Spanish monarchy would be reborn, better and stronger."

Degulado commended her. He flattered her by saying she'd made her argument well, and that it was consistent with the *Quixote*. "Far truer than anything Marxists have tried to do with the book."

With a long ring, the bell cut off whatever Degulado was preparing next.

"We have run out of time." The professor began gathering his smoking paraphernalia and papers.

On the way out, Degulado asked Myria if she wanted to get a coffee. Lance was almost to the door when Degulado asked him if he would join them. Myria eyed Lance apologetically.

"Sure," he said.

"Come along then," Degulado said.

"Sure," Lance said. "Yeah, great idea."

"How very nice of you, professor," Myria said.

Myria's world shrank to demitasse size as Degulado and Lance talked in heated voices about politics. Her coffee cup was her whole world. She looked into the milky shallows of her *café con leche* and thought her own thoughts. Her opinion wasn't called for or regarded. She was a bit pissed. She had been the one to rescue Cervantes from the Marxists.

Degulado enjoyed his ripostes with Lance. He and Lance, their heads nearly touching, appeared to be enjoying one another's company exceedingly, exclusively. At one point, Degulado patted Lance on the back. At one point, Lance laughed until tears streamed down his cheeks. At one point, Myria decided she was ready to go back to the residence. She was tired of both of them.

"I should get going," she said to the professor. "Thank you for the coffee."

"Before you do," Degulado said, "I want you to understand how much you impressed me."

"Nice of you to say," Myria said.

"Your classmate here may ask why you are so well prepared."

"He's smart enough to figure it out," she said.

Degulado cackled, the cackling leading to a coughing fit. "We'll see if he does," he said, once he'd caught his breath.

Myria was halfway down one of the picturesque blocks of barrio Santa Cruz when she heard urgent footsteps.

"Hey, there, girly." It was Lance. He put a hand on her shoulder, slowing her to a stop.

"Girly!" She laughed, derisive. "I'm not a girly. I'm not even girly, for that matter.

"Hey now," Lance objected. "Nothing meant by it."

"No, no," she said. "You don't get off that easy."

"You're going to make me pay?"

In a merciless tone, she replied: "The revolution is not yet won, comrade. Not until the revolutionaries realize how demeaning it is to call women 'girly.'"

"I stand corrected."

"Is that an apology?"

"It is," he said. "I beg forgiveness."

"Good," she said. "We can be friends, then."

"I would like it a lot, Myria—if we could be friends." Nervousness had crept into his voice.

"You sure about that?"

"It's just that—"

"What now? I haven't read my Hegel sufficiently?"

"Hegel, nah," Lance said. "We just met. You and me, we haven't hung out much."

She frowned. The presumption! The ego! He imagined she wanted a relationship. And he was already backing out! Backing out of a relationship that wasn't real, only imagined, on his part.

"It's no big deal," she said.

"Now hold on there, Helen Reddy."

She sighed and began walking.

"Okay, that was flippant." He sounded exasperated.

She turned. "How about calling me by my name? Is that too intense for you? Why not call me Myriam?"

"Myriam," he repeated cautiously, as if her name were a new piece of clothing he was trying on to see if it fit.

"You got it."

"I do," he said. "I won't forget it."

"Okay," she said.

"I did want to ask you...." He stumbled over his words.

"Ask me what?"

"How did you know what Degulado was on about? I mean, the way you pulled that stuff about the *Quixote* out of your...."

"My hat?" She laughed. "I didn't pull the answer out of a hat. I read the syllabus. Did you?"

"I guess not," he said.

"You think Trotsky's History in three volumes is going to get you through Professor Degulado's course? Or Marx? Or Bakunin. All of history's tragic revolutionaries?"

"Bakunin...."

"I know, I know. He wasn't a Marxist. He was an anarchist. Frankly, I'm all for anarchy. Respect the individual. End class warfare."

"You're not going to believe me," he said, cheeks flushed.

"I... doubt it," she said.

"The day you came into class, that first day, do you remember?"

Myria couldn't say she did.

"You were, like, the only girl I wanted to talk to," he said, still flushed.

"I was?" Genuine surprise there.

"You were. I saw you and you seemed so..."

"So what?"

"Nice," he said, "cool. But kind of wild, tormented. You never smiled. You wore black on black. You rarely spoke. I'd think, 'Why is she so sad?' Every time I saw you, I'd wonder, 'What happened to her?' Honestly, you seemed in real need of a hug."

Who was the tragic figure now? Myria, the *solterona*, pitiful, swathed from head to toe in black denim—a tragedy of a girl, not at all unlike a character from a Lorca play, one of those morbid spinsters who make a cult out of longing and rejection.

Myria, la solita. Myria, the unwanted. Myria, the discarded, alone and pining, in a strange and remote city.

A far cry from Helen Reddy.

"Guys are always so verbose," came her reply, and it was meant to be as acerbic as it sounded.

His eyes widened. They were riverbed brown. It was the first time she noticed the color of his eyes.

"Please! I'm not sad, Lance." She was. "I'm not in need of rescuing." If only. "I can take care of myself." Barely. "It's all good." It wasn't.

Lance leaned over, his breath in her ear. "Whoever it is, I'll kick his butt."

"Ha! You are funny." She was laughing.

"Seriously," he said. "I'll whoop his sorry ass."

"It's not necessary."

"Just let me at him."

"I don't think that's such a good idea.

"I'll tear the guy apart."

"You're beginning to scare me."

"Am I? 'Cause I could take care of this for you. Just let me at him."

She shook her head. "Not necessary. Got it?"

He laughed, and she together with him, and he wrapped an arm around her shoulders, and he pulled her in close, squeezed her firmly.

It was actually wonderful being hugged like that.

Wonderful until Killian showed up.

"What do we find here?" he asked.

Myria felt the slide of Lance's hand down her back.

"I don't know, Killian. What?" Myria flashed.

Killian smiled, satisfied. He'd rattled her. She had a nearly irrepressible urge to strike him. He looked to Lance, who didn't appear addled, and whose hand made itself at home on Myria's ass. "Gawd, talk about being alone in desperate company," Killian said.

"No, Killian, that would be you," Myria retorted.

Killian laughed antagonistically. "Lance, beware. She throws herself at everyone."

"I'd like to throw something at you now, like a brick," Myria threatened, "because that is how thick, stupid, you are being."

"No different from making out with you. Now that was painful."

Myria didn't respond. At his worst, Killian was annoying. He taunted, pestered—was generally obnoxious. But after that wretched incident in Morocco, and now this! Myria wanted him hurt—more than hurt.

The Inquisition had come up in her Golden Age Literature class. It happened during a discussion of the *Quixote*. Some students were appalled by the famous knight's cruelty. One of Myria's classmates pronounced the book "gross." She was referring to the passage in which the famous knight concocts a potion of rosemary, oil, salt, and wine. He mixes the ingredients together and cooks them for a long time. He asks for a flask to put the potion in but there is none at hand. He must settle for a cruet. He stands over the cruet and recites more than eighty Our Fathers, the same number of Hail Marys, Salve Reginas, credos. He drinks almost a full quart of the stuff. Don Quixote immediately vomits the entire contents of his stomach. He sweats profusely. He suffers horrendous pain. He is stricken with spasms. Ill as ill can be, he falls into a deep sleep. He may be dead. When he awakens, he pronounces himself cured of his injuries, strong enough to go into battle. Sancho thinks his master's recovery a miracle. He begs him to let him try his potion. Alas, poor Sancho is also taken ill. Nausea overtakes him. He faints. He comes to. He faints again. He shits his pants. He believes he is going to die and that Don Quixote is to blame. Don Quixote chides him. No one who has not been dubbed a knight could possibly benefit from the elixir.

"Gross, really gross," the student had said.

The student next to the girl said that Don Quixote was a homicidal maniac.

"But he drinks the potion too," a student remarked.

"He's nuts," the student said.

Degulado had drawn on his cigarette and said: "Don Quixote may have been mad but Cervantes was not. The author is alluding to the Inquisition, and most possibly a method of torturing heretics known as the water cure."

"It's very simple," the professor went on. "Clamps are placed on the victim's nose. It forces him to open his mouth in order to breathe. A rag is stuffed down the throat. Water is poured into the mouth and the victim must either swallow excessive amounts of water or choke to death. "

Myria wanted Killian choked. Drowned, in fact.

CHAPTER

TWENTY-TWO

CURSES

Worn out and agitated, Myria paused under the doorjamb before venturing down the dim-lit corridor to the common room. She could hear Cristina blaring on the tele. The women played the television so loud she could hear the gasping sobs of the heroine as the novio pleaded with her in his consoling basso.

If only the novio knew. He'd be horrified. His kind tended to be that way. Traditional. Religious. He'd definitely be sickened. He might even vomit. Probably not. He'd take the news like a true man, stoically. He wouldn't permit his feelings of revulsion to interfere with the obligation he felt for Cristina. As a man of faith, that was. He'd never abandon her to her fate. Never. He'd have to have a long talk with God first, though. Well, not directly to God. Catholics didn't pray directly to God. They prayed to the saints or to the Virgin Mary. He'd pray to the Mary because she was above all the other saints. She had also been a woman once. A mere girl, actually, younger than Cristina when the angel—what was his name?—came to her. Of all the saints, she would be the most understanding. She had been in the same predicament. He'd pray for her to give him strength. Alone. In a cathedral. On his knees before the big altar. The really big altar. Enormous. Grand. Very grand. On his knees, his hands worked into a single fist pressed to his forehead, he'd have one of those long talks that characters on soap operas have with the Blessed Mother. When he was convinced his pleas had been heard, he would genuflect and stride out of the cathedral into the sunlight.

But the novio still didn't know.

Myria decided she wasn't in the mood for Cristina at the moment. She needed to be alone. She said a quick "*Hola*" to her housemates on her way to her room.

She dropped her knapsack on the floor, and ignoring the mess of clothes, books and papers on the bed, lied down, cursing Killian until she fell asleep.

Amelia knocked on her door later in the day. It had to be Amelia because none of the other women visited Myria in her room.

"An American called," Amelia said. "I told him to call back because I assumed you were resting."

"Was it Killian?" Aside from Sheffield, he was the only guy who had the residence phone number.

"Yes," Amelia said. "He repeated his name to me three times just in case I didn't get it the first time. What an annoying person your Killian is."

"My Killian! Oh, no, he's not my Killian."

"Good," Amelia said. "It seems as if you are finished with him."

"Oh, I am. I am so finished with him."

"Good," Amelia said. "Life will be less complicated for you."

"But what if he keeps calling? He'll keep on calling. He's like that if he doesn't get something he wants. How do you get rid of a person like that?"

Amelia shrugged. "What does it matter? He is dead to you now."

CHAPTER

TWENTY-THREE

KILLIAN, AS ALWAYS

Myria hadn't given up on the idea of transferring but the director set up so many obstacles that she was stuck in Sevilla. All she could hope for, if she wanted to return to the States with something to show for her year abroad, was to hunker down, do her work, and have nothing more to do with Killian.

She went to her classes. She joined Samantha and Port for coffee. Killian was always there. He did what he could to get her to speak to him. Her replies, curt and cold, fended him off. He would flirt with Samantha instead, or bicker with Port. If he tried to catch Myria's eye, she looked away.

"You're mad at Killian, aren't you?" Samantha asked several days after what Myria began to think of as the Lance debacle.

"Sort of," she said.

Lance continued to sit next to her in class. He and Degulado wrangled. Their arguments had done much to lift the professor's spirits. Myria sat, a glum shadow at Lance's side, unable to muster the energy to participate.

Lance.

He caught up with her one day after class.

"Is everything all right?"

"Right as it can be," Myria said. She was afraid he would bring up Killian. Instead, he asked her out.

She smiled, teeth closed. She looked best when she smiled with her teeth closed. Otherwise, her chin would double up. "Sure. I'd love to."

"I could come by your place."

"I don't have a place. I live in a female-only residence."

"Are you kidding?"

"Not kidding." At least he didn't make the usual jokes about convents and virgins.

✉✉✉

"What about him?" Myria countered, after Samantha asked her about Lance.

"Killian said you were seeing him."

Myria sighed. "Killian is crazy."

Samantha nodded sympathetically. "Killian is crazy. He's not boring, though. Lance is so boring."

Myria couldn't help but wonder. "I didn't know you two were friends?"

"We're not," Samantha said. "Lance tried to date me when I first got here."

"I see," Myria said. Every guy had tried to date Samantha when she first arrived in Spain.

"He's not my type," Samantha said. "You get it."

"Not really," Myria said.

"He's so full of himself."

"Really? He seems like a nice guy."

"You haven't spent an entire afternoon listening to him talk politics," Samantha said.

That sounded like Lance, the Lance Myria knew from class, the Lance who she went out with the night before. He had asked if she

minded if they just took a walk. She was all for it. The broad river
with its arched bridges. The lustrous night sky. The waxing moon.

"You just said you went out with him."

"One time," Samantha said, "and I swear it was the most boring
date of my life."

"It couldn't have been that bad," Myria said. "The most boring
would be…I don't know, like the guy is dead or something."

"Okay, he wasn't that bad," Samantha said. "But he almost
bored me to death."

"You're funny," Myria said.

Samantha scrutinized her for a moment. "Killian was right then.
You are going out with Lance."

Myria fessed up. "You got me."

"I don't see you as a couple," Samantha said, her voice pure
puzzlement, eyes round with surprise.

"Crazier things have happened," Myria said.

Amelia also wanted to hear about Lance. She had found her
sitting on the cot when she'd returned from her date.

"Can he kiss?" Amelia asked, moving over to make room for
her on the cot.

Myria sat. She buried her head in her hands. She grinned into
her palms. When she raised her eyes, she was still smiling.

"We almost got arrested," she said.

¡Carajo!

Damn.

"But we didn't," Myria said, quick to assure her friend.

"Obviously not," Amelia said. "You would not be here if you
did. You must have been fucking in the streets if you were almost
arrested."

"Not in the street," Myria said. She and Lance certainly hadn't
been fucking in the streets.

"Where then?"

"Under the Puente de Triana," Myria replied. She was thoroughly and happily ashamed of herself.

"Everyone gets caught there," Amelia said. "Hundreds of girls have sacrificed their virginity under the Puente de Triana."

"I'm not one of those girls," Myria said.

"You mean you are not a *puta*?" Amelia laughed.

"I meant I'm not a virgin," Myria said, laughing too.

"You are completely wrong," Amelia said. "You are a virgin in Spain unless you are keeping something from me."

"That's one way of looking at it," Myria said. "And you know I never keep anything from you."

"Then you have lost your Spanish virginity," Amelia said, satisfied.

"So I have," Myria said.

"It would have been better if he were Spanish," Amelia remarked. "But it will have to do."

CHAPTER

TWENTY-FOUR

WHERE?

Myria heard the news from Samantha. The kind of news that feels as if you had just been thrown from a bridge; news that causes your heart to pump like a rapidly flooding bilge; news that gets stuck in your throat so you can't swallow; news that makes you feel faint, sick, afraid. Horrible news.

"Where is he now?" Myria asked.

"He's still in the hospital."

"In the hospital you said."

"I visited him last night," Samantha replied.

"How did you find out?" Myria asked.

"Port told me."

"How did Port know?" Myria asked.

Samantha responded: "He and Killian were supposed to meet at the train station. Killian had talked Port into going to Madrid with him for the long weekend. Killian never showed up."

"Killian wasn't there?" Myria asked.

"Port waited for him. He never came."

"Oh, shit!"

"Port decided he'd flaked out. They bought their tickets in advance, a hotel booked—everything was all set."

"What did Port do?" Myria asked.

"He went to Madrid without him," Samantha said.

"He went without him! Didn't he realize something was wrong?"

"He thought...I don't know what he thought," Samantha said.

"I can't believe Port went to Madrid without him."

"He did," Samantha said.

"That is so messed up!"

"You can't blame Port," Samantha said. "What was he supposed to do?"

"But," Myria said, "it doesn't sound like Port. It sounds more like something Killian would do."

"Well, Port did. He went to Madrid."

"If he went to Madrid, how did he find out Killian was in the hospital?"

"When Killian didn't show up at the Institute."

"After Port got back you mean?"

Samantha explained. Port had gotten back from Madrid. When she saw him, she asked how it went. He said he had a great time. She asked how he and Killian had gotten along. Port told her that he wouldn't know because Killian hadn't bothered to show up. Samantha said she hadn't seen him around either. Port told her not to look so worried. But she was worried. She suggested that Port stop by Killian's to see what was up. It turned out that Killian was in the hospital. He had been found unconscious outside a club. He had gone to see some punk band. He stepped outside to get some air or something. A bunch of guys followed him into the alley. They beat him within an inch of his life. He was really roughed up. He almost died.

Myria listened without interrupting. She saw with piercing

clarity her friend standing in the empty classroom, the sun shining in through the window, glancing off Samantha's blond hair. Myria listened closely to the troubled waters of her friend's words, coming in fits and starts. Near tears herself, Myria averted her eyes, not able to bear further the blanket of sadness that covered Samantha's face. Instead, there was the callous play of light through the open window, the nervous bird flutter in the trees, the indifferent shadows gathering at the far end of the room. How many times had she wanted Killian to die? How many times? The floor began to feel unsteady, as if it might move out from under her, setting her horribly, horribly adrift.

CHAPTER

TWENTY-FIVE

SAILS

If you push the people who need you far enough away, they
will sail on without you. The thought often came to Myria
after decades of hearing nothing from Killian. He left no wake.
The currents gave no indication of where he'd gone. At a time in
which everyone was plugged into the Internet and most anyone
could be found on some social networking site, he had managed
to disappear. Myria assumed he simply didn't want to be found. He
couldn't be dead, and not because the idea was unimaginable, but
because the dead announced departure from the world through
certificates, obituaries, actuaries. It left her wondering where he
might have landed. Europe? Africa? Asia? Something told her he
had to be in some far off place to be unreachable. For someone
who insisted on being the center of attention, Killian had pulled
off the perfect disappearing act.

India was a good guess. Myria could easily picture Killian in
India.

Often, she thought of Killian while she was at the beach. It was a mystery to her why she had these sudden surges of remembrance. She had more than enough to think about. She scarcely had time to think at all. Or bathe, comb her hair, put on unwrinkled clothes. Her twin boys, those two adorable, look-alike tykes, swallowed her whole.

Myria, the harried mother. She and Lance were living in Queens. When she mentioned to other mothers she married a professor, the responses came in tones of flat-out envy.

"You are lucky. If he were in medicine, you'd never see him."

"I wish my husband were a professor. He'd be home more to help out with the kids."

"My husband works on Wall Street. You have no idea. And ever since the crash happened, his hours have only gotten worse."

How utterly wrong those people were. Clueless wives who had no idea what was involved in being a professor. The university careerist, ever fearful of not making tenure or being promoted, was driven to enslaving himself. He spent enormous amounts of time and effort prepping for class, teaching the class, arranging office hours, supervising doctoral candidates. He was also required to grind out papers, fly hither and thither to attend high-profile conferences, and publish lest he be crushed like a bug. There were also the faculty meetings, a caucus of petty grudges, backstabbing, and power plays that required the skills of a chess master to survive unscathed. The professor had scant time for his family. His wife was left on her own to scrape and scramble, fend and forage.

Before Myria married Lance, she supported wholeheartedly his desire to embark on an academic career. She supported him because she was clueless. They began their marriage as a couple but his job turned her into a wife. Lance's job stole her identity and prospects because having children was still a career killer.

Caught off guard by the swiftness in which Myria, the mother, replaced Myria, the independent woman, she had plenty of regrets, and was not at all above feeling bitter.

"Sometimes, I'd like to disappear," she would say, slamming the top of the washing machine shut. "You have no idea how good you have it," she would say to the cat, dumping food in its bowl. "What if I vanished?" she would ask the anchor on the morning news. "What about that?"

Or, she would call Lance at work. There was that time he let her call go to voicemail. "If you don't call me back in five minutes," her message went, "I am going to buy a one-way ticket to Paris, take the kids with me, and you will never see us again."

When he called back, she repeated her threat.

"Myria, you have to calm down. I was teaching. I have a full load today."

"You think I don't know it?"

"So if you know it, why are you calling me?"

"When are you coming home?"

"I'm not sure. There's this thing."

"This thing? This thing?"

"Faculty meeting."

The babies were wailing in their cribs.

"Are the boys okay? I can hear them crying."

"Now you hear them crying? You didn't hear them crying at eleven last night, and again at one o'clock, and again at six."

Silence followed by throat clearing. Finally: "I'll see if I can get out of the meeting."

"Good. Because if you don't walk through this door in an hour, you may as well not come home."

Myria hung up on him.

During those days, when the boys were not yet three months old, and colicky, Lance did what he could to be supportive. When she screamed at him, he calmed her down. When she broke into tears, he took her in his arms. When she was too tired for sex, he didn't complain—and would go take a shower.

Myria was not always exhausted and depressed. Twins were a lot of work. They required the patience of a panoply of saints. But, they were also her identical cherubim, her matchless wonders, her beloved sprites. Myria never regretted the boys. She regretted that she had let motherhood turn her into a hag.

"You are not fat, Myria. You're as smart, beautiful and sexy as the day we met," Lance would say when she despaired of ever feeling like herself again.

"I wear mom jeans."

"You look great no matter what."

Beach season made her feel even more of a hag. Myria never had a bikini body. She did keep vigil when it came to her weight. If the scale was on the upswing, she sacrificed, sometimes fasted. Pregnant with twins had meant eating for three. After the boys survived the perilous trip down the birth canal, Myria continued to eat for three. The twins turned two when she began to lose the big baby belly. Another year went by before she fit easily into a size twelve. It took five years to be able to stand naked before a mirror and not feel as if the mirror were her mortal enemy. Myria's inflated misgivings over her body/herself had finally shrunk to manageable proportions.

During those five years, Myria lost touch with a good many of her friends. She had Lance, the twins, relatives and no one else. Samantha moved back to Colorado. Port lived with his wife in Westport. Other friends lived closer. Their crazy, busy lives made getting together difficult.

Killian, she had forgotten. Memory hadn't made a ghost of him. Reverie didn't conjure him. Recollection excluded him. She kept no photographs to remember him by. People on the street didn't remind her of him. If she saw Killian again, would she recognize him?

She was at the beach with Lance and the kids when she found herself thinking of Killian. Lance was splayed out on a towel, snoozing. The boys were coasting on their bellies over the waves.

Myria yelled at them not to swim out too far. The cold water had turned their lips blue by the time they ran up to her. She wrapped them in thick towels.

"Are you hungry?"

She traipsed up the dunes with the two boys to the concession stand for hot dogs and ice cream cones. They sat down to eat at one of the picnic tables. Myria could see in the distance where the cleave joined horizon and sky, and remembered.

Killian was going on about Lance, nagging at her and launching insults at every opportunity.

"What do you see in him?"

"I'm not going to talk to you about Lance."

"No, really, I want to know."

"Ask me if I care."

"Do you? Is that it? You actually have feelings for him?"

"I actually have feelings for him."

"You don't."

"Okay, I don't. I don't have feelings for him."

"But you've slept with him."

"I'm not doing this, not again."

"It boggles the mind how you could sleep with him. He's so unattractive."

"He is attractive in his own way. Besides, pretty boys are boring."

"Pretty he isn't. He's almost deformed if you think about it."

"What the fuck is wrong with you?"

He hectored. She scolded. He attacked. She fought back. They were miserable together, acting out their sordid emotions: envy, anger, deceit, obstinacy.

If he was gloom, she was doom. Or vice versa.

And yet, Killian had never wanted to break it off with her. Break it off as in the two of them stop drinking, drugging, and clubbing. It was a ritual between them. No matter which city she was living in—New York, Boston—he would show up on a whim and say: "Go put on something fabulous. We're going out." Out they went, all night long, on a mission to oblivion.

Myria gathered up the twins' ketchup-smeared trash. She wiped their messy faces with a paper napkin.

She was twenty-five or six, or twenty-seven before realizing she couldn't keep up with Killian. No one could keep up with Killian because there were no limits. She had arrived at that stage when she felt there had to be a limit or else her life would completely self-destruct.

There was a Bowie song that used to remind her of Killian. *Rock & Roll Suicide*. How many times had Killian passed out on the wall-to-wall carpet and still did too many drugs?

He had other problems.

"It's just so miserable? Can you imagine trying to explain something like that to a doctor? I could die thinking of it."

The more he spoke, the more she wanted him to stop speaking. What could she say? How do you console someone who tells you he is impotent (as Killian put it)? He explained his troubles in detail she didn't want to hear as they hurled in a cab down Riverside Drive. It would be morning soon. He had finally met someone he wanted to "do it with" and he couldn't. He was afraid he might lose her.

And then, that horrible day when Samantha urged Myria to go with her to visit him in the hospital.

Samantha hadn't exaggerated the extent of Killian's injuries. It was as if the guys who jumped him wanted to kill him. Swollen, bandaged. One eye was completely shut, a black sack. The other eye, less swollen, but so bloodshot it seemed to weep red tears.

Like a battered Cyclops, he watched her out of his one eye.

Samantha had brought in a clutch of balloons. There must have been a dozen bouncy skins in fanciful colors round with helium. She presented the unruly bouquet to Killian while encouraging him with her sunniest smile.

He smiled. The balloons bobbed on their ribbons in his clenched hand.

Samantha settled herself in the chair at his bedside. She chattered about meaningless matters.

Myria hung back.

Killian turned his red eye on her. "Tell her to come in," he said to Samantha.

"Killian wants you to come in."

She went and stood at the end of his bed.

He released the balloons. Colorful globes taut and fragile, ready to burst at any moment, floated to the ceiling, where like confused planets they bumped against one another.

"What's up?" Lance asked on the drive from the beach back to Queens. "You're so quiet."

"What am I thinking about?" Myria said. "Killian, I guess."

"Really?"

She and Lance were living together in Boston. Marriage was still some years away. Killian called and called. He barraged her with phone calls.

"Myriam, you never come to New York."

"It's because I don't live there."

"I could come up."

"Don't do that, Killian."

Lance was in the kitchen making paella from a box. He cooked more back then. Pancakes on Sunday mornings. Spaghetti during the week for lunch. Tuna melts at midnight.

"Myriam, if I leave now, I can be there tonight."

"Tonight is out of the question."

"Come on, Myriam."

"I'll call you."

"You always say that."

"I promise."

The next day the phone rang. She looked to Lance for help.

"It's Killian. I can't talk to him."

"Don't answer the phone."

"He'll keep calling."

"Tell him to leave you alone."

The phone stopped ringing.

"He doesn't listen to me."

The phone began ringing again. A swift and sharp sadness took hold of her. Why was he so needy?

Lance answered the phone. Myria saw to the paella. Lance wasn't long.

"Was it Killian?"

"Doesn't matter."

That was the last she heard of Killian. It was anyone's guess where he was now. Myria doubted that she would ever see him again.

Sometimes, when Myria was at the beach with Lance and the kids, a ship would appear in the distance, one of those tall ships, a clipper, proudly set at full mast, all sails flying, heading out to sea.

Away from her.

About the Author

Kathryn A. Kopple is a specialist in Latin American Literature (Ph.D., NYU). She is the author of Little Velásquez, a novel set in 15th century Spain.